URBANA FREE LIBRARY

3 1230 00405 5964

URBANA FREE LIBRARY
(217-367-4057)

DISCARDED BY
URBANA FREE LIBRARY

DATE DUE		
APR 05 2010		

D1264830

While the Music Lasts

While the Music Lasts

ALICE McVEIGH

URBANA FREE LIBRARY

ORION

Copyright © 1994 Alice McVeigh

All rights reserved

The right of Alice McVeigh to be
identified as the author of this work has been
asserted by her in accordance with the
Copyright, Designs and Patents Act 1988.

First published in Great Britain in 1994 by
Orion
An imprint of Orion Books Ltd
Orion House, 5 Upper St Martin's Lane, London WC2H 9EA

A CIP catalogue record for this book is
available from the British Library

ISBN 1 85797 939 7

The Publishers gratefully acknowledge
permission from Faber and Faber Ltd to
quote lines from the following:
Four Quartets by T S Eliot
The Hawk in the Rain by Ted Hughes
Collected Poems by Sylvia Plath
Choruses from The Rock from The Collected Poems 1909–1962 by T S Eliot

The Publishers gratefully acknowledge permission from J. M. Dent
to quote lines from the following:
Sometimes The Sky's Too Bright by Dylan Thomas
I Know This Vicious Minute's Hour by Dylan Thomas

Typeset by Deltatype Ltd, Ellesmere Port, Cheshire
Printed in Great Britain by
Clays Ltd, St Ives plc

For my two sisters,
Kathy and Helen

– 'music heard so deeply
That it is not heard at all, but you are the music
While the music lasts.'

T. S. Eliot
'The Four Quartets'

I

A Decent Sort

. . . O never give the heart outright,
For they, for all smooth lips can say,
Have given their hearts up to the play.
And who could play it well enough
If deaf and dumb and blind with love?
He that made this knows all the cost,
For he gave all his heart and lost.

Yeats

Warren Wilson, having swallowed two hundred and nineteen pills, balanced the last pill delicately on the bones of his wrists. In truth he looked all bones, a lean, stretched face locked on to a narrow body, but all he noticed was the lines of his hands. He had once, he thought, been proud of his hands. Tapered, strongly sculpted, they had made his living from twenty-two to forty-two, from what he considered the beginning to the end. And tonight, tonight was the end.

He moved neatly, almost fussily, transferring the emptied prescription bottles into a row by the bed, then adjusting, as precisely as a director on a film set, the angle of his new and, he recalled, expensive suitcase. There would be nothing messy, nothing dramatic, nothing left to chance. He would tie up the ends of his life and present it, a perfectly wrapped parcel, to the silently grieving God in whom he had long since forgotten to believe.

There was no malice in his thoughts, or rather, because no feelings are exempted, the smallest possible portion of malice. He knew of course that Caroline would suffer, that his son would suffer – even, conceivably, that Isabel would suffer – and these sufferings he regretted, as much as it was possible for him, in his present steadiness, to regret anything. His wounds were already scabbing, closing over. His certainty had, in completing him, liberated him from his guilt. In his mind he was already gone, and the rhythmic, assured movements of his body felt like a widening sliver of sunrise, the first gestures of spring. His impatience, his illness, had left him, and his restlessness with it; he was well; he was recovered, he was moving on.

He put his spectacles into their leather case, the lid snapping down with a satisfactorily completed sound, and the room was ready, except that the violin case was still open. (How many hotel rooms, he wondered, as he surveyed it with a twinge of nausea; how many evenings of solitaire, of drinks with the brass; how many tremulous and embarrassing sexual encounters? He had looked out over the skylines of how many foreign cities? And all for what?) Not that it mattered, he reminded himself. Not that any of it mattered now.

He removed the violin from its case with a softened, trance-like movement. The room may have been ready but he was not ready. He had a last farewell to make.

It was an old violin, 1775 Italian, carved into ripe, incandescent perfection by one of those makers whose name, without incurring an indrawn whistle from concert-goers, provoked a startled respect from fellow musicians. What a beauty it was! – hardly cracked, worn smooth at the edges by generations of fingers, the varnish the same rich darkness as Isabel's hair, the lines seamless, a living, breathing, perfect thing. Someone else will learn to love this, he thought, stroking its belly, just as someone else will always be running their fingers through Isabel's warm hair. A little dart of pain here, centred in the stomach, the finger's motion arrested.

But I will not see it, he told himself: I shall be home, returned to the timelessness of the beginning, suspended in the act of unbeing. I shall have completed myself; abdicating, I shall have, in the only way open to me, entered the music.

2

After tonight, there will be no more endings. I will have guessed the riddle and won the prize, which is truthfulness.

The violin vibrated under his hand – his sleeve had just brushed the D string. A polished, stylized, crafted, wooden box, that was all: how strange that it should feel so human, so meaningful. The music of nebulousness, the winds of time – these would prove his music soon, the rustlings of the blood inside the womb.

The weakening was beginning; his head spun slightly . . . They would say, of course, that he was depressive, and why not? He had suffered his breakdown, paid his union dues. He had laid his sacrifices at the feet of enough mad gods; he too had once believed in music, in justice. He could hear the voices already: 'Happened ten years ago, poor chap, but the weakness always lingers, and of course that old business with Isabel . . . Wonder if he felt much pain, seemed all right in Detroit, didn't he? All that touring's hard, and who the hell will tell the wife?' The guilt of those who'd never really liked him, the misery of those who'd neglected to show their affection; he suddenly felt sorry for them all. It wasn't a bad orchestra, no worse than most, and he had friends here. He could pick up the phone now and they would come – William, Clarence, even Piotr. In a few minutes it would be the arm around the shoulders, the clean cry of the American ambulance, the hot white hospital lights. He shook his head, which felt increasingly dizzy. Not that way. No.

Oh there were people, many people, who liked him, respected his dedication, were pleased to have him around. Pleasant old Warren, middle of the firsts, a reserved, self-possessed, over-precise little man with his mistakes (his experiments with addiction, his infatuations) well behind him. You remember Warren – fellow always banging on about Giotto frescoes, the one with that little ritual of putting his violin away. Married, not too unhappily, with one averagely disappointing child. God, but I never heard he was depressive, who'd have guessed it, bloody hell.

He heard the voices, noticing, with an academic interest, a coldness in the centre of his bones. No, he had no illusions about orchestras; he'd seen too much for that. The shock would last a week, the mourning a fortnight, references to 'that tour when – ' for a couple of years before – oblivion. It would be the same, he knew, even for the most prominent members of the orchestra, for the loathed genius who led the cellos and the empty-headed beauty in the second violins, for the leader of the brass pack and the self-important chairman of the players' board. It had been the same for Mirabel, for Henry, even for old Eugene. It was only human to pass over, to move on. It was self-defence, self-preservation, too obvious to provoke resentment or despair.

He found his fingers groping for the bow. He hadn't thought to play but in his dreamlike state it felt only natural: his choice of music, his own last rites. What to play? Not Bach – too God-infused, and not Beethoven, lest the intensity drag him earthwards. It must be Mozart; the Adagio from the G major concerto would be right, the suspensions achingly resolved, the motion limitless. In his now bloodless fingers the nerves would flicker one last time, and in his heart he knew he would remember everything, forgive everything. In his hands the violin, that instrument of torture over the last few years, would become again a clear singing thing, the sound even, warm, all hungers appeased.

As he played the images rose up in his mind – the gigantic heaving swell of Adrian's birth, the keening of seagulls over the shore, the sun skimming over the edge of time's horizon, her face, bending over him, that long, longing look over the brandy glasses . . . A stab in his chest and he laid the violin down – too late too late for that – sweet Jesus the pain! He was falling, flying and the door's opening whooshed in his ears like the roar of the sea.

II

The Collection of Hearts

I think the full tide of human existence is at Charing Cross.

Samuel Johnson

Isabel, being Isabel, never attempted to take any news calmly. Upon hearing that Warren was hanging onto life by a hospital sinew, she gave, as her reputation deserved, a fair imitation of hysterics, and became the focus of attention for the remainder of rehearsal. Members spent their time divided between being shocked and trying to recall what exactly had occurred between her and Warren fifteen years before. Half imagined grimly less, and half, still more grimly, more than had actually happened.

When she found herself alone, however, Isabel discovered that she was, limelight apart, even more shaken than she had pretended to be. She forgot the recent Warren Wilson, with his pinched face and finicky gestures, and mourned, with the excess of a nature given to excess, the Warren she had known years before.

Oh, he had never been handsome, exactly, but his body had been more compact, less attenuated, and his countenance so peculiarly expressive that his narrow features and too-delicate limbs had been forgotten. How odd it was that she had never noticed him changing! And how gradually he must have changed; how subtly time had thinned his character, his boyishness, away! Looking back, she searched for the moment when his lively movements and poetic fancies had slipped into hesitancy, nervousness, that rather old-fashioned primness. The trouble was, there didn't seem to have been a moment, or else she had forgotten it; it was too long ago.

She turned to the mirror herself, to search for the girl that she had been when first they met. Yet it was hard to discern much alteration in Isabel, so jealously had she guarded her beauty, rising in the night to remoisturize her face, toning her muscles religiously into the most becoming lines. A few wrinkles had dared to ruffle the smooth cream of her face, but she was sure that she had never carried herself better, dressed herself more becomingly, looked much more desirable than she did now at thirty-nine. For a moment she allowed herself to imagine the time when she would only be a 'well-presented woman of a certain age'. How she dreaded those years! Pushing back her hair, she dismissed her image, content to live in the present, as was her preference – the future too nervy, the past too complicated for definition. Vain she certainly was, but Isabel was an emotional creature and no one could blame her if, after honing her make-up to perfection, she ruined it all by a sudden cloudburst of tears for the loss, not of the recent Warren Wilson, but of the Warren who had slipped away unnoticed over the years.

Wiping the tears hastily away (tears dried the skin so horribly) she dredged up her diaries – extravagantly written but possessed of a certain undefinable style – of that early period, the period before she had concluded that life was for living rather than for writing about. It cost her some time to find the place where she first mentioned Warren, but then she found herself, as always, equally entranced by her extrovert verve and by what she secretly thought of as the movie script of her life.

Another terrible day's travelling; coach-lag setting in with a vengeance and all of Italy looks remarkably dusty and dry and like other bits of Italy. Chatted to a tolerably amusing fellow with the most marvellous snapping eyes, new violinist named Warren (awful name). Some of the brass are already calling him rabbit warren but I think nicknames are bloody. Warren tells very droll stories, also quoted poetry at me, which I never fail to find affecting – though Bob laughed very nastily and whispered 'Pansy' to me – which I'm sure he isn't, just a bit young and delicate for all this. Still, he's got to get used to it as he's taken the job, and I can't see him converting the firsts to poetry! He was appalled at the amount of drinking that went on in Padua, having yet to learn that it's really about the only outlet for tension left to us, not to mention its uses in speeding up the boring travelling bits.

Friday. Another mad day's travel to Rome – sat with Warren, failed however to inspire him to poetry. He did quote something equally worrying though – Socrates, I think, or was it Plato? Foresee a sticky end for said Warren, though his eyes have a peculiarly sweet tilt to them and his lashes are quite gorgeous. Skin marvellous too, though a few extra pounds wouldn't hurt, ditto a little grey around the temples. I told him so, impulsively, and he blushed to the tips of his ears and didn't speak to me for about ten minutes. Good Lord, you'd think he'd never received a compliment before, which may even be true, as he's new to the profession and Cambridge (my dear!) was never like this.

He seems half-repelled, half-seduced by the whole touring experience – raves about the Mahler, in ecstasies about the Strauss, but in a state of total mystification about the ways in which orchestras work, relationships between members, etc. When someone mentioned Roger being with Aline, I almost heard his jaw drop; and he awards us women such respectful attention that he is quite the general pet already. We are, to be honest, rather more accustomed to jokes and gropes than to held-open doors and chairs being pushed in after us. It was generally agreed in the ladies' changing room that, as he is still youthful enough to die young, he can't live long . . .

Sunday. There was a party last night and, even I must admit, it was quite a function. The chianti was everywhere, at

7

the official reception and in about six adjoining rooms at the Sheraton. Julian was being an absolute boor, at one point trying to remove L's bra, but Roger soon put a stop to that, as the only person he permits that kind of behaviour is himself.

Warren got talking to Piotr about books. He never stops talking about books – and of course you can't stump Piotr on books; he's not only read them, he's read them in the original Latin or Hindustani or whatever. They very nearly out-talked the party, because people had either paired off for rather more private larks or had staggered off to bed by the time I spotted that Warren and Piotr were still at it, talking, I believe, about *Adam Bede* and the implacability of destiny. (I string along with that line of thought, and presently proved it.) I was too tipsy to retire, but not tipsy enough to give in to the obstinate advances of Julian; I joined the literary guild for protection (Piotr knew, but Warren hadn't a clue, of course). He was still talking about Fate when Piotr – he does suffer, poor boy – got his first indigestive pangs of the night and charged off for his tablets . . . It took Warren longer than you would suppose to grasp that his lecture had failed to grip his new audience.

'Didn't mean to bore you with all this,' he said suddenly.

'Oh, you weren't,' I lied politely, Julian-conscious, for he still, like the troops of Midian, prowled and prowled around. Warren must have drunk something despite the overriding interest of his discussion with Piotr, because what came out next astonished me.

'I suppose you're too beautiful to care much for books,' he said, and I had to ask him to repeat it, less out of gratification than because he had spoken so softly I could hardly hear him. Anyway, it was a pushover from that point; I've never found seduction simpler. He came to my room (for a drink, would you believe), and protested just a shade too energetically when I proposed he sit on the bed. He seemed worried about what anyone would think who might come in – as feeble an excuse as I've yet struck and yet, you know, I believe he meant it. I had to kiss him first, and I made such a spectacular job of it that

8

I wondered whether I hadn't overcooked the goose – but only for a moment. *Then* I was knocked flat by the force of all that pent-up emotion. He was not nearly as inexperienced as I'd supposed, either that or else so sensitive that it made no odds.

Anyway, when I woke up I was alone and incredibly thirsty. Part of me was absolutely dying to tell the girls, but I didn't want him teased – and there was some part of myself that wanted to keep him separate, as something too surprising and precious to bear daylight, or competition: a type of selfishness, I suppose.

He passed me a note as we got on the coach, but chose to sit elsewhere. Already he looks different to me, his face leaner, his bearing more masculine, more commanding . . . I couldn't make head or tail of his note. It said:

'Why, what could she have done, being what she is?

Was there another Troy for her to burn?'

Suddenly dissatisfied, Isabel flicked through the next few pages; she remembered it all. How Warren had avoided her, captured her interest and then had captured her, to everyone's astonishment, for the duration of the tour. And how, on her return, she had simply moved back in with Joel, as though it had never happened, which of course it never had, as touring never manages to quite connect with real life . . . She only needed to skim over the meeting in Victoria Station; she recalled it all, more clearly than she would have believed possible. How tense his face had looked when he saw her, how bright the patches on his thin cheeks!

'I thought you weren't going to speak to me again,' he said.

'Don't be absurd; you've joined the same orchestra, remember?'

'That wasn't what I meant.'

'My sweet creature, you mustn't take it so much to heart. We were on a tour. Things happen on tours which – '

'So now I don't matter, is that it?'

I was surprised at his ferocity. 'Of course you matter. But

you can't be jealous of Joel; that would be ridiculous. We've been living together for nearly two years.'

'You mean, I suppose, that he's been a more durable diversion that I have.'

'I mean, if you want to be technical about it, that there's been some level of commitment for rather a long time. Does that satisfy you?'

'No, it bloody well doesn't! You're worth ten of that soulless clod; do you want to throw away your whole life? Commitment, indeed! Isabel, I want you to marry me!'

I stared at him. 'You're proposing to me in the middle of Victoria Station?'

Warren made an impatient gesture. 'Where I propose to you is not the issue! I am proposing to you, yes; it is Victoria Station, yes. Who cares where it is? I only care about you. Marry me.'

'You must be mad,' I murmured, very moved. I had often imagined being proposed to, sitting by the sea, or overlooking cliffs, on a moonlit night, or, very possibly, in some rosy dawn, by some eminently unsuitable celebrity. I had not imagined Warren, white-faced and imperious on Victoria train station, but I seem to have a rock-bottom level of common sense which saves me in such crises, despite all my layers of vanity and weakness. I prefer fantasy, when all is said and done, but reality, when imposed, almost always finds me equal to it.

'Listen, Warren, I am terribly fond of you and always will be, but I – I'm not the type to get married. I just don't see the point, somehow. The idea doesn't appeal to me. I'm sorry to disappoint you – I'm terribly touched. To be honest, nobody's ever proposed to me before – but I couldn't possibly marry. You or anybody. You must believe me, because if I was the kind of girl who wanted to get married, you would be the kind of person I would choose. Really. I do mean that.'

'Oh, thanks,' said Warren harshly. 'I'm only good enough for the odd fling on some awful tour. Not in Joel's class, obviously. You wouldn't contemplate any level of commitment to me.'

'You're crazy to be jealous of Joel,' I told him. 'Absolutely crazy. It's Joel who should be jealous of you, and probably will be, too, once someone tells him, as somebody is bound to . . . I know this is new to you, and all that, but honestly it happens all the time, and you'll probably feel this way over and over again. It won't just be me, I'm sure of that; it's not in human nature to fall in love just once. The thing's addictive, like caffeine, or alcohol. You're too warm and generous to avoid it.'

Warren half-bowed, a brittle light shining in his eyes. 'Thanks very much,' he said. I caught at his arm; I couldn't bear that he should leave me like that.

'Oh, I am truly grateful to you for – feeling so much. It does mean a great deal to me, whatever you may think.'

Warren didn't draw away, as perhaps I had expected. Instead he pulled me to him with an almost painful intensity and said: 'If there's ever anything that I can do – ' And I, half-amused at the notion, and half-shaken, allowed him to kiss me.

And that, thought the older Isabel, returning the diaries to their drawer, had been that. Ten years later, Warren had met and married the insipid Caroline, while she, Isabel . . . Oh, she would never marry now, she'd seen too much of it. She had married none of them, of course, and perhaps she had loved none of them either, except for one – and it was hard to remember, all these years later. For the sake of her self-consequence, she wished to believe that she had loved them, but the notion of ever having been fatuous enough to love Clive – Clive Dunsmore of all people! – was too damaging to her self-respect to contemplate.

No, she had been flattered or bored or seduced into imagining that she had loved the others for a time, but that was all. Perhaps she had only ever been in love once, perhaps

Warren had been right when he had said to her, 'The desert is squeezed in the tube-train next to you, the desert is in the heart of your brother.'

'What on earth do you mean?' she had asked sharply, but he had only smiled his thin, twisted little smile and turned away. Poetry, always poetry! Isabel had felt a woman's impatience with the impracticality of the stuff. Why couldn't people simply say what they felt as she always did herself? – or nearly always. It had occurred to her some while later that perhaps Warren had not meant to insult her, that he might have been referring to his own feelings, and yet this notion too failed to satisfy her. She knew he thought her heartless, superficial, unthoughtful, and perhaps she was some of these things – but so were the other members of the orchestra, surely! Why did he sit in judgement only on her? For a time she was cool with him, and then, Isabel-like, contrived to forget it entirely.

As she sat on her bed, the older Isabel tried to recollect other times she had spoken to Warren; there had been thousands, surely, since she had joined the orchestra fifteen years ago. She recalled one evening in particular. He had been giving her a lift to some rehearsal or other, while she had been feeling low, terrible.

'I seem to spend my life drifting from person to person,' she told him. 'I don't think I know exactly what I'm looking for, or how to spot it when I find it. I know, I ought to by now, what I don't want, but that's as far as I get.'

'You drift because you're afraid of loneliness,' Warren replied, not looking at her. 'And what you're looking for is peace within yourself, separate from other people. You'll never be freed from your fears of loneliness until you come to terms with that.'

'Don't be absurd. Why should I ever be lonely?'

Warren made an impatient gesture. 'You always miss the point! I don't know why you are the way you are. Maybe your father preferred your brother to you. Or maybe you were too spoiled to adjust to not being absolutely everyone's darling now. All I know is what you do, and that is to collect people. You collect hearts, do you realize that? Do you have them tacked up on some wall, your monstrous collection, your trophies? You know, I can almost imagine it . . . It's almost obsessional, an insurance against being unloved, or against being alone. But the point isn't why you do it, Isabel, but how you could help yourself by changing. You don't seem to be able to realize that.'

'A collection of hearts,' Isabel murmured, rather caught by the phrase. 'Do I still have yours, Warren? Despite knowing me so well?'

Warren's mouth tightened. 'We're friends, Isabel. You know I'm always here if you need me. I told you that once – in Victoria Station, if you remember.'

'But do you love me? Not as a friend. I need to know, Warren.'

'I've been married for three years!'

'Is that my answer?' she inquired, half-amused but half-affronted.

'No,' Warren admitted, refusing to look at her. 'You know the answer as well as I do.'

His face was already too thin, remembered Isabel, already a little stretched and drawn-looking. But she had kissed him all the same, her friend, her brother, her trophy. It was scarcely credible that he might soon be gone, might even at this moment be slipping away – Warren, who had always been there for her, Warren, for whom unfaithfulness was simply not an option. And she didn't bother to try to smother the tears this time, because her make-up was ruined anyway, and because she knew it was too late to say yes in the middle of rush-hour on Victoria Station.

III

David

(Five years earlier)

Someone just outside his window had decided to dig Athens up and start over, and despite Roger's feeling that something along these lines ought to be attempted – and even his grudging pleasure at this evidence that the hour had produced the man – he woke up fretful and cross.

The previous night had not helped his temper. Roger Ash could not be accused of being the sort of orchestral conductor who shirked his social responsibilities; this was particularly the case when these included the entertainment of a fetching young soprano possessing not a syllable of Greek. However, their evening together had scarcely begun before Roger had elected to drown his companion's whine in the dregs of the local retsina. Singers! Vain, whingeing, self-important, self-deluded hypochondriacs, the lot of them! In which observation there might have been a good deal of solid truth, except that Roger, hypochondria excepted, was otherwise a pattern of the species himself.

The phone rang, interrupting his undiluted contemplation of his aching head. Conductors like Roger lived for the call of the telephone. It was for The Call that they studied extra scores into the night, polished their every orchestral contact, and took their agents – idlers and scroungers to a man – for expensively simple lunches in London. The Call – Abbado down with flu in Tokyo, Muti axed by food poisoning in Rome – that would propel them from the second rank to the first in one long effortless stride. The Call from a recording company, having made the executive decision – intelligently, without a doubt – that Roger Ash was a name to conjure with.

However, it was not The Call. It wasn't even his agent

Irene, chomping her everlasting Churchillian cigars. It was Paul Ellison, the principal oboe of his orchestra, the Orchestra of London, ringing in his secondary capacity as Chairman of the Board. The two men possessed a healthy mutual respect, a respect based on detestation and unsullied by a single gratuitous act of goodwill. Roger suspected – rightly – that Paul was angling to replace him with a more charismatic and gifted conductor; and Paul feared that Roger had the power or the energy to circumvent him.

'Terribly sorry to trouble you so early.'

'Been up for hours,' growled Roger untruthfully. 'Checking out the bloody Ligeti for next week. Is anything wrong?'

'Well, there is a problem. The principal cellist you selected has withdrawn.'

Roger groped in his memory. So many fantastic cellists, so many nationalities. Which had they actually chosen in the end? Paul, irritatingly, anticipated his lapse of concentration.

'You remember, the Scottish fellow. He's been offered more money elsewhere – the Royal Sinfonia is my guess, but he's being cagey, wouldn't say. Anyway, that leaves us with the decision again, and we're under time pressure this time. He's made us look like fools.'

'Sorry, I can't put my finger on my notes,' said Roger, shuffling a few sheets with the letterhead of his hotel on them. 'Just remind me of the top candidates again.'

'There was the Japanese girl, but the section hated her. There was the Yorkshireman, but he was voted against by the other string principals. There was Tranter – terrific technique, great sound – and the young Israeli, Schaedel. It really has to be one of those four, unless we decide to go through the whole audition mess again.'

Roger's soul revolted at that. Nineteen more Dvořáks, overly soulful unaccompanied Bachs, hazardous attempts at the Schumann, and dawn raids on the Shostakovich: so many cellists, thought Roger, so little time. But he was suspicious of

Paul's pat analysis. Paul clearly wanted Tranter, and that in itself was worrying. Hadn't Paul been at music college with Tranter?

'I liked David Schaedel myself,' he said, trying to remember whether he had, through the woolly mists of Athens humidity and the taste of retsina fumes in his mouth.

'Schaedel, um, yes,' said Paul doubtfully. 'He's not got Tranter's experience. The section liked Tranter quite a lot.'

'Marvellous bow control though, and loads of soloistic flair.'

That was safe enough. Hell, music college graduates had that, these days. 'Besides,' added Roger, trying to recall whether it was true, 'I liked Schaedel's attitude. Lots of attack, punchy.'

'The Union'll go berserk. Yet another foreigner plumb in the front of a London section, taking jobs away from British players.'

'Well, yes, but just imagine the publicity. Young Israeli solo sensation, tempted to London for a shot at glory – that sort of angle. Go with Schaedel, Paul. He's definitely the one I'd prefer.'

There was a pause at the London end, interrupted only by the spirited resumption of attack by the man with the pile driver. Roger was able to interpret the silence, correctly, as the sound of a bullet being bitten. Paul wasn't strong enough – yet – to stand against Roger, and, if Roger Ash had his way, he never would be.

'I'll put it to the Board,' said Paul at last, which meant surrender.

Roger suddenly found himself, hangover apart, in an intensely good humour. 'I never really cared for the Scottish chap anyway,' he said, 'brilliant though he admittedly was. Seemed an egotistical type of bastard, on the whole.' Which would, in the history of orchestral appointments, have gone down as one of the truly ironic remarks, except that neither of them knew it.

'It seems such a pity,' said David Schaedel, gazing around him with some disfavour, 'that English women should be, on the whole, so particularly plain.'

'Do you think so?' inquired William.

'Who can think otherwise? They come in but two types – the washed-out and, of course, the too-fat. The slim ones are washed-out, colourless; the fine-complexioned girls are too fat. There are of course also the exceptions, who manage to be both too pale and too big, but these, I grant you, are quite rare. Now in Israel, most of the women, indeed most of the people altogether, have a darker glow to the skin, a better tone to the muscle. You will observe my forearm. This is a good example of my point.'

William Mellor could not be accused of being a temperamental soul. Now fifty-five, he was mature, well-judging, well-respected and collectedly in control of his feelings. The fact that he felt his temperature rising on this occasion was mainly because his new cello principal had been with him, including his first rehearsal, for the last six hours without remission, and there was no rescue in sight. The forearm held out for his inspection, moreover, was still extended. He was clearly expected to say something, so he said it.

'Very fine indeed,' he said, with a smile. David tucked his elbow out of sight, satisfied. Indeed, he felt pleased with life altogether. His new section were not bad players; and the impression he had made on them was obvious. In truth, they were probably too overawed by his skill; later, he must teach them that, although naturally to be looked up to and venerated, he also intended to be their colleague. A fine line to draw, this, but his duty . . . It was at this point that David was startled out of his meditations by an apparition across the floor of the pub, a girl so exquisite in colouring, so well-formed, so –

'Who,' demanded David, 'is that stunning creature?'

William followed his gaze across the crowded pub. Useless

to deny that one girl stood out among the others, her beauty vibrant, expressive and yet to his eyes overlaid with some sense of foreboding, some warning signals: the movements too self-consciously enticing, the smile too swiftly torched or quenched; the sweep of eyelash vulnerable across luminous skin. Useless to deny her superiority, but there was still something unsettling about her. William knew Isabel only slightly, but wished all the same that David had singled out one of the other women – an unreasonable, even absurd possessiveness, he realised, and pushed the thought away.

'I suppose you mean the dark girl,' he replied. 'Her name's Isabel Bonner.'

'She is actually in the orchestra? I did not observe her, as surely I must have, had she been playing.'

'Isabel sits on the last desk of violas,' said William shortly. Some mischief in him considered adding that she was English, but he thought better of it.

Usually the soul of courtesy, William was finding David Schaedel's first day as principal a considerable strain. David had started by shaking the hand of everyone in his new section, at the same time generously informing them that he expected loyalty and support at all times. He had immediately inquired about changing the players' crucial pecking order and then proceeded systematically to destroy the bowings, worked out through the ages and enshrined by obdurate tradition, of Brahms' Fourth Symphony.

The talk at the rehearsal interval had been principally of lynching Roger Ash, although slow-working poisons and boiling oil had also claimed their supporters; while no one, strangely enough, had admitted to missing David's weaknesses during his trial period the previous autumn. In the pub following that first disastrous rehearsal, the atmosphere had blackened still further. Paul Ellison had disclaimed all responsibility in a row with the cello section, who had departed in high dudgeon, leaving David in William's hands, as being the only man diplomatic enough for the task. Not that David was conscious of these machinations. On the contrary, he informed William, his reception had far exceeded his expectations.

'The goodwill of the section,' he said, 'I take for granted. Of course, at first they are overwhelmed by their good fortune, but later, later it will hit them, so! Almost I could see the gratitude, the surprise, dawning in their faces during the first rehearsal. I was moved, I confess, very moved. I did not expect such a reaction – or perhaps, to be honest, I expected it, but not so quickly. My section in Manchester – '

'Did you enjoy working in Manchester?' inquired William, quenching the desire to laugh.

'In some ways it was good for me,' pronounced David. 'I arrived from Israel with all the equipment – the technique, the talent naturally, as well as that little something special which, you will agree, is so rare. And in Manchester I added leadership: the ability to command respect as well as admiration. Manchester gave the – polish, the finesse, to my abilities. However, all my section there were aware that my playing demanded the wider stage; we often spoke of it. The cellists, naturally, were upset when I departed; there was the party for me, and other parties after as well; there was a cake, and many things were said about me. But they accepted that I needed to move on, to progress. Also, there was another reason, a more personal reason. I would not tell this to just anyone you understand, but you are a man of the world – '

'I've been married for twenty-five years,' said William, but more in warning than assent, because he loathed gossip.

'Precisely, and you know therefore what women can be like, especially when, well, certain attributes are involved. I can tell that, when you were younger, you must have been extremely handsome yourself – even now, in a dimmer light perhaps – but, at any rate, there was a woman in my previous orchestra who fell in love with me at first sight, simply captivated, and nothing that I could do could prevent it. The poor girl, how she suffered until I agreed to move into her flat! But later, later it went wrong. You see – '

'Sorry to interrupt,' said William, who could bear no more, 'but I don't believe that you've had the chance to meet Caroline. This is Caroline Wentworth, and Isabel Bonner, both of our esteemed viola section.'

No comparable introduction could have stopped David so effectively in his tracks. He looked closely at Isabel, and his critical eye could discern scarcely a flaw. The mouth possibly – but he preferred generous lips. The floating near-black hair, the exquisite setting of the fine dark eyes, the light tan of the arm exposed to the elbow. He smiled at Caroline (a tolerably pretty girl) before discharging the full battery of his eyes on Isabel.

'Charmed,' he said, displaying his dazzling teeth. 'I am most charmed to meet you.'

'Hello,' said Caroline politely, but Isabel only smiled, too accustomed to admiration for it to make any particular impression upon her. David was certainly good-looking, but she'd heard enough about his arrogance to dispose her against him. Besides, her heart was full of Clive, the boyfriend whose lateness in meeting her had been the cause of her coming to the pub. Mercurial, and temperamentally inclined towards extremes, she felt misery clawing at her. Besides which, she had no desire for her discussion with Caroline to be hijacked by the new principal cellist. William guessed enough of this to feel guilty at having co-opted the two women, but David was unconscious, and Caroline – caught by a little flutter of admiration – his ally.

'Let me get you a drink,' said David. 'No, please, I insist. You, Caroline, what would you most particularly like?'

'A shandy, please,' said Caroline promptly.

'And you, Isabel?'

'Thank you, red wine,' replied Isabel, in resignation. Her eyes flashed a signal of reproach at her friend, which was observed by William, though Caroline misinterpreted it.

'He *is* rather gallant, isn't he? Didn't someone say he was Israeli? They quite often have that swarthiness, I think, plus the flashing eyes. I'd imagined he was Spanish, or perhaps Italian.'

'I'm sorry, Isabel,' said William in an undertone. Isabel glanced up at him, startled at having been understood, though the unhappiness still clawed her.

'It doesn't really matter. Nothing matters very much at the moment.'

'My own feeling,' David was saying to Caroline, 'is that a cello section – or even a viola section, for that matter – is like a ship. Perhaps you have never thought of it, but so it is: the captain who is the principal, his lieutenant, a boatswain perhaps, and then all the sailors who must all pull together. A happy analogy, do you not think? It is my own. Discipline is the most important part, but it must be administered with skill and authority – and tact. Tact is so important and must never be forgotten! The hardest part of leadership is being tactful. There was a player for example in my Manchester section who always – but always – jumped in early. At first I handled this very badly; I said privately to this player, "You are too early, you rush the beat," but this was a mistake. He continued to mistime his entries, so then I realised my error. I called the section together and said – mentioning no names, you understand – that anyone who came in early would be instantly moved to the back of the section. After that, believe me, there was no problem, though sometimes perhaps I felt a little slowness in coming in behind me. Still, that was a lesson to me in how to make the ship run smoothly, a lesson I will not forget. I hope always to be able to learn from such mistakes.'

William, who as associate principal was the new 'lieutenant' of David's ship, had suffered a distinct sinking of heart during this narration. He was about to offer some change of subject to Isabel, when he suddenly noticed her face raised glittering towards the door. A heavy-set fellow carrying a motorcycle helmet had entered and was pushing his way towards them.

'Clive!' said Isabel, rising up and kissing him. The man shoved back his hair gloomily.

'Thought I'd never bloody find you. Didn't you say you'd wait?'

'I did wait,' flashed the girl. 'I waited half an hour. Didn't I, Caroline? I waited for ages.' But Caroline was absorbed in David's description of his audition, and did not attend.

'Oh, sod it. Let's get out of this,' said Clive. 'I left some gear on the bike and don't want it getting nicked. See you outside.'

Isabel slipped on her coat. 'Goodbye everyone, and thanks for the drink, David.'

'But you hardly touched it,' objected David, although she was almost out of the pub by then, moving like water through the crowd. 'Never mind, it will not be wasted,' he added philosophically, adding the remains of her wine to his glass. 'I think I was telling you, Caroline, about what Roger Ash said to me at my audition. "I can tell," he said, "that you have tremendous solo experience, naturally. But what can you tell me about your orchestra background?" So I told him, I said – '

Perhaps there were hidden depths, thought William, his mind still bent on Isabel and her yobbish-looking boyfriend. There had to be some reason for being selected by a girl like Isabel, a girl who could, quite literally, pick and choose. Or perhaps it was a purely physical thing, the animalistic attraction of youth that he'd chosen to obliterate from his own memory. But the explosion of radiance in the girl's face when she had seen Clive in the doorway argued differently, and everyone knew that Isabel's myriad moods were near-reflections of her feelings, whose motives might be argued but whose strength could never be denied. She was a difficult, fascinating creature!

David, meanwhile, was telling the enraptured Caroline about his early concerto triumphs. Seeing that he might himself depart without disruption, William made his excuses and left, closing his coat against the chill January night.

IV

Trial by Orchestra

(from Piotr's private files)

The person I blame is Roger Ash. If Roger hadn't been too busy placating his third wife about that Tokyo business; if the appointment hadn't coincided with the negotiation of his own new contract; if he'd exercised a smidgeon of sense or a scintilla of judgement, everything would have been different. The conductor of an orchestra, hang it all, has a responsibility. The conductor of an orchestra has a Vision – don't give me that kind of look – that's what he tells the press, doesn't he, when he's appointed. A Vision for the Future, no less. A Vision of Excellence, I kid you not. Though if Roger Ash ever had a Vision, which, mind you, I doubt, it'd be leggy, fishnetted and swishing one of those rather complicated leather thong efforts. It was because of Roger's ruddy Vision we got David wished on us in the first place. And because he appointed David –

But let's impose some order on the proceedings, though to do so goes calamitously against the grain. Let's start where the year started, the year that was to go down in Orchestra of London history.

The trouble began with the dignified retirement of the previous cello section principal, Felix Price. Under his leadership – and it was leadership, make no mistake, both hands on the wheel – the cello section had been knitted into a unit reckoned by the *cognoscenti* to be the finest in the country. Once he had honourably retired, mainly in order to splice obscure types of roses onto different sorts of roses, or so it was rumoured, the rot set in.

First of all we had the night-watchman style of William, one of nature's number elevens if ever there was one. It wasn't that

William didn't look the part – tall, elegant, with a mane of silver hair and the most marvellous sculptured face – Hollywood casting, so far as looks went. He was simply too charming, too accommodating, not nearly ruthless enough. His solos were eloquent, even inspired, but as generals go he was a non-starter. Leadership gone, we cellists, notoriously a disparate bunch, started to go our own ways, with the decline of the unison pizzicatos being particularly marked.

Mind you, I won't have William blamed. For a start, he has a noble soul, and n. souls are at a premium in any orchestra, but especially ours. Secondly, he is, was, and ever shall be, my best friend, the person – perhaps the only person – with whom I can be entirely and irreverently myself, completely and astonishingly honest. And besides, William had his own problems at this time, not excluding a wife crippled with a progressive nervous disorder.

At any rate, I was the third cellist of the stricken section, as well as William's confidant. I was also fated to become intimate with the man appointed to the principal cello job over his head, during this splenetic and salacious time. Against all odds, and nearly all advice, our conductor Roger Ash (a perfectly unspeakable man) selected David Schaedel, an Israeli cellist, for the post. Roger must have been dazzled by his technique, which was little short of wizardry, because David, unlike every other Israeli I personally have ever met, was notably short on soul. Indeed it was a matter of lively dispute within the section whether David possessed a soul; the jury being perennially divided on the subject.

But, whether or not in possession of an accredited soul, David boasted many other qualities. First, he was vain to a degree I have never previously witnessed. A slim, tanned, curly-topped youth, he combined a striking muscle structure with a profile enchanting from the left and, as he himself remarked, even more delightful from the right. (This was due to the nose being just crooked enough to interest. Wistful were the speculations that arose about the origin of this injury, but the occasion was never as far as I know determined). David spent an inordinate amount of time thinking about his appearance, whether buying clothes, having his hair styled or procuring professional facials. The shirts he wore were a particular irritant – always silky, in the most outrageous colours, turquoise, mustard, tangerine, scarlet . . . He worked out daily, to keep up the tone of his quite gratuitous muscles, and always practised in front of a mirror, less to keep an eye on his bow arm than to gauge the effect of his every gesture on a possible audience.

Besides which, he was superstitious to the point of lunacy. David deferred most of his movements to a middle-aged woman of dubious origin, who lived, if lived is the word, in a most insalubrious area of Manchester. This soothsayer, whose name I inevitably forget, not only did Tarot cards, read palms and foretold astrological trivia, but decreed, with the assistance of an imagination a fellow artist could not esteem too highly, exactly what would happen to David. Even when she got it wrong (which was rare, as she was clever enough to leave almost everything open to interpretation) he never failed to believe her. I have known him to miss important concerts rather than travel 'across water', which, as he lived south of the river, meant going pretty much anywhere. I have even known him to extricate himself from relationships, if his conquests should be dignified by such a title, rather than disregard a Mancunian warning of 'trouble from dark beings, be they man or woman'.

I recall him once inquiring anxiously about the colour of my eyes.

'I don't know,' I told him, 'judge for yourself. Hazel is what it says on my passport, though I've never been satisfied as to what hazel is.'

'They look brown to me,' he said, with utter dissatisfaction. 'I call that brown.'

'You disappoint me inexpressibly,' I teased him. 'I like to think them odder than that, and very much more amusing. If you look closely there are strange lights in them, greenish lights, and flecks of every colour you can imagine.'

'Well, they're dark anyway,' he retorted, as if that solved everything, as for him, of course, it probably did.

It was Old Eugene who told me why he had been asking, and strangely enough I date David's distrust of me more or less from that date. Not that everything wasn't coming to a head anyway, of course.

Roger had lost confidence in David by February, and privately came close to admitting his error in appointment. Old Eugene, who had sat next to me at cello four since before the Flood, had been shoved back to number five in order to make way for David's favourite, who had scooted up from nowhere. The fact that said favourite was a grisly player and my personal bane did not deter David one whit. Perhaps he was secretly hoping I would get annoyed enough to depart in peace.

If so, he was disappointed. The promotion of Adam Halloran, a poser and a sycophant, only hardened my own determination to subvert David's little plans. The demotion and humiliation of Old Eugene, a battle-scarred veteran with an outstanding number of friends in the orchestra, upset nearly everybody. But what really turned David's unpopularity into the kind of situation crime writers dream of – or perhaps they don't, as that number of suspects would prove technically unwieldy – was his behaviour to Caroline.

Now let me first declare not an interest but a lack thereof. I am, to put it mildly, gay, and Caroline is the kind of girl whose innate girlishness grates upon me. I see no point in denying that she irritated me to the point of rudeness, but nobody, tragically, asks the sub-principal cellist for advice in choosing a viola player. The point is that Roger Ash, after first allowing in Isabel, further muddied the waters by selecting Caroline for the vacancy in the viola section.

Not that Caroline is a flirt in Isabel's class. No, Isabel is the genuine article, from her Cleopatra looks to her Gucci handbags. Isabel is addicted, to love and sex, to pain and power. Isabel is irredeemably passionate, charming, insecure. Isabel is restless, reaching, searching – though what she seeks I don't suppose the girl herself knows. There are so many musicians like that, people who spend their lives looking for something always just beyond their grasp. And when they find it . . . But I grow distracted. We were, were we not, discussing Caroline.

Caroline is a mild and good-natured creature from Shropshire, plump but, I am assured, comely. Comely to David at least, as became rapidly apparent. Besides which, Caroline only told him what he wanted to hear – for example, how fabulous a player he was, and how bitterly misunderstood by such as I. Caroline worshipped David; when he played solos she went weak at the knees, and when he stood alone for the audience's applause it was pretty to see her tremble.

Her devotion did not go unrewarded. After mature consideration of at least a couple of hours, David bedded her; nor were the results of this audacity so displeasing as to preclude a repetition. After unceremoniously dumping the girlfriend he'd left in Manchester (there were reports, one trusts unfounded, that he did the deed by fax), David moved in with pretty Caroline; the fact that her flat was rather superior to his doing nothing to deter him.

In theory domesticity should have calmed the dear boy; in practice, such was not the case. Not a bowing (the hallowed bowings of St Felix of the roses) but David had to alter it, much to the distress and dissatisfaction of the section. And not only that. Not a rehearsal went by without David's wasting as large a part of it as possible in pointless discussions with fellow principals about phrasing and interpretation. And not a day went by in which his drifting little eyes didn't alight upon a woman, whether audience, administration or orchestra, other than our unsuspicious Caroline.

This was the situation then, some months after David's

appointment. He had got rid of his former girlfriend and captured Caroline. The cellos were being stirred to mutiny by the unequal treatment given to Old Eugene, who was popular, and to Adam, who was not. There were rumblings of earthquake-like discontent from the double basses (bullied to victimization point by David, who regarded them, all too obviously, as serfs of his cello section). Roger Ash had reached the point of demanding, like a fellow dictator of former times: 'Oh, who shall rid me, etc.' The hour, I told myself, had produced the man. I was ready, even willing, to do anything, short of murder, which would oblige him.

It was at this strategic moment that Hochler appeared, blindingly polished shoes included, to carry the baton while Roger was being inflicted, for the betterment of his bank balance, on some fellow-sufferers in the Oslo Philharmonic.

V

Verklärte Nacht

(from Isabel's diaries)

He wasn't particularly good-looking; a typical middle-aged middle-European banker type, neither tall nor short, neither fat nor thin, wearing an expensive suit in a faintly old-fashioned style. The world is full of men like this, I thought; they're the stalwarts of every city company, the backbone of every law firm. They only baulk at running their own businesses due to a native conservatism, an innate distaste for risk. They generally have stable if uninspired marriages, and are devoted to their children. This particular specimen probably had a second home in France and a taste for old wines. His gait suggested that, when younger, he might have ridden horses, but we are into the realms of serious speculation here.

I often amuse myself with analyses of guest conductors. There's little enough to occupy the mind of the last player in a viola section; to be truthful, this is true of all non-principal string players, unless the player's one of those irritating types who spend half their lives following up errors in the score and pointing them out to their betters. Intellectual boredom is why you tend to discover back-desk strings well up in Open University courses, active in orchestral politics and generally itching to run the place. Hormonal, I expect; isn't everything these days?

But I am of an exclusively imaginative disposition; studying bores me while committees only make me impatient. I wish I found my work harder, but I have as my first hobby the study of human nature, and find it absorbing enough. Conductors in particular interest me – a peculiar crew, upon the whole – but it isn't often that I find a conductor actively nerve-racking. This conductor shredded my nerves into little pieces.

There was nothing at first to suggest an outcome so spectacular. After making and docketing away the first impressions previously recorded, I settled into his idea of rehearsal routine, something which differs so wildly from conductor to conductor as to be impossible to categorize. Hochler took effortless control of the orchestra, courteously squelching the usual time-wasters, speaking directly to the guts of the bigger sections, treading through the Beethoven without either fussing over details or skating over technical considerations. It was in the middle of the Schoenberg that I realized that my bemused consideration had drawn his attention – in fact, that Hochler, not content with being observed, was watching me.

Now back-desk players are not, as a rule, overjoyed at being picked out by the great and the good. The whole skill of playing in the back of a string section consists of melding so smoothly into the sound – whether the section is (musically speaking) bullish or effeminate or any point in between – that it is impossible for a conductor to spot the cracks. I began to wonder whether I was sticking out – the cardinal sin – or looking too interested, another unprofessional move. I took the edge off my fortes, and started a political discussion with my (rather reactionary) desk-partner. These little ploys failed. The conductor's eyes still seemed to be focussed on me, searching, reaching into me.

I hadn't noticed Hochler's eyes at first, or else that German banker's façade had misled me. His eyes were extraordinary, multi-coloured, depthless, and seemed to be probing un-opened areas of my own – nothing so crude as appearing to notice my body, but nonetheless filling me with an uneasy sensation of raw and sensual power. The first time this occurred, I dropped my gaze, overwhelmed with embarrass-ment, and mine is far too exuberant a nature to be easily embarrassed. This happened during one of those earth-shattering moments in *Verklärte Nacht*, and I remember thinking that he was conducting the piece as if he'd lived it. Perhaps he had; at any rate, he elected to remind us of the plot.

'For any of you young people who have not studied the score, this is a story of a couple, a man and a woman, who go on a walk together. During the course of this walk the woman tells the man that she is going to have a child but' – and this is the point or nub – 'that the child is not his.' Here he paused, just long enough and not a smidgeon longer. 'So then the man says O.K. – and that is it.'

I cannot describe to you the drollness with which Hochler delivered this speech. Those of us who had subconsciously expected Teutonic metaphysics were particularly diverted. He turned around and surveyed us calmly, upon which the laughter dried up.

'Letter M,' he decreed and pressed the starter pedal again.

By the next day, I had forgotten Hochler; I was tied up in knots about my boyfriend Clive, who had, according to an informant in his office, been showing unmistakable signs of friskiness with one of the secretaries. I was trying to take my mind off the subject by chatting to one of the orchestra's nobler souls – there are a few of these in every orchestra, generally lurking in the back of the second violins – when I became aware of Mr Hochler having materialized behind me.

'Hello,' I said, as it is contrary to my foreign policy to be overawed by conductors, however exquisite their musicianship or intimate their glances.

'Good morning,' he replied, with just a hint of a bow, and shimmered podium-wards. 'That man simply terrifies me,' remarked my companion, and I agreed with him.

The orchestra departed for an out-of-town concert that afternoon. Coming back to the concert hall pick-up point I drove past Mr Hochler walking alone, emanating a distinct impression of wistfulness and isolation. I turned around at the traffic lights to watch him until he was out of sight, head slightly bowed, hands jammed into his Savile Row pockets.

That separateness, I wondered: was it the by-product or the cause of his career? And I felt an absurd longing to comfort him. We're in the same boat, I thought; none of us is entirely alone. And I leaned back, feeling as if some barrier had been silently smashed to pieces.

The concert, in a smallish town, was poorly attended – indeed, at the beginning of the second half, from which most of us were omitted, we perched in the audience, roughly doubling their number. I nearly collided with Hochler at the start of the interval. He had conducted so well that, observing his gaze wrapped around me, I impulsively exclaimed, 'You deserve better!'

'So do you!' he responded, seizing both my hands. The expression in his eyes was so intense that, filled with irrepressible elation, panic and nervousness, I was almost sorry I had said anything. Besides which, as everyone knows, it's excessively bad form for a tail-end viola to hob-nob with conductors. Cursing myself for my stupidity, I managed to avoid him during the second half, before returning to the orchestra coach for the long trip back to London.

Absorbed in my own thoughtfulness, I was taken aback by hearing Lucy discussing Hochler directly behind me – Lucy being our requisite local nymphomaniac, a delightfully proportioned girl, further boasting a complete lack of subtlety.

'I liked his arms first,' she explained in a confidential undertone guaranteed to carry the length and breadth of the coach. 'I don't usually go for hairy arms, but when he rolled back his sleeves in the second Schoenberg rehearsal I thought, hey ho, sexy arms. So, I asked him what he was doing for lunch. Let's see, that was the day he arrived.'

'So he was a goner,' suggested Mirabel, a horn player with some experience of Lucy's operations.

'No, don't you see, that was the whole point. He wouldn't come, said he had work to do. Well, that fired me up; I couldn't stop thinking about him then – terrific eyes, have you noticed? I accused him of being stand-offish and he just laughed and said he was free on Tuesday. Well, I dressed fit to kill on Tuesday; you might have seen – my designer green top, little black skirt – and met him for lunch in town. Tried everything – the frontal assault, the brushing-up-against-by-accident, the implied suggestion, everything. He wasn't biting. He just sat there and talked about Munich, didn't even sweat.'

'Perhaps he's gay,' said Mirabel.

'Think I'm daft?' demanded Lucy contemptuously. 'It's all there, under complete control. He was playing with me, kidding me along. He knew the game all right. I've never felt so cheated in my life.'

'Perhaps,' said Mirabel thoughtfully, 'there was some signal that you missed.'

'Signal! Oh, he gives off signals, all right, but it's as if he can't help it, or they're meant for somebody else. Believe me, I know. There's something strange about him.'

'Yes, he can actually conduct,' quipped Mirabel, not without some bitterness.

The last concert in the series was also out of London, though at a better venue. Four of us left town early, to explore a stately home near the concert hall and search out a riverside restaurant. The dinner was particularly successful, at a candle-lit pizzeria, and I was in a relaxed frame of mind when I suddenly felt the peculiar unease that comes with being observed. I turned around to find Mr Hochler acknowledging us in passing, his eyes fixed intently upon me. Seeing him again made me almost too uneasy to eat, and I resolved not to let him unsettle me during the concert. It's perfectly possible for an experienced player to follow a conductor's every gesture without ever looking up; indeed, it's a necessary skill during demanding passage-work. I vowed not to catch his glance, whatever happened.

Naturally enough, I failed. I managed the Schoenberg,

mainly through the luck of being in the second viola section, but in Beethoven's Seventh I got fatally caught up in the music. I forget exactly what Mr Hochler did in the Finale, but it was something deliciously spicy, which pleased me. Involuntarily glancing up, I noticed him watching me out of the corner of his eye. And I couldn't help smiling at him, or perhaps he smiled first and it was catching. And it was one of the good moments, the ones that make the whole thing possible and genuine, even worthwhile. The moment of comradeship – doesn't have to be a conductor, normally isn't – that tells you that we really are in this together, lifted by the strength of the music, beyond time, language, distances, no longer strangers, or perhaps we never were strangers and in that moment simply recognised each other.

I didn't see him after that, didn't really want to, somehow. That rounded, perfect moment, leaning together against the music: that was enough. I may never see him again. Which would I suppose be a shame, because each of us is only allotted a few really good conductors in a lifetime, and, though the pleasure of working with him felt not unmixed with danger, that's surely true of many of life's richest enjoyments. At any rate, we were discussing him after the last concert, two double bass players and I – I can't remember whether I have in these diaries immortalised Nancy and Annette. They're rather attractive and empty-headed, rivals on the double bass, and, more occasionally, rivals in other areas as well.

'I'm so glad to have unloaded Hochler,' sighed Nancy. 'I didn't like to say anything, but I'm sure he had a thing about me, poor man. He just stared at me throughout the concerts, with the most incredible single-mindedness. It very nearly put me off my playing.'

'How can you say that?' interrupted Annette, laughing. 'It was me he was after, believe me. Couldn't take his eyes off me, and gave me the most beautiful smile once, in the middle of the Beethoven. Really, Nancy, you are vain.'

'Oh, he *smiles* at everybody,' scoffed Nancy. 'It's that

smouldering look that *means* something. He has a way of looking at me – really, it's quite frightening – without the shadow of a smile, an almost terrible seriousness. I can hardly describe it.'

'That's funny,' retorted Annette, 'I can. As if he was thinking about undressing you, incredibly slowly, but nothing lewd about it, almost sadly, as if he couldn't help it. There's something quite extraordinarily sexy about him, though you could scarcely call him handsome . . . What do you think, Isabel? You were directly in front of us. Which one was he focussed on, Nancy or me?'

'Sorry,' I replied. 'Can't help you there. I was too busy with the notes to pay attention to him, to be honest.'

You could say that I saw something even as far back as this. You could say I saw the year fanning out dangerous before me, though I did nothing to stop it. I remember wanting to confide in Warren Wilson, about Clive, about Hochler, but our own history seemed to get in the way. Perhaps, once you've put someone through what I once put Warren through, the tenderness between you always has a slightly rancid texture; there are lines you can't bear to cross, subjects of too much resonance to touch on. What I needed I suppose was a woman friend – but I've never had a close woman friend. I passed Warren that night, wishing, even longing to talk to him, but delicacy made me pause, and Warren walked on.

VI

Torelli v. Mirabel

(from Piotr's private files)

Then came the Torelli débâcle. Now I can't tell you offhand whether Antonio Torelli beats his mother, is unkind to animals or plays the piano rottenly. However, I am in a position to authoritatively state that the boy cannot conduct. Some years ago, I kept lizards, though deciding in the end that captivity was unfair on these swift, elegant, cleverly painted creatures. However, I would say at a venture that any one of my lizards, except possibly for Fafner, who was always outstandingly dim, would have been more of an asset on the podium than Antonio Torelli.

Torelli was a composer, one of those neo-Romantic, quasi-minimalist, Pre-Raphaelite and pan-nationalist composers who regularly infest *The Late Show* and are the bane of an orchestra's existence. Almost everything about Torelli was fake. He had divided his life between Switzerland and London, where he had perfected the most toe-curling Italian accent. He claimed that his father, a Swiss civil servant, was a Venetian glassblower, which was actually only his hobby on occasional weekends. His influences, he suggested, ranged from Palestrina to Rossini, but were on the balance of evidence far more likely to have been Andrew Lloyd Webber with an added dollop of the bongo-drum school. Not only that but he felt it due to his heritage (his grandfather, after all, had been born in Palermo) to display his artistic temperament at least four times daily, regardless of wind or weather.

David liked him. They had lunch together before the first rehearsal of the new Torelli commission, and sources close to them admit that a possible new cello concerto might have been touched upon. Their meeting was conducted in an atmosphere of uniform cordiality or, at least, such was the case until a waiter proved slow with Torelli's mousse, which he dashed to the floor in a fit of temper, probably making a fetching and artistic pattern upon the carpet.

The rehearsal of his latest opus was always bound to be fraught. We'd had a tiring recording the day before, the afternoon felt more like morning, and a particularly hungover morning at that. I noticed that Clarence, the second bassoon, looked particularly ill and run-down, also that Isabel was in a state, so nothing new there. Her boyfriend – Clive somebody – by all accounts wasn't working out, though by the look of him (extraordinarily muscle-bound) he worked out quite often enough to be going on with. About the only really cheerful-looking person about the place was the rough-and-ready third horn, Mirabel, but *that* didn't last long into the rehearsal.

The piece was one of those meandering efforts so beloved of the Arts Council, modishly pretentious and creakily old-fashioned by turns. We could have polished it off in half an hour with a proper conductor, but Torelli was historically suspicious of letting any conductor loose on his work, his suspicion not surprisingly coinciding with an occasion where a conductor made a judicious if unauthorised 'cut' of about a third in one of his pieces. Anyway, Torelli reckoned he was a vastly underrated conductor himself.

'Conducting,' he once said in an interview, 'is – how you call it – instinctive. It cannota be taughta. It cannota be learned.'

As the rehearsal wore on, I kept wondering how hard the boy had tried. Time after time he tried to bring in the horns – third horn first, then the principal. Time after time, good old instinct let him down. At one point I could have sworn that his left hand was beating in four and his right in five, which is quite extraordinarily difficult to do, if you've never tried it. *Malheureusement*, however, his piece was written in the time of three. The poor horns stood no chance; the accompanying troops of strings faded into dispirited silence.

'Try it without the horns,' suggested David, and the black look with which Torelli welcomed this proposal suggested that one great cello concerto had just gone the way of all flesh.

'The horns alone,' snarled Torelli. 'Uno, due, go! The third horn! Horn numero tre! What is your name?'

'Mirabel,' replied that individual, without a tremor.

'Mirabella, you are terrible! In alla my life, in orchestras on five continents – five! – I have never meta such incompetence! I give you the beata, I getta no sounda. I give you the next beata, you come in too late – fortissimo, fortissimo, you come in late! I tear my hair, my hairs are torn! I fire you from my work! You go away from my lifa, play in your owna bathroom! Play in a pizza parlour, play on the Northern Line! Where is the manager, the orchestra manager? I needa the manager.'

Susan was already on hand, calm and sensible, but she wasn't given a chance. It was a race between Henry, bitter at the insult to his horn section, and Mirabel, but the race was no contest.

'Listen to me Mr – whatever your name is,' said Mirabel, in such commanding Australian tones that he glanced up in sheer amazement. 'There isn't a horn player in London that could make that entry. There isn't a horn player in the entire world that could make that entry, and the reason – yes, there is a reason – is your beat. You haven't got a beat, mate. You haven't even got a shadow of a beat. Your beat reminds me of my grandmother kneading bread. Your beat reminds me of my best friend's toddler trying to reach something too high for her. Not only that but I think you must be some kind of Bible freak, because your right hand sure the hell doesn't know what your left hand is doing. You want your piece performed – and I'm sure I don't know why, because it's rotten – you get yourself a conductor. A conductor with a beat. That's my advice to you, you can take it or leave it.'

And she stormed offstage left, to a chorus of applause and shuffled feet. Personally, I haven't cheered so much in years. It wasn't just that Torelli had been unforgiveably rude and was hilariously incompetent; it was the pent-up vengefulness of orchestra towards conductors, the feeling of the oppressed towards their oppressors. Oh, I know they're not all like that, but that's sometimes how it feels. Them and Us. Their glory, our serfdom. Their money, our backs. Believe me, I know.

Susan stepped forward into the whirlwind. This was a mistake, as her best friends might well have counselled her.

'Mr Torelli,' she began, and didn't get another word in for minutes. Insults and curses, maledictions on his fate, applications to the Holy Mother, concerts on five continents and upstart horn players – Susie bore the brunt before our fascinated gaze. I especially liked the incandescent bit where the Italian accent became weaker and weaker until it careened out the window altogether, to be superseded by a lively mixture of Swiss and English swearwords. Oh, it was a great day, a memorable day – for everything but music.

In the end Torelli was strait-jacketed away, pink and sputtering, the orchestra released. Whereupon David saw fit to lecture his section in general, and your correspondent most specifically, on giggling and other 'unprofessional behaviour'. Can't say I listened, personally. Old Eugene had just passed a note to me from Isabel.

'Want to play quintets at my flat tonight?'

I turned around and gave her the thumbs-up. Quintets, Mozart quintets but not omitting or indeed stressing the two Brahms, were exactly what the nerve-ends required. An inspired idea . . . And some hours later when the Brahms did start, Warren leaning over his violin, Caroline and Isabel weaving their viola lines together, and it was my song, my bit, my shout, I felt amazing. The music poured out of my instrument in a great liquid stream; there were meadows and mountains in it, fields and rivers, the music was a river itself, leaping over little waterfalls and catapulting down valleys. Nothing can touch you at a time like that; all the niggling irritations of life are flooded away. You're not even mortal, caught up in that wide glorious flow; no, you're God and all his angels and you know you'll never want to come down to earth again.

VII

The Dragon's Will

(from Isabel's diaries)

I did the dragon's will until you came
Because I had fancied love a casual
Improvisation, or a settled game
That followed if I let the kerchief fall:
Those deeds were best that gave the minute wings
And heavenly music if they gave it wit
And then you stood among the dragon-rings.
I mocked, being crazy, but you mastered it
And broke the chain and set my ankles free;
St. George or else a pagan Perseus;
And now we stare astonished at the sea,
And a miraculous strange bird shrieks at us.

Yeats

It began, as such things always begin, out of misery. Clive had finally, out of selfishness or kindness or whatever excuse came first to hand, told me the truth, and the truth had beaten me.

Oh, let's be honest, here if nowhere else. It wasn't as if I hadn't guessed, even known, that he was unfaithful; if experience has taught me anything, which I sometimes doubt, it's that everyone is unfaithful, in their fashion. No, what made it so bitter was the resonances Clive's words stirred in me, the recognition of a loss that spelled defeat. And perhaps some part of myself had imagined that, at some point, after waiting long enough, Clive and I might marry, give my mother a heart attack, conform, just for once, make a change. I'd even gone so far as to imagine it: myself in cream (white wouldn't suit me), my younger sisters in yellow (which wouldn't suit them either), daffodils all over the church, a spring wedding, complete with trumpets. Somehow, having imagined it made it seem worse, a bleaker betrayal, very nearly a broken engagement. Besides which, being on tour and being told on the phone made it harder to bear. There was no one I could feel comfortable talking to, no one I could trust not to subtly blame me. There was of course Warren, devoted, trustworthy, but his eyes would reproach me unbearably and we would both know, beyond all truthfulness, that I was using him.

Instead, I spent two hours before the dawn writing Clive a letter that I knew I could never actually send. I have a theory (and my one-time therapist quite agreed with me) that we should all be forced to write, completely honestly, no holds barred, for an hour every day. It's possible then that murders, beatings – everything we so enjoyably deplore in the morning paper – would sink without trace. At any rate, the exercise of writing, gouging it out of the system, did help me. I arrived at breakfast limp but comforted, an extra dose of make-up obscuring puffed eyes and a pallor excessive by anyone's standards.

Warren stared at me, undeceived as usual. I could practically watch his mind whirring, deducing, weighing the evidence – wrongly, I suspected, in this case. Not that we could have spoken of it without discomfort. We both knew, and I knew clearer than usual that morning, how ruinous caring even a little is to the nervous system. I sometimes wonder how Warren, given the acuteness of his sensibility, ever survives anything.

We flew to Lyons after breakfast, and I was grateful to find myself seated next to William on the flight. William was undemanding, unpredatory; William would let me be still with my wounds. I longed for peacefulness, even as my brain rushed, bruised, around the same cage. The truth was, as perhaps I'd always suspected, that Clive had never had any interest in me as a person. I'd tried to imagine that he was afraid of becoming emotionally entangled, but I didn't believe it. For Clive I had been a status symbol, a diversion, a turn-on, and anything else you can imagine which lessens in attraction with time. My mind was the only part of myself which had never held any appeal for him. And in this he was so strikingly similar to my previous lovers that I felt sudden tears slipping out of the corners of my eyes. I remember wondering whether I was only capable of attracting the kind of man who had no genuine interest in people, Warren excepted of course. Or perhaps – even worse, that I'm only attracted to people who are unable emotionally to answer me. I flicked the tears up onto my temples, casting a quick glance at William to check that he hadn't noticed.

But William had noticed. A distinguished-looking older man, the cello section's aristocrat (Winchester and Oxford, for his sins) there's very little which escapes his notice. He's one of the few members of the orchestra whom I suspect of knowing about the strange and resonant misalliance I had once slipped into with Warren. He's also probably the only one I would trust not to tell anyone about it.

'Are you all right?' he asked in a low voice.

I nodded and turned back to the window.

'If someone's making your life difficult – ' said William abruptly, and as abruptly halted. He was thinking of Roger Ash, the principal conductor, I suppose, or Paul Ellison, another of those men (every orchestra possesses some) whose hobby is playing women like practising scales, first up then down then on to the next one. I'd had my troubles with Roger in the past, and Paul has more than once indicated his availability, but, even in my single phases, I could never help remembering Paul's wife, that pretty, tight-pinched face. The face of someone who keeps trying, in the teeth of the odds, but who's been made to suffer for it. Something in that face has never left me; I don't know why not. I roused myself to respond to William.

'No, nothing like that. I'm just a bit tired,' I lied, summoning up a smile.

'I've often wondered what it must feel like to be a woman in this orchestra,' he said thoughtfully. 'The power lies so obviously elsewhere.'

'That's true of back-desk players in every orchestra,' I admitted. 'We never know where we are, or whether or not we'll be needed at all. Some players thrive on it; the rest of us adjust. It's all part of the deal, I suppose.'

'Did you ever try for a higher position?' he asked, bending his still-glowing brown eyes towards me until I forgot his age, forgot the fact that he'd become a grandfather, forgot everything, turning to the window as if it offered some escape. Such an ordinary question! – and such extraordinary feelings.

'Long story,' I said, breathing more quickly.

'Sorry,' he said.

'Don't worry about it.'

The silence between us pulsed, a warm, almost palpable thing, as if some dangerous admission had been made. The engines roared down the runway; the plane churned doggedly off the ground. Other people's voices rose around us, cocooning us against observation, doubtfulness.

'I always thought,' I said dreamily, 'that by the time I was thirty I would have my whole life straightened out. That I would understand everything, and believe in nothing; that some part of me would have completely grown up.'

'And I'm in a position to tell you that it will never happen,' said William, with a little smile.

I don't remember much about the next couple of days. We toured Luxembourg and France; I didn't record anything here because I didn't feel up to it. I was down, very down, and hit the valium I still carry with me, just to get through the concerts. It tends to make me feel dozier as well as calmer, however, so I expect it was the fault of the tranquillizers that I wound up confiding in Mirabel.

Mirabel's the newish third horn, the first ever female in that section, more or less appointed over Henry's dead body.

Australian, attractive in a mannish, confident sort of fashion, but solidly built and easily five feet ten. I remember when she first came we were all amazed to hear that she was straight; but in fact she's married, to some scientist, mathematician, something along those lines. However, the point to remember about Mirabel, other than the fact that she's generous and warm-hearted and a fantastic horn player, is that she has absolutely zero tact. There's a bulldozer-like simplicity about her which is both winning and frightening — frightening because she's afraid of nobody. Roger Ash — any conductor — she'll take them on. That's probably why the men in the horn section like her. She says the things they might think, all right, but have too acute a sense of self-preservation to put into words.

Anyway, I ran into Mirabel in Strasbourg, in the hotel lobby. She'd missed the rest of the horns — they hunt in packs, as a general rule — and we agreed to have a meal. I remember thinking, here's one person who'll never tempt me to reveal all, but it just goes to show how wrong you can be, because Mirabel was in strangely mellow mood. A conductor could have messed about with whole bars of phrasing and she wouldn't have minded. Softened, that's what she was. It turned out to be her wedding anniversary; and she waxed lyrical about her angel-in-scientific-disguise husband and how devastated she was to miss being with him on the day.

I don't suppose, off-hand, anyone could have conceived a story more likely to affect me. Here I was, mourning the marriage that would never happen, and along comes poor Mirabel, unknowingly unleashing every valium-blocked tear.

We finished up in her room, talking till three in the morning. She couldn't have been more supportive, once I'd told all — or more indignant with Clive. It made me feel almost peaceful, to hear her railing against him — not in the vindictive way some women in the orchestra might have, but with a heavy wallop of generous spirit. I felt drained the next morning, but more resigned; I didn't regret confiding in Mirabel.

Not, that is, until my attention was drawn to the not-so-useful side of her hot-headed nature. Mirabel, who couldn't keep the knee operation of her great aunt to herself, had a field day with Clive's rejection of me. By mid-morning the brass and winds were all abreast, the strings baying in hot pursuit, with the last (probably Clarence, who inhabits another world) bringing up the rear somewhere around evening. Nor was there any secret about how Mirabel viewed the situation. No, Clive was deceiving himself if he supposed that Mirabel, having once spoken to him in the Barbican car park, ever intended speaking to him again.

Around noon I became aware of a tidal wave of orchestral interest bearing down upon me. This betrayed itself in all kinds of ways, from messages of support which I could just about cope with, to attentions I could more happily have done without. Specifically, I became target-practice for Paul Ellison.

Writing this now, weeks later (I get so behind with my diary on tours), I don't know why it became more than I could bear. It's often like that abroad: time becomes telescoped, intensified. Days seem to last forever and minor feelings become magnified wildly beyond their normal scope. Perhaps I'd hoped to reduce these effects with the pills, but towards the end of the week I was simply drifting. In theory, I could have been scooped up by almost anybody; in practice, no one but Paul would have tried. To somebody like Paul, always alert for a chance to turn any situation to advantage, the knowledge of my break-up with Clive simply represented opportunity.

We happened to be at a party, a reception thrown by the sponsors, thick with wine and cigarette smoke, French civic dignitaries and altogether too many speeches. The concert had gone well and Roger Ash was responding in that halting pigeon-French which so endears him to the natives, when Paul suggested to me that we slip out. Easily enough done, as we were on the end table – and in a few moments we were breathing the clear night air. The combination of the chill and the drugs and the wine and the concert made my head light; for the first time since unburdening myself to Mirabel I felt practically well, practically normal. Paul slipped his arm around me and I remember thinking that he felt more solid than I'd imagined – still, must be forty by now, and the thick, wavy, red-gold hair that he'd always been so vain about had become trimmed with flecks of grey.

I wasn't ignorant of Paul's almighty conceit even then. It was simply that various factors at the time made me feel tolerant of his faults. And, physically anyway, he hasn't many. His hair is still pretty fantastic, and (more crucially) he knows how to use his eyes, his hands, his body. Most of all, he knows how to play on his deep, expressive voice. A phenomenal first oboist by profession, he employs his voice like the lower strings of a cello, every nuance virtuosically calculated, which is to say, so well calculated as to sound improvised.

'You're so beautiful,' he breathed – which is not a sentiment that I ever tire of hearing. The more beautiful you happen to be born – and I was born fairly spectacularly beautiful – the more beauty comes to matter to you. It's the Marilyn Monroes who obsessively dread old age and the loss of their attractions; Mrs Jones down at the laundromat would scoff at such a notion. Beauty can become part of our identity, like a job or a family or a vocation; its desertion can feel like redundancy, even death. My share of beauty is still present, still slogging away at the same stand, but the sun is just dipping over the horizon and nothing living lasts forever. I shivered in the night, as Paul tightened his arms around me.

'I was watching you tonight,' he said, 'while you were playing. Your face got rosier towards the corners of your mouth in the fast sections, as if a torch lit underneath was waxing and waning. And towards the end of the symphony the lights and the heat had unspun individual curls on your neck until the tendrils stood out like dark little springs. I wanted to touch your hair so badly tonight.'

Not unpoetic stuff, you must admit. Perhaps there's an art in seduction as well as playing the oboe; or perhaps seducers see differently from the rest of us. Of all the people who had observed me that night – audience, conductor, fellow players – how many had seen what Paul had seen? The temptress, the collector, as Warren would have put it, was satisfied. Oh, I knew what Paul was up to; but I didn't much care. I wondered briefly whether it was Clive I was missing or this – the kick of erotic uncertainty, on with the dance.

'You may touch my hair now,' I told him softly.

We had wandered far enough from the patio for the lights of the reception to have dimmed. Paul pulled me towards him under a tree and kissed me with a good deal of expertise. His hand slid up my back inside my blouse and I was just beginning to wake up to what was going on when a large figure loomed up out of the darkness. I pulled frantically away from Paul with a little cry. All kinds of horrible fancies flitted into my tipsy brain: 'Musicians found murdered in Strasbourg Park', 'Fiend axes symphonic duo' – Then I saw that the axe fiend was William. My breathing eased, but Paul's didn't.

'What do you mean, rearing up like a bloody ghost?' he demanded.

William regarded him steadily. 'I walked up from the concert hall,' he said calmly, but with an undertone of contempt it would have been hard to miss. 'I didn't see that anyone was here. I'm sorry I startled you, Isabel.'

My head had cooled and, summoned up by William's attitude, I saw again that image of Paul's wife, the lines of restrained misery cut into that pointed face. William turned to leave us, but I caught his arm, suddenly certain.

'Wait, I'm coming with you.'

'What!' expostulated Paul.

'I'm ready to go back. I – feel better now. Goodnight, Paul.'

Unsurprisingly, Paul failed to respond to this. He swivelled on his heel and plunged deeper into the darkness. Leading me back towards the patio, William did not return my pressure on his arm; he looked serious and tired. When we reached the patio, from where the noise and heat of the reception rose to meet us, he gently disentangled his arm from mine.

'I know you're rebounding, Isabel,' he said quietly, 'but you don't want people talking about us as well, do you?'

I stopped him. 'Please, William, wait!'

Courteously, he paused, but he didn't look at me.

'I wouldn't have let him,' I pleaded. 'It was only loneliness. This week has felt so unbearably lonely.'

'You don't have to make excuses to me,' he told me, his hand still on the door. 'What happened out there has nothing to do with me at all. I absolve myself of responsibility. If you left Paul, you chose to do it; your decision, your free will.'

'That's not true, that's – only partly true. I left because you woke me up to what was happening, and I'm – grateful to you, that's all.'

'Listen,' William said, suddenly turning on me. 'You may be unhappy; you may be miserable. But you don't need to sacrifice your self-respect. There's more to you than this – febrile aimlessness, Isabel. Don't waste yourself on people who only want to use you at a time like this. You know what Paul is as well as I do – better, perhaps. People suppose that men like Paul love women, but the truth is that they hate, fear and despise women, except as an adjunct to their own satisfactions . . . This has been the pattern of Paul's life; he's become addicted to the game. It's all too easy for us to slip into such self-destructive behaviour, like the women who marry three alcoholics in a row, or who continue to choose the kind of men who abuse women. You're caught in a pattern yourself; you're trapped just as much as Paul is. If you're honest with yourself you'll spot it, even break through it. That is, if you confront the truth, if you can summon enough nerve.'

'What pattern do you mean?' I asked him.

He looked at me as if surprised by the question. 'The desire to fail with men – the longing to be used.'

He left me. I yearned for him to stay, but could think of

49

nothing further to detain him. I followed him inside after a moment, walking slowly, completely dazed. I watched him leaning down to discuss some boring cello situation with David Schaedel, saw him cornered by two of the sponsors' wives. I don't think I'd ever noticed before how broad his shoulders were, or how the smoothed-out silver of his hair became him. Warren came up to speak to me; I hardly heard what he was saying. His keen eyes, questioning me, weighing me up, made me momentarily nervous; I knew it was useless hiding anything from Warren. But that didn't stop my own gaze from following William, as if he was the last hope left to me on earth.

Behind as usual. So far behind that to recall everything will be a struggle. The tour progressed into Belgium. Mirabel, informed of my annoyance, apologised for broadcasting Clive's rejection on the six o'clock news. Of course I forgave her. She's too direct, too passionately Australian, and yet – I trust her. I trust her more than I trust myself. Her integrity is perfect. What does it say for the rest of us, when a character of such radiant, such transcendent honesty proves more a handicap than an advantage? What does it say about honesty itself?

Paul, meanwhile, refused to give up: he called me at two in the morning, a few days later, after a late concert and still later meal. I fobbed him off with meaningless excuses, wondering afterwards why I hadn't told him the truth – that I'd seen through him too far to let him near me ever again.

I couldn't get William's words out of my head – worse, I couldn't get William out of it. Whether we were just filing on to a plane, lounging around a hotel lobby, or playing a concert, I was conscious of him, aware of every turn of his cello bow, every line of his back. When he spoke to other people, went out for a meal with the iridescent Piotr, said a few kind words to Caroline, I registered him: not just the minutest physical details – the unusual thumb curve, the faint bruising under his eyes – but the subtlest mental shadings too. When he looked especially worn I noticed it, and when people mentioned him I felt my every sense straining towards the sound. I felt shy about speaking to him myself, guessing that his knowledge of my weakness must have condemned me forever in his eyes – yet I cherished every polite nod of greeting, every time he opened a door for me, beyond all reason. Can I spell it out more clearly? I was completely infatuated with him. The years between us – previously reckoned an insuperable barrier – were nothing. He understood me; the headiness of that outweighed everything. The knowledge of his wife's nervous disorder occupied my conscience in a way unmistakeable to one as versed in the signs as I was. I was in love; long before he spoke to me again, I was beyond saving.

It was almost the last night of the tour before he next spoke – really spoke – to me again. I had been drinking in the hotel bar with Warren and Clarence, while observing Paul's perfect readiness to improve Nancy's self-image. I wondered vaguely whether he'd succeed, and I thought how strange it is that we can, in the space of about a week, go through so many changes of feeling and sensation as to regard as a near-stranger the person that we were before. I wouldn't have allowed Paul to kiss me that night for thousands of pounds; yet the previous week, in the darkness, I had completely surrendered to the pleasure of it.

William entered, saw the group, and seemed on the point of going out again when Piotr forestalled him. Clarence, just getting another round, paused on his route to ask what he wanted to drink, and he eventually joined us. I can't remember how the others drifted away, or why William stayed behind. It's all a blur to me until I said: 'Thank you for the other night.'

He made a dismissive gesture; I noted, hungry for every lunatic detail, the trickling of tiny lines along the muscles of his hands.

'I have forgotten it,' he told me.

'I haven't. Not a word.'

He had probably merely meant to be gallant, and was taken aback by my sincerity. It propelled him however, as it was meant to, into a higher gear.

'Warren was talking about you the other night,' he said. 'You and Paul. He said something like this: "My observation suggests that we put a higher value on the people who refuse to recognise us. There's hardly a man in the orchestra who doesn't treat Isabel with more affection and respect than Paul does, so naturally enough she prefers Paul." '

I flushed. 'I don't prefer him.'

'Perhaps not. It was simply a notion of Warren's. He is observant, you must admit, in a general way.'

'I can't deny that Paul is attractive – was attractive – to me. It wasn't until the other night that I realised – '

'I don't feel I'm the right person to hear this,' said William quickly. 'I spoke out of turn to you the other night, said things I had no right to say. I'm friendly with Paul and mean to stay friendly with him, for professional reasons. He's given me to understand that he regards my behaviour the other night as uncalled for. I told him that it had nothing to do with me, but he didn't seem to believe me.'

'But it did – it did have something to do with you,' I told him passionately, and could say no more. William sat looking at me in a puzzled fashion; and I felt so unbearably fond of him that I leaned over and kissed him. His lips were warm, too warm, the warmest I could remember. I had to will mine to break away, regretting the contact, regretting the separation. I saw his knuckles whiten against the table and felt myself flushing. It wasn't possible. He wasn't the type. But my pulse pounded a different message, of fear and elation and complete and utter certainty.

'Sorry,' I told him.

'No trouble.'

'I think – I think it was the wine.'

'We will say,' said William lightly, 'it was the wine.'

But it wasn't, I knew. I watched his hand unfold itself securely against the table. It was a strong hand, a strong person, the kind of adult proof against my impulses. But when I looked up I found he was emptying his weighted eyes into mine, and when he spoke I didn't know whether or not to be reassured.

'There's no point in lying to yourself,' he said softly. 'Not about Paul, not about me. You must know how I feel, Isabel, though I've no right to feel it. The power is in your hands. A single word, one look, would be enough.'

I raised my eyes wordlessly from his hands. The poetry had stealt over me as he had spoken, along with the old recklessness. If love was a foreign country, let him be my interpreter; my conscience, so long quiescent, stirred and was still. I felt the rush of blood that accompanies danger and I watched as he submissively lifted my wrist to his lips, as though he had been dealt a blow that he scarcely deserved.

The tour over, the next few weeks brought a series of vexing and irritating situations. Clive had moved out in the interval, taking a number of my possessions with him; some of these he returned, after legal threats, some I never saw again. Some I felt almost relieved not to see again, the flotsam and jetsam of a relationship which seemed by then to have belonged to the Middle Ages.

The orchestra had fewer concerts than usual, or perhaps it merely seemed that way. William took leave; his wife was worse. She was periodically worse; multiple sclerosis seems to do that to its victims. I tried to push him to the back of my mind. When I remembered what he'd said on tour – and I did remember, every day I remembered – it seemed that only one construction could be put upon his words. Yet I couldn't believe the construction. I wonder now, looking back, if this wasn't because I almost didn't want anything to happen, that I was in the mood for an idealized, courtly romance, the kind of ritual that Warren had seemed to provide when we were younger. I wanted a complete change from the Clives and the Pauls – to break the pattern, as he had put it himself. Well, I'd certainly done that already. I'd fallen for someone older, deeper, more sensual, more controlled, and I couldn't have him; his marriage, his marriage stuck in my throat. I was miserable; and I could tell that he was miserable too.

When he came back, I read it in his face, in the studied way he avoided the usual pub after concerts, in the weary lines of his eyes. But he actually said nothing. It was Piotr, his friend (and that friendship one of the oddest in the orchestra: the philosopher and the voluptuary, the lion and the fox), who exploded at me. Yet even Piotr's explosions had style. An avowed anarchist, a writer *manqué*, lost, I sometimes thought, to everything except gay sex and the more prurient strands of human interest, he let me have it between the eyes.

'You bloody women,' he said. 'With your bloody manipulations and your trivial campaigns . . . You reduce me to tears, you know, but you'll drive him to madness. He can't take it, the way your eyes soften when you watch him, the way you make your dress swing when you walk by. You do these things; I've seen you; I don't miss much. He enters a room and you're plugged into a socket, lit up, there's a vibrancy around you. What the hell do you want with him, anyway? He's not your sort, Isabel; he's nobody's plaything; he doesn't deserve it. Oh, I know women's ways; you want to tear him down, teach him to water your pretty little feet with tears. And it might just work too, because he's sore tried with his wife and it's all there in his nature, coiled up and ready to take off. But there's a greatness in him that you could no more own than you could own the world, Isabel. He's greater than all the rest of the band put together. He's been worn down by more trials than you could very well imagine – believe me, I know. And I know that any victory you might have will last only as long as it takes him to get up off the floor and flagellate himself for it. Move on, Isabel. You've gone clean out of your class.'

54

I couldn't understand why this speech made me feel so fragile. The insults fell away from me, the jeering, misogynist tone washed over me. The authentic voice of Piotr overrode these, hard though he fought against it, the authentic worry of someone who loved William like a brother. I think my tears frightened him, unused as he is to being seen through by other people. I kissed him on the cheek and left him staring after me across the instrument storage room. I walked into the ice-clear sunshine – March sunshine, that rarest, most refreshing of varieties – convinced that he was right, that nothing could happen, that I was freed, freed from the weight of desire I'd been carrying, freed from the longing to conquer and be conquered.

How peculiarly wrong we can be! We were playing in the Barbican not a week later when I knew that nothing had changed. William had arrived in a very odd mood, reckless, funny. I saw him teasing David in rehearsal, something he normally never does (and which David, lacking humour, never even recognises), and caught his eye. Instead of turning away, he smiled at me, so mischievous a look that I was gone again, disastrously gone, completely elated. I had become pure desire, a single, drowning momentum. I saw him sitting in the darkened auditorium before the concert and joined him; then I lied, leaning back against my seat.

'I dreamed about you last night,' I told him.

'Was it good?' he asked impishly. 'Did you enjoy it?'

'How do you know what I dreamed?'

'I can guess.'

'You're extremely impertinent.'

'You brought it up. I need never have known.'

'And you still don't know. It's all guesswork.'

'My dreams,' he told me with a flash of intensity, 'happen all the time, not only at night. I carry you with me every moment, the way you move, the way your voice lifts when you speak, everything.'

I should have become used to his startling switches from

55

light into darkness, but still he took me by surprise. My heart jumped sideways, the way it does, and the hall seemed breathlessly still, the far-away noises of people rearranging music and tuning harps suddenly distanced, muted by shadow.

I turned towards him, just caught the stage light reflected in his dark, pain-shaped eyes.

'Kiss me,' I begged him, but he was already there, his mouth closing down on my words, and I was nothing but the nerve-ends of sensation, everything else blown warm away. And I knew I must have him, if it killed us both, if the world itself went into meltdown. It was so terrifying, so certain, that had he pulled me down between the rows of seats I would have made no objection – but he forced himself to stop, stood up, passed his hand over his forehead.

'I'll call you,' he said, almost inaudibly, and walked steadily along the rows of seats and towards the stage.

The orchestra was free for the next two days, and I thought he'd never call me. Piotr would argue him out of it, I thought; his wife would sense something odd about him; something would happen to prevent it. But he did call, late on the second day. His voice sounded formal, businesslike, but I'd learned by then how swiftly it could alter.

'Isabel? William. I called to apologise. I – I was going to write, but it didn't work on paper. I'm very sorry about the other day. The situation with my wife is . . . unusually difficult, or perhaps it only feels worse, feeling – having grown to know you better.'

His voice had already warmed; I thought again how powerful a tool it was, but rough-hewn, not oiled, as Paul's was. Like an unfinished sculpture which still says enough.

'I don't want an apology,' I replied quickly.

'And what you want, what you seem to want, I can't give you, Isabel. I can't. I want you, you know that, but I could no more take you than I could sweep the moon down from the sky. My feelings, which are just about containable now, would completely finish me. Choose someone else, for both our sakes. I can't answer for the effect you have on me.'

'I can't do that.'

'Why not? So beautiful, so flamboyant – everybody wants you. You don't need me, Isabel; you're still young. This is nothing but an overreaction to your mistakes with other men. Believe me, you'll be grateful for resisting this someday.'

'Grateful! For being rejected by the first person I've really loved!'

'You imagine you love me because I'm safe. But I'm not safe, not any longer. You've changed me, or time has changed me, or the orchestra's changed me, but I'm not the person you imagine I am. I'm as capable as anyone of using you, to show that I'm still attractive to women, to prove to myself that the passion I've restrained for so long is still capable of firing. I'm warning you off me, in the clearest terms I can use. Find an undamaged man, someone gentle and kind. Don't let any of us use you anymore.'

'I don't want you because you're safe,' I told him, wondering whether it was true. 'I love the danger, the precarious balance of forces inside you. I love the struggles you're going through, the very conscience that's berating you! I couldn't give you up if I wanted to, and I don't want to.'

'My dear, you haven't tried. Have you thought what people would say? The horrible comments, the sniggering gossip? Have you considered how it would look to the outside world?'

I don't believe I had, strange though it seems now. I'm always so obsessive about appearances, which is why I was so furious at Mirabel for presenting me to the orchestra as a rejected lover (which is, of course, exactly what I was). I wondered what Mirabel would think if she knew about William – she would be shocked; there was a streak of antipodean puritanism in Mirabel. I imagined Piotr's contempt, Caroline's surprise, how bad Warren would feel. I felt a flutter of panic, but the memory of William's lips, strong enclosing shoulders flicked it away.

'I'm past caring,' I admitted.

'You're not in my position. Think how it would look, at my age, with my wife's illness.'

'People would understand. Everyone knows how – impossible it must be for you sometimes.'

'Do you think I actually want people to understand that?'

The cry was from the heart. Poor William, with his private wounds – except that nothing is private in an orchestra, and everyone knew that his wife had been practically bedridden for years. I remember the first time I heard it, wondering how a marriage could survive anything as terrible as that. Later, admiring William's strong-mindedness, I supposed it might be possible. In his tone now I heard everything: the impossibility of bearing it, and his determination to bear it anyway. 'He's greater than the rest of us put together,' Piotr had sworn, and Piotr was right.

I lack nobility myself, but, like Piotr, I am attracted by it. Wasn't it his lines of suffering that had drawn me to William in the first place? He had become reshaped, defined by pain, not, as most of us would be, into fretful weakness but into character and strength. There's simply nothing more attractive than that, to my mind; nothing more deserving of admiration.

'Oh, William,' I said impulsively, 'Piotr was right. I'm not fit to speak to you.'

'Piotr said what?'

'Never mind. Forgive me. All this is entirely my fault. All you did was express an interest in helping me and then I – I suddenly realised what you were like.'

'No, no, you idealise me. I'm exactly the same as everybody else.'

'I'll try to believe that, for your sake. I'll try not to make it any harder.'

'Thank you,' he said quietly, and rang off.

★

You know the rest, must have guessed it. It wasn't that I hadn't meant what I told him, or that there was a moment – or any moment I could identify, at least – when I realised that there was nothing I could do. It was simpler than that, too simple, as simple and wordless as possible, a matter of a pause outside my hotel room, a single look exchanged and my leaving the door ajar behind me. I heard him follow me but was afraid to turn around. He lifted me; I smothered a little cry. Once he'd put me down on the bed he peeled off each layer of clothing lingeringly; his concentration almost frightening me. Then his fingers started spreading my hair out behind the pillow, pulsing along the line of my back, following the curve of breast, just caressing the flesh of my inner thigh. I was burning long before he joined with me; I was aching with surging sweetness; and I knew in that completion that this was a pivot point, the end, the beginning, of everything, and that I would never know light without darkness again.

VIII

Watcher on the Balcony

– music heard so deeply
That it is not heard at all, but you are the music
While the music lasts.

T.S. Eliot

She was there every week when the orchestra played, sitting in the same seat, a slim, still little woman in her middle thirties. Piotr, who awarded everyone, in and outside the orchestra, nicknames of merciless brutality, had christened her Pym's Delight, seeing in her primly folded hands and shapeless grey coats a typical Barbara Pym heroine. In this however he did her an injustice, for, although she regularly assisted at vicarage jumble sales, she did so purely to oblige her mother, and, although unmarried, she was guiltless of an obsessive interest in clergymen.

Elinor Jay was a romantic. A personal assistant by day, in one of those anonymous City firms whose activities, while pumping the lifeblood of the economy, make for dull reading, she became by night the heroine of her own lively imagination. She had first attended an Orchestra of London concert on a blind date with one of her brother's estate agent friends. Not having been taken to any concert since her schooldays, she had been enraptured by Tchaikovsky's *Romeo and Juliet*, by Alfred Brendel's piano playing, and by the collection of beautifully dressed men (and, more occasionally, women) before her on the stage. She began weaving stories about them, captivated by the extraordinary variation in the apparent involvement of the performers, the characteristic differences in playing styles, the complete experience.

At work the next day, she telephoned and took messages hardly conscious of what she was doing. On her way home she stopped in a record shop and with reckless extravagance bought four compact discs of the orchestra she had heard, including one consisting entirely of works by Webern which, from that day to this, she could never bear to listen to. This recording included a picture of the orchestra; she pored over this, trying to recall which of the players' looks had particularly appealed to her. From that concert onwards, and despite an irrevocable distaste for estate agents, Elinor Jay was addicted to the Orchestra of London.

Two years, a change of job and a succession of still less interesting blind dates later, her situation remained unaltered. Her brother had given up any notion of marrying her off; anyway, she seemed perfectly content with her life, consisting as it did of office routine, visits to her mother, the occasional dinner with married friends, and the Orchestra of London. Elinor attended every concert the orchestra gave in town, unless her mother, Pinner's premier hypochondriac, insisted she was ill and claimed her attendance. She became a 'Friend' of the orchestra, which entitled her to a jogging outfit in a particularly vile shade of pink and tickets to a couple of cocktail-type functions a year. She took to fundraising with a convert's zeal, button-holing her acquaintances to complain about Arts Council policy and the lack of government support for music. And she bought recordings, every CD the orchestra made, regardless of her own musical preferences – though these too had developed; she was quite capable by then of preferring Mahler to Bruckner and middle Beethoven to late. Yet it was more than the music itself which obsessed her.

Occasionally, on her way back to her car after a Festival Hall concert, Elinor would glimpse an orchestra member, dressed like anyone else (or rather worse), walking to the artists' car park or Waterloo Station. At first she was disconcerted by their very ordinariness, even disappointed. Later, their apparent normality excited her, and she toyed with the idea that she might accidentally meet a player, even one of her favourites. She rushed out of the hall in order not to miss any chance, then dawdled around the stage door as the musicians hurtled out. They usually separated almost immediately into those sprinting for trains, heading towards the car park, or aiming for the nearest pub. However, fortune blessed her on one of these occasions, for Piotr was expecting a friend from Yorkshire. He spotted 'Pym's Delight', and, being in whimsical mood, accosted her, with a familiarity that robbed her of breath.

'Good evening,' he said. 'I wonder if you might have observed, in this vicinity, a rather Pickwickian character? The person to whom I refer is a gentleman, most decidedly a gentleman, about fifty years of age, of robust and rubicund aspect, his entire bearing suggestive of a quite astonishing performer on the bass trombone. I was to have met him here, fully fifteen minutes ago.'

'No,' said Elinor, feeling rather dizzied by this level of discourse. 'I haven't seen anyone answering that description. For that matter, I've never seen anyone answering that description in all my life.'

'Dear lady,' replied Piotr with some severity, 'allow me to observe that, until you have, you cannot have met a really fine bass trombonist.'

'I cannot accuse myself,' replied Elinor, 'of having met a bass trombonist of any variety whatsoever.'

'You astonish me! I had not thought it possible, in this enlightened age! One supposes, at least, that you have met hordes of the numerous if mediocre cellists who ply their humble trade, if asked, in every nook and cranny of this dark and treacherous land?'

'Not even that,' admitted Elinor, fascinated by his archaic and liquid patterns of speech.

'Allow me in that case to present myself. I am Piotr,

anarchist, sub-principal cellist, homosexual and sufferer from chronic indigestion, more or less in that order.'

'My name is Elinor Jay,' said Elinor faintly. She had never to her knowledge met either an anarchist or a homosexual before, and the mixture seemed at once too rich and too thrilling to bear. She wondered for a moment whether Piotr was entirely serious, but there was no flicker of amusement in his high-boned features. He regarded her attentively before rebuking her.

'That is not a particularly adequate response. Couldn't you at least attempt to match the indigestion?'

'I – I come to all the concerts,' she said weakly.

'I know that already. It has been noted, and will, no doubt, be taken down and used in evidence against you on the Day of Judgement. What else do you do?'

'Do you mean that you've actually noticed me?' Elinor gasped, almost stunned. It had never occurred to her before that the orchestra could see as well as be seen, that their concentration on the music could be less than total.

'I notice everything,' said Piotr. 'If you play as efficiently as I do, my dear Elinor (a most suitable name, if I may say so), then the leisure required to observe human nature is usually forthcoming. There was a young man in the audience tonight, fourth row stalls, with a complete Shakespearean tragedy written in his face . . . You, however, wear your trials most lightly. I enjoy the particular stillness you possess; self-sufficiency is a quality one cannot admire too highly. Loyalty – you never miss a concert – ditto. And imagination – because your imagination is all too evident – is too rare and delicate a thing to be lightly praised. Sometimes, principally during the more luscious movements, you give the impression of being in the middle of some delightful dream.'

'Piotr, my dear fellow!'

The greeting came, all too obviously, from the missing bass trombonist, and Elinor, her head still spinning, was about to turn away, when Piotr, neatly disentangling himself from his friend, introduced her.

'Sam, this is Elinor Jay. Elinor, allow me to present my aforementioned fellow musician, Samuel Archibald. I trust you will do us the honour of joining us for a short drink?'

The annals of personal history are dotted with such moments, turning points in our lives whose significance can only be seen years, sometimes decades, later. All Elinor's instincts, her ingrained prejudices, the deeply grooved behaviour patterns of a lifetime – the very Conservative Party and church in which she had been brought up, threw up their hands in horror at the very idea. Yet against that there was Piotr (anarchist, homosexual, the acquaintance of ten minutes); there was something about Piotr that she liked. And her fascination with the orchestra gripped her ever more securely.

'Thank you,' she heard herself saying. 'I would enjoy that.'

It was perhaps fortunate for Elinor that she had, of all the orchestra members, first encountered Piotr. Piotr had many faults – he would himself have admitted to dozens – but he was genuinely interested in people. He treated Elinor with the exaggerated courtliness of bygone ages, teased her with calculated judgement, and, in the course of a couple of drinks, won her over entirely. His friend was another 'character', as she termed it to herself, witty, well-read, and particularly excitable on the subject of nineteenth-century Dutch painting. As he spoke, whole new vistas of aesthetic experience opened themselves before the personal assistant, a world in which ideas and concepts, performance and expression played a part undreamed of in the artistic cul-de-sac in which she'd grown up.

As Elinor walked back to the underground she was a mass of shattered prejudices and burgeoning hope. She had not observed that Sam's artistic raptures were based more on enthusiasm than on expertise, or that Piotr had been simultaneously amusing her and (in the form of the Shakespearean tragedian, no less) marking down his prey for later in the evening. She felt as if her life, after thirty-five years, was actually opening before her, awash with excitement and opportunities.

To her disappointment, a month's hiatus followed, during which the orchestra toured the U.S. and fulfilled a number of recording contracts in studios. These weeks seemed meaningless to Elinor. In desperation she attended a couple of concerts of rival London orchestras; she was too inexpert to make musical comparisons, but found that other orchestras failed somehow to impart the same sense of characterful individuals to her. She attended meetings, which seemed even duller than before, of her local Conservative association, and scandalized her local vicar by disapproving of his homophobic sermon. Her mother complained that she was abstracted and listless during her visits, and her boss asked her whether she was quite well.

'The same as usual,' she told him, without thinking.

'Perhaps you'd like a little break,' he suggested.

But she could think of nowhere to go, and no one to be with. In the end, she stayed, wondering if this was a breakdown, and, if so, what one was supposed to do about it. She felt as if her character was falling into pieces like a bad jigsaw puzzle, with unfamiliar shapes and edges that failed to fit. She felt newly made, fragile, only held together by bits of glue.

Upon the orchestra's return in late February, she went early to her seat, her heart jerking with excitement at seeing all the familiar names in the programme. Then she noticed, almost with disapproval, a new name, a new and important name. They had replaced the ex-principal cellist; William Mellor was being listed second again. The newcomer had a foreign-sounding name – could he be German? – David Schaedel. She kept her eyes on the right-hand side of the stage and was probably the first in the audience to see him.

Lord, but he was beautiful. Not tall, but exquisite, small-waisted, strong-shouldered. Dark without being swarthy, his head was perfectly poised upon his neck. His face reminded her of Greek sculpture, wide-browed and sensitively moulded, the mouth sensual to the point of weakness. His only imperfection was his nose, which was slightly crooked. Elinor found herself pleased about his nose; without that, he would have been too absurdly handsome. There had to be a limit to everything, she felt, from the depths of her puritan tradition, David Schaedel's beauty included.

She knew instinctively, almost before he put bow to string, the kind of cellist David would be. Here was none of William's reserves of emotional strength, or Piotr's casual brilliance. A purist would perhaps have been struck by the staginess of David's show – it was hard not to see it as a display, so dramatic was it and so extrovert – but Elinor was completely dazzled. The power and authority, the passion and explosiveness, caused her in the first few minutes to abandon her former idols and become mesmerized by the new principal. Her favourite instrument was now combined with her favourite performer – William, Paul, Piotr, even Roger with his saturnine glamour seemed grey and lifeless in comparison. Piotr glanced up and smiled at her; she was both touched and censorious. Certainly David could never have noticed her; his whole being seemed caught up in the Brahms piano concerto.

The second movement took Elinor entirely by surprise; one of the most eloquent cello solos in the repertoire unfolded beneath her; she was transported into a realm of pleasure so close to pain as to be almost indistinguishable. To think of all those wasted years when such sounds were strangers to her! She was aware she prized these moments all the more fiercely for that . . . David's face took on a becoming flush as he played his solo; he was conscious of the critical ears of his colleagues, but to Elinor he seemed to be playing only for her. She left the hall that night hardly aware of where she was going, her head entirely encompassed by David Schaedel.

She didn't meet him until, in one of life's little twists, she won him in a raffle. This happened at one of the Friends of the

Orchestra of London's cocktail functions: Roger Ash himself called one of her numbers out. She hesitated a moment before claiming it; she dreaded feeling conspicuous; but curiosity got the better of her. As she moved forward, Elinor hoped it wouldn't be something 'for two' so that she would have to confess her single condition; she also remembered to hope that it would not be yet another lurid orchestra sweater. In the event, both fates were spared her.

'Well done,' said Roger, smiling charmingly. 'You've won a free performance in your home by the orchestra's string trio. Give my office a ring on this number to arrange a date, will you?'

Elinor returned to her place, clutching the precious sheet of paper. In her wildest dreams she had never imagined anything as wonderful as this: to have three string players from the orchestra in her flat, playing for her! Her head a torrent of possible friends she might invite, furniture to be rearranged, and dinner menus (was one allowed to treat the players as guests? – she couldn't bear to treat them as anything else), she slipped away from the function.

On the day agreed, she pleaded illness at work and spent the entire afternoon in meticulous preparation. She had invited two married couples whom she had reason to believe were not entirely unappreciative of classical music; it was a perfect excuse to pay off her debts of hospitality to them. By the time everything – food, wine, the flat, her own (normal and, she felt, rather dull) appearance – was ready, she found herself ridiculously nervous. What would she say to the players? Would they think her musically ignorant? What if the social mix didn't gel (what if the sweet didn't gel)? What if they got on to politics? Surely they couldn't *all* be anarchists. And whom would the orchestra send? Politics aside, she rather hoped for Piotr; he was so marvellously unselfconscious.

Whom they sent, of course, was David Schaedel. He was the first to arrive, with Caroline and Warren not far behind.

Elinor answered the door and was completely deprived of speech.

'Am I in the correct place?' asked David, his intonation pleasingly Israeli.

'Oh, yes. Yes, you are. I'm – Elinor Jay.'

'Miss Jay,' said David, inclining his head over her hand.

'Come in, do. But please, just Elinor. No one calls me anything else.'

'And I,' said David with conscious grandeur, 'am David Schaedel, the principal cellist of the orchestra.'

'Oh, I know who you are,' said Elinor artlessly.

'Do you? I am an extremely recent appointment. I was only confirmed in the job in January. I can assure you, it was a difficult thing to bring off. My situation was in the balance until the last moment. Believe me, the competition is terrific for such a job.'

'I'm sure it is. But you play so wonderfully well – '

David was flattered. 'Perhaps you refer to my Brahms solo?'

'The piano concerto. Yes, I was there. I – I'm always there. I have tickets to all the concerts.'

'Ah, my colleagues,' said David, spying Warren and Caroline. 'This is Warren Wilson, of the first violins. Also Caroline – I have forgotten her second name – Caroline, of the viola section. We have here a Miss Jay, first-class patron of the orchestra. She heard the concert the other night, you will remember, my Brahms solo.'

Warren and Caroline entered, murmuring greetings, and politely shook Elinor's hand. Elinor began to recover, her face flushed almost into prettiness. She recognised Warren and Caroline, but was not overawed by them.

'Caroline Wentworth, isn't it? So pleased that you could come.'

Warren inserted the business-like note. 'You're having quite an intimate party, the office said. Just a few friends.'

'That's right. Two couples I happen to know, and you three. I hope this room will be large enough.'

David made a dismissive gesture. 'The space – that is no

68

problem. The acoustic will be abominable, but we will overcome this.'

'What we chose was Mozart and Beethoven, a divertimento and a trio,' added Caroline. 'Does that sound too much for your guests, or about right?'

Elinor had no notion of how long such trios might last, but hastily agreed. 'That sounds perfect. Can I get any of you a drink?'

'Have you wine? A reasonable wine, a good claret?' asked David.

'I have a claret; I hope you might think it a good one. I'm not very clever about wines.'

David was pleased. 'I will tell you everything about this wine. What will you try, my friends?'

Warren was already intent on setting up music stands and parts. 'Oh, anything for me.'

'Anything non–alcoholic, please,' said Caroline. 'It's very kind of you.'

David followed Elinor into the kitchen, while Warren leaned towards Caroline. 'He's beginning to drive me around the twist, with his Brahms and his wines – and all the way down in the car he was moaning about that cat.'

'Well, he worries about seeing cats, at least he does if they're black ones. I wonder if Miss Jay has a cat; she looks the cat type.'

'I really can't stand much more of him. It's the colossal ego of the man! Did you notice that he answered what he'd like to drink before asking you?'

'Can't say that I did, to be honest. Anyway, what does it matter?'

'It's not bloody polite, that's why it matters! I can't believe it's normal in Israeli society.'

'No,' said Caroline doubtfully, 'but then, David's a genius. There are different sorts of rules for geniuses; at least, I think so. You can't expect them to be quite normal. His superstitious streak, for example. The trouble is that he's overly sensitive to psychic vibrations. I heard him telling Isabel.'

'Psychic vibrations, my left elbow. The man's mad.'

Elinor and David returned with the drinks. Elinor handed one each to Warren and Caroline, then came back in with her own.

'This is quite a tolerable claret, Elinor, you will be pleased to know,' said David. 'Your wine-seller is a good judge; you may rely on him.'

'I do, believe me. But I'm so glad that you like it.'

The doorbell rang and shortly thereafter Elinor emerged to admit two couples into the room, Sidney and Jane, John and Bryony.

Sidney was a well-meaning, if hearty, car salesman with a rather condescending wife, Jane. They were both about forty, and inclined, in the kindliest possible manner, to patronise Elinor. John and Bryony were gentle churchgoers, of much the same sort of age.

'So these are the musicians!' exclaimed Sidney with that joviality which was worth thousands a year to him. 'Good Lord, you seem young to have made it to the top of your tree!'

Warren flushed. 'Yes, well, it's true that the more established members tend to be married and settled. They don't normally volunteer for this kind of fundraising evening the way we do.'

Sidney guffawed. 'Fundraising! And I thought we were going to get a little free music here!'

'Oh, you are, sir, definitely,' said Warren with a smile. 'Miss Jay won us at an event in aid of the orchestra's benevolent fund.'

Jane was examining Elinor critically. 'You're looking extremely well, darling, much better than at the Bensons' party, when you looked so peaky. I didn't think that green print suited you, a bit too youthful in style perhaps, but your old blue looks simply lovely. And the flat looks wonderful too, it really does. Are those new curtains, the striped ones?'

John turned to Caroline. 'So. How long have you three been

playing together?'

Caroline wondered, as she had wondered before, why this question was never asked of her regular quartet. 'Oh, fairly long,' she said vaguely. 'There are several chamber groups within the orchestra, though we don't get a chance to play as often as we'd like.'

'I'm just so sorry our youngest couldn't be here,' put in Bryony. 'She's a little angel and adores music. Do you know, she was trying to sing before she could talk? At least, we thought it sounded like that. At any rate, she's only been studying clarinet for two years and she just got a very high pass indeed in her grade two exam. But that must seem like absolutely nothing to you people, who must all have got grade eight years ago!'

'Not at all,' said Caroline diplomatically. 'She must be very hard-working.'

'What are these gradings you speak of?' interrupted David.

Caroline was swift to explain. 'David is from Israel, where I don't suppose they have national music exams.'

'In Israel we have many, very many, music competitions. I myself won no fewer than seventeen competitions during my youth in Israel. They were not all equally important, you understand, but that will give you a picture of the way it was run in my country.'

'Quite,' said Jane, who had overheard this. 'Oh, yes. I had always imagined Israel such a musical country. All those Jews, of course; Jews are nearly always musical, aren't they? It's their main claim to fame, along with banking and those rather peculiar little hats.'

Caroline broke in before David could catch this, but David was not in the least discomposed.

'Perlman was from Israel originally, wasn't he, David?'

David selected a stick with a square of melon on it. 'Yes, that's true. Once I played a solo recital near the place where he was born. I remember I played the Kodály solo Sonata; it did not go badly. I recall that the reviewer – '

Warren, responding to a question of Sidney's, spoke rather louder than usual in an attempt to avoid hearing David. 'No, it's not a Strad; my violin isn't particularly old, as violins go, but it's a nice, even-sounding instrument.'

'And what would a handmade violin like that set you back?' inquired Sidney tolerantly. 'A thousand pounds, something like that?'

'Actually mine cost me rather more than that, though I got a very good deal on it.'

Sidney was interested; although he had shone at French at school, money was his favourite language. 'What? Three thousand or thereabouts?'

'I actually paid twenty-two thousand for mine, but, as I said, it's not made by anybody really famous.'

Sidney whistled. 'No! You could buy a fine car with that kind of money, real wheels. Jane, this fellow paid twenty-two thousand pounds for his violin!'

'Is it a first violin or a second violin?' asked Jane, inspecting it doubtfully, but Sidney's mind had careered elsewhere.

'Say, what sort of car are you driving, Warren? I could do you a deal, that is, my garage is running a promotion on the latest four-wheel-drives. You could part-exchange whatever you're running – '

'You mustn't get the idea that I'm very well-off. I drive a nine-year-old Ford and I'll still be paying off this violin twenty years from now.'

'Oh. Shame.'

'It is,' said Warren, not without irony.

Meanwhile Bryony was staring intently at David. 'You know,' she mused, 'I'm sure I've seen you somewhere before.'

'This is possible,' agreed David. 'Do you take the *Strad* magazine? They did a little article about me once, a couple of years ago.'

'No, I don't read foreign magazines. But there was a model – the spitting image of you – in that knitting pattern magazine I borrowed from Elinor. Elinor, do you remember?'

Elinor blushed deeply. 'No, I'm afraid I didn't really notice any of the models.'

'Oh, but he really was so like! The gorgeous boy in the stunning Argyle-type pattern. He really might have been you, David. I'll send it back to Elinor and she can show it you at one of your concerts. I know she never misses your concerts.'

'No,' said David thoughtfully, 'it was not me. I have never modelled. However, one of the most important sculptors in an exhibition asked to take some photos of me – from the right, the right is my better side, as they say – for some studies he hoped to do. I do not know what became of these photos; I never heard.'

Elinor took Warren aside.

'I don't know whether you might not like to play now, so you could relax and have dinner afterwards.'

'Are you planning on our joining your guests at dinner?' he asked in surprise.

'Only if you don't mind,' said Elinor hastily.

Warren was far from pleased. His idea had been to get Caroline away from David's influence before any further harm could be done. However, there was something in Elinor's face that made him feel suddenly protective of her.

'Oh, of course not, delighted,' he told her. 'Well, I'll get the troops going now then, if that suits you.'

So it happened that Elinor's dinner party became a concert. The trio played extremely well, though it must be admitted that the whole was somewhat outshone by David's individual contribution. The obvious admiration of Bryony, and the palpable if less wide-eyed admiration of Caroline and Elinor inspired him to new heights of posturing. It was all too easy for David, thought Warren, fighting jealousy. To be foreign, handsome and glamorous was surely enough without being quite sickeningly talented as well . . . Warren wondered whether he was observing David truthfully; David appeared to him so odiously self-satisfied that he was convinced that a sensible girl like Caroline would be able to see through him. But she didn't, that was obvious. Perhaps he was exaggerating

David's vanities – or perhaps, as a man, he was immune to David's charm. That was another possibility.

Elinor's mind was similarly distracted during the recital. With the lights on, in her own front room, she was unable to lose herself in the music the way she could in the darkened concert hall. Her guests – John and Bryony soporific, Sidney a bit restless, Jane subtly admonitory – worried her; their slightest movement seemed to her to denote deep levels of boredom. (In this she was in error: they were all entertained, although Sidney was entertaining himself by doing complicated commercial transactions in his head).

She was also embarrassed. Whether she looked at David or forced herself not to, she was so conscious of him as to be unable to enter into the music the way she loved to do. His beauty, incandescent from a seat in the audience, was so unsettling close to as to unbalance her brain. It was bewitchment: there was Bryony, usually so sturdy, and even the rather superior Jane, regarding him with a pensive wistfulness Elinor had never seen before. The viola player too – what a pretty girl she was! – was attracted; that was clear enough from the way she played. God had no right, thought Elinor, to create anything so frighteningly near perfection. It must sow seeds of dissatisfaction everywhere.

When the concert was over, Jane heaved a sigh.

'That was simply marvellous,' she said, and having checked on a few musical terms beforehand, added, 'Your codas were magical.'

Bryony, not to be outdone, announced that the slow movement had almost reduced her to tears, and that her little ones, had they been there, would have been inspired to practise beyond all reason. John, unable to think of anything musically pertinent, asked David in a kindly fashion whether he didn't find a cello rather a large object to cart around, while Sidney bettered this by announcing that he hadn't enjoyed music so much since the last time he'd heard the theme to *Ski Sunday*.

David Schaedel dominated the dinner-table conversation after the performance. Even Sidney deferred to his opinion on the various wines, and Jane insisted on repeatedly referring to the situation in the Middle East. As the dessert was cleared away, she followed Elinor into the kitchen.

'Your trio is really too divine,' she said, as Elinor set the coffee machine in motion.

'They're not my trio; they're just the group that the orchestra sent.'

'Caroline is so sweet, and Warren so well-mannered, and honestly I think that David's going to be famous. I don't pretend to be a musical expert, but even I could see that right away. Charisma, the genuine article, plus the most marvellous fingers. There'll be no stopping him.'

'They're a very talented group,' agreed Elinor, wondering why mere praise of David should cause her stomach to tighten so strangely.

'And now,' said Jane briskly, 'we need to talk about you. Sidney and I are quite worried about you.'

'I can't think why.'

'You'll be thirty-seven this year, and are still making absolutely no effort to get married.'

I'll only be thirty-six, thought Elinor, and then realised it made no material difference. The point was, did she want to get married?

'I'm content as I am, Jane,' she said mildly.

'If you want my opinion, you aim too high. I was just the same. Nothing but the most delightful, handsome, clever man for me! But then I met Sidney and all that didn't matter anymore.'

'No,' agreed Elinor, thinking of Sidney and wanting to laugh. 'I can see that.'

'Now Sidney's been a wonderful husband, and I think that, once you get married, you'll wonder why you didn't trouble for so long. And all you need in order to get married is a little care and attention. It wouldn't exactly hurt, mind, if you

75

were just a touch more vivacious, but really men would as soon have a dullish, gentle sort of wife, most of them. A different hairstyle, some proper make-up – well, any make-up really – and a more interesting wardrobe should do it. I'm absolutely certain that, once someone actually noticed you – '

They had neither of them noticed David until he had stood in the doorway for some time. Then Elinor, turning, saw him, and her cheeks flamed. Jane, equally discomfited, started busily pouring out the coffee.

David was quite at ease. Entering the room, and casually putting his arm around Elinor's unresisting waist he said, 'Miss Jay, I have a message from Warren; he prefers no coffee. Also a message from me: you are already quite delightful as you are.'

With that he awarded them both a flashing smile, and left the kitchen. Jane, speechless, took charge of the coffee, while Elinor leaned weakly against the sink. Her heart was full. David didn't despise her – that was enough.

This evening undoubtedly marked a turning point in the relationship of Elinor with the orchestra. Before then, Piotr aside, she had been unable to contemplate the players as normal people, as fathers with teenager trouble and women whose washer-dryers were capable of breaking down. The dinner party altered this completely. It was not that the musicians' mystery disappeared; it was simply overlaid with at least a shade of reality. If Caroline chanced to be looking into space between movements of a symphony, Elinor now knew her well enough to suppose that it was David Schaedel and not Bruckner's Fourth that was occupying her – Equally, if David left the stage arguing heatedly with Piotr, she could surmise that matters other than musical interpretation were the cause.

All this did not make the orchestra less fascinating to Elinor. If a little knowledge is a dangerous thing, then a little knowledge of a particularly handsome young cellist is a more dangerous thing still. Human nature is so generously constructed that our first impressions, if favourable, seem fated to be overlaid only with still more agreeable impressions; we find it easier to reject data that contradicts any good opinion we have formed than to accept it.

Elinor was not stupid; she was not even outstandingly inexperienced. She had dodged the goodnight kisses of enough estate agents to be aware that attractive men are not always unselfish. Thirteen years, even in an outstandingly dull City job, are enough to teach any intelligent young woman these truths. But any romantic is vulnerable to a passionate infatuation, especially when caught up with the glamour with which Elinor had impulsively invested the orchestra.

That part of her mind still capable of judgement told her that David had been odiously self-satisfied at her party, that he had shown only a modicum of interest in any conversation of which his talent formed no part, and that his manners would have scandalized her mother. But she had gone beyond judgement. Her love of the orchestra had crystallized into love for a single member, who happened to be David Schaedel. She woke up wondering what he was doing, and tossed at night imagining whom he might be with. She worked herself into a nervous tremor when he had a solo, and wrote an eager letter to the critic of *The Times* when he displayed only a lukewarm enthusiasm for him. When she visited the orchestra's favourite bar after the concert, she blushed if she caught his eye, cursing herself like a schoolgirl for her weakness. It did not take Piotr long to make a successful diagnosis, or to make haste to alleviate the symptoms.

'It's time you got your head straight about David,' he told her one night.

'I can't imagine what you mean,' said Elinor haughtily.

'No? Well, as a gentleman I'll have to take your word for it. Otherwise I could have sworn that you pinken every time he enters a room, and plunge into conversation with anybody handy to cover it up. It's no good, Elinor; I'm too old a hand to fool. As for David, you don't know him. You've only seen his public face. The truth is that he's a vain, superstitious, ignorant, superficial, selfish, rude, arrogant, grasping, irritating and sex-mad egomaniac. If I had a pound for every minute in his life when he wasn't thinking about himself, I would have two pounds. He doesn't even play very well. Oh, I know what you think, but, with due respect, you don't have much of a clue, musically speaking. Roger Ash is sick as mud at appointing him, now he's seen through the cheap glitz of his solos; and the cello section was sick as mud to start with. As a cello leader, he's a bloody terrific golfer, and I hear, though I have not observed his play myself, that his golf is lousy. I am scanning my brain with a laser searching for a good point about David, and all I can come up with is that he isn't bad-looking – I suppose one would really, in all fairness, have to call him handsome. Beyond that he really is one of nature's worst blunders. Shake it off, is my advice. Take a long look at him – no, on the other hand, that might work to his advantage. Avoid looking at him, and think hard about everything I've said. It's your only hope, as far as I can tell,' concluded Piotr with a sigh.

Elinor couldn't help laughing. 'Honestly, Piotr, you are a joker.'

'I wish I was joking,' said Piotr solemnly. 'Believe me, my dear, when I say that I'm not. Once a year, on a Tuesday night at ten-forty, I tell the truth, then at midnight I almost invariably turn into a pumpkin. It was a curse laid on me in my cradle – '

'You make libellous comments about everybody. I wonder what you say about me when I'm not here?'

'My reputation comes back to haunt me!' exclaimed Piotr melodramatically. 'But, honestly, Elinor, you must know that he's been with Caroline ever since he dumped that girl in Manchester.'

'I never believed it was his doing. Why, he told Caroline himself that his heart was broken.'

'Well, I didn't see his fax personally – '

'Don't be absurd, Piotr, no one could possibly dump someone by fax!'

'David could. But never mind, I can see that nothing I say will make the smallest difference.'

And yet, for all her bravado, Elinor secretly agreed with Piotr. Her infatuation was permitted by a wilful blindness hard to account for in one so intrinsically orthodox. But perhaps Elinor secretly believed that she'd behaved conventionally for long enough, that a little hero-worship couldn't seriously hurt her; perhaps, intoxicated by the pleasures of obsession, she didn't care.

It was at this strategically critical moment that Elinor's mother suffered a stroke and died. This was a terrible blow to Elinor, who had scarcely for a moment believed, despite her mother's protestations, that there was anything wrong with her, and it proved crucial in the life of her estate agent brother, who immediately deserted his family in Croydon to join an Italian monastery.

Beyond these ramifications, her mother's death left Elinor suddenly and shockingly well-off. Nothing in her mother's lifestyle or habits had ever suggested that she was a woman of means, her husband's life insurance and collection of old paintings having topped up a considerable and well-managed inheritance of her own. She had moved, complaining of ill-health, from Conservative function to church hall jumble sale, only pausing long enough in-between to observe that her children never saw her, even if they were actually present. A perfect specimen of a certain breed, she had never spent a tithe of the amount she owned, observing that foreign holidays were a peculiar waste of money and only likely to lead to stomach trouble. Stringent rationing during the War had instilled in her such a hatred of waste that she had used almost nothing in her life, and she had arranged her belongings to be divided with scrupulous fairness between her two children upon her death.

The news that she was now the proud owner of the red-pattern tea cosy made Elinor smile – if her mother only knew how she had loathed it! Even the humblest of her mother's possessions seemed to have been meticulously itemized and allocated to either Elinor or Oliver. But the money! The money dazed them all, even Oliver's wife, who confessed as much to Elinor.

'I feel so guilty about the money,' she sighed. 'It doesn't seem right taking it without Ollie. The whole thing has come as such a shock. I thought there'd be enough without it to keep us going – he doesn't want a bean, you see, nothing – but now this! There's a fellow at the tennis club . . . I'll have to fight him off with sticks if he hears about this money. And Ollie just sits in Pisa with this blissful smile on his face and says he couldn't be happier. It's like something on telly. Life isn't really this mad, is it, Elinor?'

And Elinor could scarcely answer her. The conservatism inherited from her mother, already weakened by her connection with the orchestra, was at war with wild and surreal dreams of what all this money could do for her.

('You shouldn't stop working immediately,' her solicitor had counselled her. 'Give yourself time to think about it. But I really can't imagine your staying in a job like yours after this – exposition. Indeed, you needn't work again if you use your funds sensibly. Let me give you the name of a friend of mine, clever chap, accustomed to managing largish accounts – ')

Elinor had never liked her job, but the idea of quitting terrified her. What would she find to do during the day? Of course, she could afford to go to all the concerts in the world now, but would she have to move? Her neat little flat, with everything ordered and organised, had never looked so appealing. And yet, and yet . . . If she had a house, she could hire half the string section, on her birthday, to play *Siegfried Idyll*! If she had a big enough house, she could give concerts in it! Her heart failed her at the amount of cleaning such a house would require, until she was lifted with the heady notion of hiring someone to clean it for her. She wondered if she was rich enough to have her name listed at the back of orchestra programmes, and wasted some minutes considering whether E.W. sounded altogether more substantial and sophisticated than Elinor for the purpose. Most of the patrons did rather run to a lot of initials . . .

She appeared at the orchestra's favourite pub after the next subscription concert.

'My round, Elinor,' said Piotr. 'Would you like your usual?'

'I mustn't let you buy,' said Elinor quickly.

'Too late. Done it already, except for yours.'

'A shandy then, just a half. But Piotr, you mustn't buy me a drink again.'

'Too late to go on the wagon now, my dear,' said Piotr solemnly. 'The demon drink isn't so easily swept aside as that. What's all this backsliding, anyway? Have you come to convert us to teetotalism? Been to an evangelistic meeting at Wembley, have we? Or read a rampant article in the *Church Times*?'

'Worse,' said Elinor, now used to Piotr. 'I've inherited a fortune.'

'You're right, I shouldn't have bought you a drink,' exclaimed Piotr. 'I don't buy drinks for the bourgeoisie. However, it's too late now. To anarchy!'

Elinor politely drank to anarchy.

'Have you had a death in the family?' asked Warren, who had been talking to Caroline and David on the other side of the table.

'I'm afraid so. My mother died last week.'

'Oh, what a shame!' cried Caroline warmly. 'I'm so sorry, Elinor.'

'Was it very sudden?' asked Piotr keenly.

'Yes, very.'

'And is your brother upset? We all wondered why you weren't in your usual place last concert,' added Warren.

'My brother's taken it rather oddly,' said Elinor, who didn't feel equal to fielding Piotr's witticisms on the subject. 'I had to miss the concert because of the funeral.'

David became vaguely aware that something had happened, and made inquiry of Caroline.

'I too have suffered this catastrophe,' he announced, having understood the case. 'I lost my mother twelve years ago; it was a tragedy. Even now, I do not feel that I can speak of it, the trauma was so severe. It seems as if it happened only yesterday. I had just played the Elgar for the first time – the orchestra was very poor; I was quite annoyed about it – and my mother, naturally, was there to hear me play. She had used to accompany me on the piano, you understand, when I was five or six. Anyway, not two days after the concert she had a heart attack, and hovered for a week between life and death. It was awful, a terrible time for me. I took my cello to the hospital every day and played to her for hours. However, day by day, her condition got worse. Finally they told me not to bring my cello again; my mother was dead. It was the most tragic thing; you would not believe it. At the memorial service I played the Fauré *Elegy*, also, with two cousins, Popper's *Requiem*. One of my cousins plays always out of tune, but the whole church was weeping, it was so beautiful. The effect, you understand. And then, not a month later, I won my first big competition. To think, my mother did not live to see it! So I alone know what you suffer,' he told Elinor, as Caroline gripped his hand under the table. 'Though, of course, your mother was probably not a musician.'

'No, she never learned music,' said Elinor, unable to think of a more adequate response. Piotr, who had busied himself by playing an imaginary violin during this discourse, leaned forward.

'Forgive me for interrupting,' he said, 'and permit me to express my condolences, but my curiosity is uncontrollable. How large exactly is your mother's fortune – more or less, I mean? What I mean is,' he explained to a scandalised Warren, 'that Elinor is not the kind of person to brag about a legacy. If

Elinor mentions a legacy, it's because it's going to change her life.'

Everyone's eyes turned towards Elinor, and she blushed deeply, perceiving David looking at her, really looking at her, for perhaps the first time.

'It is rather large,' she admitted in a small voice. 'I've been left more than a million pounds.'

There was a long silence, then Piotr reached over and grabbed a barmaid. 'My dear old barmaid,' he declared, 'procure us a bottle of your finest, your most exquisitely chilled champagne. Spare no expense, polish up your best, brush off the spiders spinning their webs of satin dust at the base of your bottomless wine cellar. This is an evening to celebrate.' He grimaced as Warren kicked his ankle under the table. 'Oh, I know that Elinor's much-loved mother is dead. But, and this is the point I would stress, a much-loved friend of mine has come into a fortune, and nobody deserves it better.'

'Hear, hear,' said Warren warmly, and Caroline impulsively kissed Elinor, who had turned even pinker.

'I'll pay for the champagne,' Caroline told Piotr, 'or rather David and I will, because we're celebrating too, only we weren't going to tell everybody, not having been together for very long. But you're all invited to our wedding on August 6th!'

Despite all the warnings – her own perceptions as well as Piotr's reminders – Elinor found it an effort to join the others in congratulating David and Caroline. She told herself that her feelings were absurd, that it was wonderful that David was doing the right thing by his new girlfriend, that Caroline was truly a lovely person (which she believed as firmly as she did in Free Will and the Conservative Party), but nothing could prevent her from feeling a little crushed. It wasn't that she wanted David herself, she argued, she just wanted not to feel jealous of Caroline, and it may be that there was some truth in this. Perhaps Piotr guessed what she was feeling – he was unusually gentle and attentive towards her – but she ardently hoped that she deceived the others. They were joined by Mirabel, in boisterous humour, but Warren was too troubled to hide his misgivings and Elinor seemed even quieter than usual.

Quieter too was David Schaedel. After basking briefly in the attention, he drank his champagne thoughtfully, balancing his glass on the edge of his hand and refusing to be baited by Piotr. He caught Elinor's eye only once and looked at her long and seriously, so seriously that she wondered when she would be able to breathe again.

IX

Love Letter

I knew you at once.

Tree and stone glittered, without shadows.
My finger-length grew lucent as glass.
I started to bud like a March twig:
An arm and a leg, an arm, a leg.
From stone to cloud, so I ascended.
Now I resemble a sort of god
Floating through the air in my soul-shift
Pure as a pane of ice. It's a gift.

Sylvia Plath

Margot sifted through the post. It was mainly circulars, the usual from Save the Children, nothing remotely readable except another long and rambling missive from her mother. Then she noticed, underneath the charity sheet, two professional-looking envelopes addressed to William – probably cheques. He'd been owed for a couple of things for ages.

The amount of the first cheque was huge, from a session fixer. She could hear the sound of William's razor from upstairs, like the needling whine of a hovering helicopter, or she would have called joyfully to him; in her mind's eye the new, invalid-adapted car was gathering shape. Or the carpet, a new carpet. That would give a lift to the reception rooms.

In a haze of pleasure she slit open the second envelope, but here there was no cheque. At first she thought the envelope was empty, then she saw a tiny slip of paper nestling in the bottom. There was no cheque, no letter, just three typed words like horn blasts: I love you.

The slip dropped from her scalded fingers. She bent down to retrieve it, stared blankly at the empty opposite side of the sheet, then tore it viciously into confetti. I love you. Who would send that to William, and without signing it? She searched the two envelopes, equally blanched, anonymous. They both had London postmarks, dated the previous day. There were no clues, even the address had been typed. I love you: the words resonated in her head like beats on drumflesh. When was the last time she had told William that?

The helicopter noise had ceased overhead; she could hear William's footsteps creaking in the bedroom above. I love you, I love you, was the rhythm of his footsteps, the hissing of the kettle echoing, expiring in release.

Margot, expertly manoeuvring her wheelchair, dumped the circulars, the envelopes and the confetti into the wastepaper basket. Her movements were automatic; a tidy, even obsessive housewife, all her rooms had a scalped, manicured look. A mark on the table would ruin her comfort until she'd dealt with it, and she waged a rearguard action against the elements for command of the windows. But now she felt winded, feeble, as if something was demanded of her, some command had been given that she was powerless to obey. She wanted to weep, but had forgotten how. Why should she remember? Her emotional life had been too comfortable, too settled for too long. The last time she'd wept had been when leaving her mother in the rest–home, well over a year ago. Ever since which, her own condition had, discounting one blip, seemed to stabilise – that was the cautious word the doctors liked to use. She didn't feel very stable now.

Yet the very air was persuasive against tears, the birdsong from the garden, the surging flowers, the pin–like grooming of her beige and white kitchen. Her little dog nuzzled her leg. Here was more comfort in her bewilderment, more routine to cling to.

'Yes, yes,' she told him fretfully. 'I'll feed you. You're not forgotten.'

86

He capered, as if he had never been fed before nor was likely to be fed again. She marvelled at his uncomplicated nature. Feed him, and he capered. Scold him, and he sulked. Talk to him, and watch his tail flail, as if operated independently. The lead meant walking, the keys driving, ten-thirty sleep. He was a small white dog, of indeterminate caste, and profoundly, eloquently, comfortingly stupid. Margot adored him. I love you, I love you; the drumming in her brain began again.

She heard William's tread on the stairs, in the hall, and started almost guiltily. When he entered the kitchen she looked at him as she hadn't looked at him in years – looked at him to notice him, as she might notice a stranger, someone introduced, potentially significant.

William, at fifty-five, was some eight years her senior. He was tall, strongly built, and his complexion was good. He had been lucky with his hair, which, though stone-white, was boyishly plentiful, but his features had not entirely escaped cragginess. He was careless of his clothes; and orchestral travelling had thumbed circles under the deep-set eyes that Margot had first admired. There was nothing in him to make anyone look twice – London orchestras were crammed with men of similar age and appearance.

And yet, and yet. The drumming continued, as if the torn shreds in the wastepaper basket had taken on ghostly life and were dancing invisibly before her eyes. Somebody loved him. He poured out his coffee, stirring it while still immersed in the paper. He drank too much coffee and knew it, had tried to cut back and been unable to deal with the headaches. Perhaps she'd not supported him enough, thought Margot, mechanically switching on the radio. Perhaps that was the trouble. Twenty years of marriage, her health deteriorating steadily over the last decade. Perhaps he'd felt – what, sexually frustrated? Simply bored? She tried to remember the last time they'd argued with each other. Was it really the time in the animal shelter when he'd preferred – illogically, uncharacteristically – a different breed of dog? Perhaps married life could become too contented, too mannerly; perhaps it could implode in its own placidity. A thousand silly women's articles resonated in her brain: Make Your Relationship More Exciting, How to Keep Hold of Your Man. How scornful she'd always felt of the women who read such things!

But William couldn't hide anything; she clung to that certainty. William was too genuine, too honest. If William was in love –

This was crazy; it was not William, but some Other, who was in love. Some pupil, perhaps, a student crush. A young cellist – Margot could just imagine her – delicate and idealistic, who saw in every exhaustion line evidence of a most interesting suffering. Young women are always attracted by experience and suffering. They wanted to live too quickly, to feel everything at once. It was as if, by attaching themselves to someone older, they could skip all the hard parts, escape the actual years, and skim straight through to the knowledge and confidence that they yearned to possess. Margot could remember; her memory was clearer than most. Her memory was too good, and she was terrible at social lies.

William noticed the post as he rose for more coffee.

'How's Sam?'

'No word.'

Margot felt compelled to hear him say more, to have something to latch onto.

'Mother wrote again,' she added.

Our son, my mother, she thought. Is this all we've got to fall back on? Say something, she begged him, say anything, just to halt the descending trickle of fear down my spine.

'I hope she's no worse,' he replied politely, immersed in the results of some golf tournament, but cognisant of the need to appear concerned for the old lady. Only innocence, she thought, could have been quite so clumsy, and her heart lifted again. Golf was one of William's occasional enthusiasms. He played himself, steadily though without brilliance, when he found the time.

88

'Faldo's in terrible shape. Six over par! He must be ill.'

She spurred herself onwards, a mean part of herself sensing the value of surprise.

'You had a letter from somebody else,' she heard herself saying.

'Oh? Who's that, then?' he inquired, but his mind was busy with bogeys and sand wedges, tricky lies and greens that were reckoned to be too quick for comfort.

'An anonymous letter,' said Margot, manipulating her wheelchair cleverly to avoid the edge of the new work-top. She'd taken ages choosing it, she remembered, as if the precise pattern of a work-top could mean anything! Grainy patterns, swirling patterns, geometric patterns spun in her brain.

'Anonymous,' repeated William blankly. 'You don't mean unsigned?'

'What else could I mean?'

His eyes were still beautiful, she thought, with a lurch into pity. Set eloquently in their sockets, downward-sloping. She had forgotten their brownness, the way the iris curled up and disappeared.

'Show me the letter,' he commanded in the voice he'd used to use with Sam, the voice of his father and his grandfather's father back in the cool dusty mines of Aberfan where men were men and music only for women and ponces. She felt amused, affronted. The façade was so thin, so easily breached! One moment the *Guardian*-reading libertarian, the next, dragged by the hair roots back to the caves.

'I can't.'

'You can't what?'

'Show it you. I tore it up.'

'You destroyed it? Why? What did it say? Who would write me anonymously? The idea's ridiculous. I'm not a politician.'

He was troubled; she could see that, and how was she to know that there had been a spate of unsigned lies and half-truths sent to orchestra wives a few years ago?

'What am I supposed to have done?' he asked lightly.

'It was typed,' said Margot, her voice sharpening. 'All that it said was: I love you.'

William was silent, absorbing this. When he finally turned back to his paper two strokes of colour shadowed his cheekbones.

'How completely puerile,' he told the paper, shaking it as if it was the dog and had annoyed him.

'Who is it?'

'My dear, how could I know?'

'You mean there are so many people that it could be? Is that what you're saying?'

'It sounds like a student trick,' said William calmly, ignoring the erratic rhythm of his heart. 'Just to see if I might show some interest, be available. You know how absurd students can be about their teachers.'

The mention of students relieved Margot somewhat. It had been her first thought, and she knew William well enough to trust his resistance to youthful charms. No, youth wasn't her fear. The spare elegance of the note was what she feared, the completeness of it. Was a student, however musically gifted, capable of such restraint? A blurted-out sentiment, or long pages of scrawl, would have been more her own line, when she'd been a student.

'Do you possess the hearts of all your students?' she asked.

'Perhaps one or two,' said William, with a hint of the smile which had once set her heart glowing with desire. Oh, she felt strange today, strange and weak, longing and fretful. She wanted to ask, do you love me, do I mean love to you any more? But the answer, any of the possible answers, defeated her. Perhaps, after twenty years and an illness which precluded sex, it didn't do to ask the question; perhaps no answer would really bear examination.

William wasn't brooding about it, anyway. He had substituted the sports with the business pages, his eyes scanning the figures. Margot wondered if the menopause would feel like this, shuddery and shaky and irrevocable. And all about nothing – a love letter from a smitten student!

The dog, which had huddled patiently at William's feet while he breakfasted, leaped up and performed a flawless figure of eight when his hero rose. The remains of the milk – William never finished his cereal milk – were all that occupied him, the uncomplicated little beast. Margot felt a flicker of jealousy; Toby's life seemed to her at that moment just one minor pleasure after another to look forward to, and nothing but love to collect from everybody. Love on demand, she thought, come to me; I'm the one in need of comfort. But the dog was lost in the joy of William's leftovers, and oblivious.

William went upstairs to practise. A creature of habit, he liked to do scales and studies first thing in the morning. It was this sort of dedication that had kept him at the front of cello sections all his life. He was famous for being able to sight-read anything; he was proud of that, of that and his bow control. But today he took his cello from its case, unthinking, colour still etched on his cheeks. She loves me, he thought, with a little injection of unquenchable joyfulness. She wrote because she was too impulsive to keep it back. And under this a darker swirling current: she shouldn't have written, Margot hated it, why couldn't she have waited? And deeper still the fears – fears that he wasn't worthy, fears that he wasn't young enough, that he was too dried-out, emotionally if not sexually impotent.

How many times had he seen his colleagues in such situations? Slipping, slipping and falling into the mire of infatuation or worse? Divorces and financial disaster, society's tax on misery – how many times? And he'd believed himself immune, untouchable. William? Old Will's safe as houses, his section had told each other, half-wistful, half-pitying. Not Will's scene, believe me . . . But now the theories of years, proven case histories, had to be thrown out of the window. I love you, I love you; her breasts under his fingers and his body inside hers, the flowering of her smile across the orchestra and the vibrations between them as they passed in the corridor. The very cello between his legs was Isabel and they had passed beyond guilt's excesses, beyond conscience and doubt and the sniping of other people's agendas. He loved her for the impulsiveness that had posted three words in an envelope; he loved her possessively, creatively, unreasonably. The cello glowed under his fingers; he sent the sound soaring miles away, from Ealing to Isabel's kitchen, to Isabel.

Heavens but William was playing well, thought Margot downstairs, as she tidied the breakfast dishes away. And she felt a little uprush of pity for the student, whoever she was, who had sent the note. We're never too young to be hurt, she thought, remembering. The heart is only a child, an animal, incapable of learning, only alive in the extremity of its joys and its suffering.

X

Circles in the Sky

Sometimes the sky's too bright
Sometimes a woman's heart has salt
Or too much blood;
I tear her breast,
And see the blood is mine,
Flowing from her but mine,
And then I think
Perhaps the sky's too bright;
And watch my hand
But do not follow it,
And feel the pain it gives,
But do not ache.

Dylan Thomas

At the rider's back sits dark anxiety.

Horace

Paul flew over the edge of night, watching the studded lights below the hills, the plane whistling and singing and shifting and flowing like surf beneath him. He flew over empty farmhouses, silent churches, overstuffed golf-club dinners, quiet evenings in pubs. He flew over drowsy sheep, restless horses, curving ribbons of river, all carpeted over by darkness. He left behind, flicked over his shoulder, all the orchestral irritations, his children, his marriage, the disappointment and frustration of simply returning home every day. He flung them behind him, Nancy first, in an explosion of irritable self-disgust. Yet the plane flowed on, calmly, soothingly, and his muscles slowly eased. The relief that crept over him was out of all proportion to the day's events, as if the tension and misery of years had been lifted. He was escaping, he was flying, he was coming home.

Beautifully, a ship cresting the waves, the plane turned upwards under his fingers. The controls gleamed confidently, the gauges unflickering, every inch under his control. Here, at last, he was the conductor; it was he who ordered every mechanism's movement, commanded the very moon to rise beside him. He felt powerful, more than powerful; he felt mortality slipping from him with a breaking of long-rusted chains. Flying was the only feeling in the world more thrilling than sex, he thought, adjusting his altitude – because of the danger, perhaps. One major miscalculation, one unlucky combination of malfunctions, and the little plane would tumble into the void, wing over wing, like the model planes he had collected as a boy.

The notion appealed to him. 'That's how I'd like to die,' he thought. 'No hanging around in hospitals, no embarrassing scenes, no months of dreading what was always bound to happen. Just aim at some wide, clear space and drive straight into it, nose first, then the fireball. One minute flying through space; the next – demolished, scattered, evaporated. That would be the best way. One day I'll try it; find out what it feels like.'

The remaining purple-blue of the horizon gave way as he flew towards it to a hail of faintly pulsing stars. 'It's a Mozart aria,' thought Paul, almost forgetting where he was. 'It's the slit through heaven's hemline,' but he smiled as he said it, because he no longer believed in his mother's precious heaven, his grandmother's bullying hell. He knew, as surely as that he was in command of his plane, that, if he elected to crash, he would enter a spiralling blackness as empty as the darkness beneath him, a state of unfeeling, unbeing, nothingness. No decisions, no finances, no women, no relationships, he thought – it would be heaven enough just to escape from those

94

human burdens. And, at the remembrance of yesterday's events, the line between his brow deepened and his hands tightened on the stick.

He'd returned home from work dazed with exhaustion, after a day more than usually fraught. The recording of Schumann's Fourth had gone appallingly. There had been trouble in the trumpets – the principal had flu and his deputy had suffered an all-too-public crisis of confidence. Section after section of the symphony had needed re-recording, until Roger's suave patience had been exhausted, though never the disembodied voice of the recording engineer ('Very nice, Roger, very nice indeed. I'm sure you wouldn't mind just one more effort – I think the firsts know the place I mean – '). Trouble was, nerves were catching. If one player sneezes, half the orchestra catches the bloody cold. There had been tremors in the flutes and dodgy intonation at the far end of violin fingerboards – with corresponding impatience from the understretched ranks of double-basses, among others. As the recording session fell further and further behind schedule, there appeared The Men in Suits: backers, record company producers, orchestra management conferring in corridors on mobile telephones, a spiralling morass of tension, pressure, tiredness and lack of inspiration. Once a session starts to go wrong, nothing can save it. The first bassoon blasting the second bassoon, David Schaedal trumpeting on about bowing alterations, and everybody requesting – tiredly, irritably, meaningly – for Paul to deliver up a new oboe 'A' to tune to.

As for his own major solo, the second movement *Romanze*: nobody comprehends what the first oboe suffers, he thought moodily. His reed had been on its last legs; really, he should have used the back-up, but it was too late for substitution, and the reed had been superb just two days before . . . Plus, Roger wouldn't let the line breathe properly. Never did let slow movements really breathe, no, it was push, push, push, let's get to the 'exciting' bit, no subtlety, no spaciousness, no – Paul released his stiff fingers on the car wheel. Slow down, slow down. Another speeding ticket and he'd really be in trouble.

Finally, there was the situation with Nancy. He'd spoken to her between the recording session and the orchestra board meeting. She had refused to meet him the next day, pleading 'tiredness'. Tiredness! He accused her of having someone else; she flared back that she didn't and anyway, what was that to him? 'You're the one who's guilty,' she told him. And, all the way through the orchestra board meeting, he'd wondered if it was true. His head full of guilt and innocence, betrayal and corruption, Paul drove home.

Where do you draw the line, he'd asked himself, parking the car. Had he corrupted Nancy in the first place? Had he used her? And exactly how guilty was he with regard to his wife Marion, given her avowed distaste for sex? Paul had no sympathy for those who saw ethics in terms of black and white – the prosy Warrens and Williams of this world. From where he stood it was all shaded grey, some blacker, some paler. He didn't feel guilty. Discovered or secret, successful or less successful, his affairs never caused him the least remorse. Fear, yes, trepidation, excitement and nervousness, but not remorse. Was this cold-bloodedness or only incorrigibility? And, since nothing he did seemed to make any difference, did it matter?

The house had looked empty. There had been no lights visible in the front room, and no radio coming from Marion's kitchen. Paul had dealt with his oboe with meticulous care; he was neurotic about his oboes, would let no one else touch them.

'Anyone home?' he'd called. There had been no reply, but, moving up the stairs, he'd heard voices from Nicola's room, and had felt instant misgivings.

There existed a 'good' child and a 'bad' child in Paul's family. Edward, fifteen, was a hard-working, somewhat leaden lad with his mother's long-suffering eyes; fourteen-year-old Nicola had the rebellious temper and strong passion of her father. Whether Nicola had grown more difficult in reaction against Edward's priggishness was a question Paul had often asked himself; he could have understood that, because to have an older sibling constantly held up as a model would have irritated him equally. But the sympathy he secretly felt for his daughter was more than counterbalanced by his determination that she use her life properly; indeed, Paul's strong-arm tactics with his children would have amazed colleagues more accustomed to his lax moral code and grasp of orchestral *realpolitik*. As he heavily mounted the stairs he heard the voices more clearly, Nicola's almost shouting, Marion's her usual plaintive whine. Paul's knock on his daughter's door produced instantaneous silence.

'May I come in?' he asked impatiently.

'Oh, God!' burst from Nicola.

Marion was flustered into obviousness. 'It's your father; I thought he'd be late today.'

Nicola fiercely grabbed her mother by the arm. 'Promise me you won't tell him.'

'Not – not if I can help it, I suppose.'

Paul knocked again, harder.

'Come in, Dad,' said Nicola, with overdone casualness.

Paul entered, noting the untidy state of the room with disapproval. Nicola was leaning back on her bed. At some point she'll be pretty, perhaps beautiful, he thought, but not yet. Teased, dyed black hair surrounded a discontented, too-pale face; her T-shirt looked numbingly tight, her jeans torn and frayed. Marion in contrast was beautifully made-up, an exhausted-looking woman of forty, her pinched nose and mouth spoiling a pointed, pretty face. She too was dressed too tightly – perhaps an insurance against losing Paul's interest – but the dress she had selected did nothing for her. She began fussily picking up clothes and shoes, as if that was her only purpose in being there.

'How nice that you're so early, dear,' she said, looking up as if hoping for a kiss, but Paul only frowned.

'This room is a disaster; I couldn't live in it.'

'No one's asked you to,' Nicola said pertly.

'Don't push your luck. What's all the trouble about, Marion?'

Marion spoke breathlessly; she was a bad liar, always had been. 'The mess, of course. What else?' Hastily, too hastily, she crammed some shirts into a drawer.

'What else, indeed?' Paul inquired, but Nicola remained cool. This composure was something his generation could not, at her age, have sustained, and some part of himself paid it tribute.

'Completely the wrong drawer, Mother. Do leave it to me, you'll only make it worse, really you will. I know where I want things and you don't.'

'Is that any way to speak to your mother?' Paul growled.

'Sorry,' Nicola responded, without expression. 'Now can I have my room to myself again?'

But Paul's attention was attracted by something on the floor. He stooped to pick up the condom packet, aware that both women had become very still. His voice came out controlled, too controlled.

'You're both lying to me.'

Marion spoke up. 'Yes, yes, that's true, but you know how furious you get after work. I can't bear your temper, not today. I've had trouble with the steam iron and I'm still worried about Edward; he's not really well and his eczema's been dreadful. And your mother was on the phone – her central heating's gone again and I – I thought I'd tell you later, perhaps tomorrow – '

'Stop babbling. You lied to me. You were having it out about this – this object – before I came in, weren't you? Oh, don't trouble to deny it; it's perfectly obvious. Right, Nicola, look at me.'

Nicola glanced up defiantly.

'Who is it?' he asked.

'Kevin, of course,' and Marion added supplicatingly, 'You've met Kevin, dear.'

98

'I'll thank you not to interrupt. I certainly don't remember meeting anyone called Kevin.'

'Well, you have. We've been going out for almost two months now.'

'Two months! Is that any basis for a relationship?' Paul remembered Nancy and halted, then pushed on with exaggerated strength. 'You little fool, you're only fourteen years old!'

Nicola suddenly flared. 'I'm not a fool, and this bloody proves it! A fool wouldn't have bothered to use one!'

'Listen, at fourteen, with or without a condom, you're a little fool. People get cervical cancer that way, not to mention worse things. Besides, what judgement can you have about people at your age? It isn't safe. These – objects – aren't really even safe against pregnancy. I simply can't believe a daughter of mine would be so completely stupid.'

Marion nodded eagerly. 'That's true, darling. What your father says is very true.'

Paul glared tiredly at his wife before returning to Nicola. 'Why the hell did you have to do it anyway? You remember what we said: when you're sixteen, if you have a steady relationship, you can go on the pill. When you're sixteen! If you have a long-term relationship! You're only fourteen and you've known this boy all of two months! You've deliberately disobeyed me, also you've lied to us. Well? Can you dredge up some excuse? Was it peer pressure? Don't tell me you're the last virgin left in your class. And, if you're such an adult, why couldn't you control yourself?'

'Why should I? I love Kevin and he loves me. We're old enough to do what we want. We're supposed to wait two whole years?' She leaned towards Paul, daring him. 'Besides, I wanted him! I wanted his body!'

Without premeditation, Paul slapped her on the face. Marion cried out; Nicola only breathed faster, a red mark glowing where his hand had stung.

'Why should I have controlled myself? You never do! You

just go around screwing anybody, and you're married! I can do what I like! And if you don't like it, you've only your own stupid example to blame!'

Marion was appalled. 'Nicky, it's wicked to speak to your father like that!'

'Wicked, is it? What's he got to say about it? Can he defend himself? Oh, Mother, how can you stick up for him? He's useless. I can't respect someone like that, and I don't see how you can either. I would have left him years ago. If I were you, I'd leave him now!'

'You may get your chance to leave, girl,' Paul said hoarsely.

'Are you going to prove what a great father you are by throwing me out? Oh, go ahead, hit me again – you must be dying to. I'll hold still. Here I am, hit me again. Hit me, hit me, so I can feel something, anything!'

Marion hung onto Paul's arm. 'Oh, Paul, don't. Please don't; it's so unfair to me. I can't bear it, really I can't!'

'I'm not going to,' Paul said wearily, disentangling himself. 'She deserves a thrashing, but I can't do that either.' He turned to Nicola with a strange dignity. 'What you say is too near the truth for that. I'm sorry for you, Nicola – you're like me and I wish you weren't. I wish neither of my children were like me. To be the kind of person I am is a terrible burden to put on a child.'

'Why, Paul, what are you saying?' Marion demanded, aghast.

'I know what he's saying,' said Nicola.

Paul dropped her gaze, turning savagely to Marion. 'Get that girl on the pill, or we'll be talking abortion.'

'All right.'

Paul left without looking at either of them, while Nicola sat down on the bed again, filing her nails. Marion stared at her.

'He's right, you know; you are like him. I can't read you, just as I can never manage to read him. How can you just sit there, after all that?'

'Why not?' the girl inquired, intent upon her nails.

★

All this, like the bass line to a passacaglia, ran under Paul's thoughts, as he directed the tiny plane through the long, spun-out June evening. There was more to it than that, of course, more than Nicola could possibly realise. His own battles with his father, his own struggles for teenage individuality – the styles were different, the feelings the same – rose up from some basement of memory. His father had hit him too, more than once. He could almost feel the shock on his face, that flaring of resentment and desolation. He was mad to have struck her; she would never forget it. And girls these days were not really children at fourteen, unfortunate as that was. Nicola had been fully developed, to look at, for nearly three years, and she probably had the drives and desires to match. What a stupid system it was, he thought, angry again, that enabled immature teenagers to have adult bodies! It was on a par with having to choose your career, your future, at an age when you were still almost incapable of rational thought – or going to college at a time when you were emotionally unequal to it. If we reached puberty at sixteen, thought Paul, went to college at twenty-four, and started work at twenty-eight, it would all make a bit more sense . . . He was thinking about anything, he realised, rather than about what Nicola had told him. He was desperately scouring his brain for anything other than what had most hurt him.

Respect. His child – Edward didn't count – did not respect him. And why should she? He was a hypocrite, demanding standards of behaviour in them that he could never begin to achieve himself. He had failed, as anyone would have, in keeping his marital troubles from his children's alert gaze; Nicola probably knew everything Marion did, possibly suspected even more. It was impossible to deal with a child like Nicola, who could look at you with clear eyes and see the liar beneath. It was impossible to discipline a child who saw so much, who judged so harshly.

Paul longed to be open with her, to explain everything.

'Nicky,' he imagined himself saying, 'I shouldn't have married your mother in the first place. I was young, I was going to a new city, a new job, I wanted to have someone by me. I looked for the most obvious wife I could find, a woman as near my mother as possible – barring the religious part, at least your mother isn't religious – and I married her.

'It was clear almost from the beginning that it wasn't going to work very well. In the most basic ways, we weren't compatible, though she was very attractive back then and I did – want her, fancy her, whatever you call it these days. She always put up with sex. It never did anything for her, except produce you children; she was pleased with that, pleased with her success, her production capacity. I don't mean to sound harsh on your mother, because I should have corrected my mistake before it ever came to children, but it was never going to work, I see that now. It was always going to be a mismatch, an old-fashioned marriage, if you like, me earning the bread, Marion baking it. She never cared about flying, or music, and, if I'm honest, I never cared much about the house or you children, not until you were older, anyway. Now you're grown, it's different; now I do want your friendship, your affection, and I can't have it, don't deserve it. My behaviour towards your mother has lost me your respect.

'But, Nicky, think what my life has been like – concert after concert, recording session after recording session, tour after tour. Even the most incredible music feels like nothing but pressure, pressure, pressure, to me now. And once that happened there was nothing to give my life meaning or zest, except for flying and I can't afford that every day. No one to come home to who cares about the orchestra, no one to talk to about planes, new cars, politics. And women – independent women, women who share the same orchestra, the same pressures – all over the place. Drinking with women in foreign cities, thousands of miles from you all – can you imagine that? Working with women in stressful situations, conductors who threaten and scream, soloists who can't hack it, concerts poised on a knife edge of failure . . . Can you imagine the adrenalin flow that can't just sink down again, the fierceness of the desires that overwhelm you? Then imagine afterwards, the return home. The little peck on the cheek that means nothing, the passively endured lovemaking, the pathetic attempts we both make to seem interested in things that the other doesn't give a damn about . . . It isn't enough, Nicky, it doesn't feel like enough, not for a whole life.

'So I take lovers. You all know it; you all hate it; it makes me despise myself. I accept that. But what are the alternatives? There are two alternatives, and it's too late for either of them. One is divorce, meaning separation from you all, financial trauma, the whole bit. The other is driving my car over a cliff, or my plane into a hill, and, oh God, I could just about do that now. The contempt in your face and the truth that I could never tell you . . . It's you I should have married, Nicky, someone like you. Someone with gumption and guts and nerve and brains, someone who could talk to me as an equal. No one at all or else someone like you.'

There was blackness all around him now, and the little lights on the end of the wings glowed faintly febrile. Lights in the darkness, he thought, one of his mother's sayings slipping back to him, a light shining in the darkness and the darkness shall never put it out . . . He felt dizzy with truth and pain and recognition, almost lightheaded. It was bloody dangerous flying a solo plane feeling – what? A positively lunatic attraction to his own daughter, a convulsive desire for the completely unattainable, for (his mother again) eternal damnation. Determined to swerve his brain back to normal, he summoned back the faces of Nancy, Annette, but even Nancy seemed anodyne to him, the complacent indentations around her mouth, her demure untouchability. Was it only a month ago that this desire had driven him mad? It must have been a tour craze, the kind of mental disruption that only happens miles from home.

Paul took a deep breath. He wasn't going to crash the plane; he wasn't going to die, not for a good long while anyway. Nicola knew, she really must recognise how unsuited Marion was to his needs. Nothing had been irrevocably destroyed or lost that night, nothing unspeakable had slipped out. His behaviour had been irrational, but he'd also been under a lot of strain – the Schumann recording, what Nancy had said, finding the evidence in Nicola's room. He would survive, come through all this. It was better that he knew, better that it had happened. He drew a deep breath and contacted air traffic.

'E147Z calling ground. Permission to land.'

'Ground to E147Z. Permission granted. Can you circle at 3500, that's 3500 feet. We'll be calling you in at approximately twenty-one-forty.'

Making circles in the air, thought Paul. Maybe that's all we ever do, our lives a meaningless jumble of empty circles, some smaller, some larger, leaving nothing behind but a momentary trail of smoke in the sky. Who would remember the Schumann a year from now, a few years from now? And, given time, Nancy's body would fade from his memory as the others had faded, an illusion of rightness that was really as flawed as all the rest. Perhaps he would keep searching; could he be blamed for that? People would call it cynicism, but it didn't feel like cynicism; it felt like hope. He felt suddenly certain that Nicola understood, that it was her burden too, and that obscurely lifted him.

The runway lights shone clean and straight and beautiful as he steered the plane in to land between them: two perfect lines of lights stretching into blackness, a universe ordered and controlled. The plane curved down, eased onto the tarmac, the reverse thrust vibrating thrillingly under his fingers. Paul felt a sense of physical release glow over him; he was cleansed, he was down, he was going home.

XI

Anarchist's Revenge

Never morning wore
to evening, but some heart did break.

Tennyson

(from Piotr's private files)

I tend towards the pigeon-holing tendency, and I know it. I decide that Mirabel, just to take an example at random, is a beefy example of Australian womanhood, a terrific horn player, and not someone whom I personally would wish to cross in a dark alley, and I leave it at that. But to imagine that this is all there is to someone like Mirabel is a tremendous error of judgement.

These humbling reflections followed a particularly foul murder of Brahms' immortal First Symphony by a conductor whose name I so wish to erase from my consciousness that I cannot now recall it. I was in the pub drowning memory of same when I overheard Mirabel quizzing Caroline about her engagement to David. This was what I picked up, while supposedly talking cricket with Clarence:

'– He's not the marrying type, Caroline. I'm a firm believer in types. Some men won't ever settle down. Look at Paul Ellison.'

'Are you daring to compare my David with him?'

'No, no, that is, not exactly. I just think David can be – well, impulsive, the way we all know Paul can be.'

'Yes, well, that's just artistic temperament,' said Caroline, sipping her wine. 'David never plays the same piece the same way twice; he lives off his emotions. Rostropovich is apparently just the same. Mind you, the cello section doesn't understand – how suddenly, in the middle of a concert, for example, he might realise that a phrasing is simply unmusical. They can't comprehend how he simply can't play an unmusical phrase, not to oblige anybody. It causes him so much anguish! I'm so glad I'm not a genius, Mirabel. It doesn't make for an easy life.'

'No, no, I'm sure it doesn't,' said Mirabel, her instinct for truth warring with her desire to be both useful and tactful. 'But marrying – genius – isn't easy either, Caroline. You're taking on so much more than most people. I've been married for years, to a complete saint as it happens, and I'm in a position to tell you that, even in these circs., marriage just isn't an easy option. You think you'll never feel lonely again, but you will; you'll feel everything just the same. Even in the closest marriage you can feel terribly alone, irredeemably alone! I don't know why we don't just admit that we are alone, that every device we have for pretending otherwise is just that – a device, two lonelinesses united, which might or might not work . . . As for our jobs, orchestras conspire against marriage; our whole way of life conspires against it! The only way any marriage works is with gut-rock determination and dual willingness to compromise and nerve and luck and judgement and God knows what else besides. You'll have to give till you've got no more to give, and then dig deeper. You'll have to fight each other's despairs; you'll have to give support until it feels like blood. And comes the day, when you forgive enough and care enough and dig deep enough, comes the day you know it really is for ever and ever, world without end, which is what we all promise in the first place and only time can truly deliver. And this is a good marriage, Caroline, this is success!

'Elaine, my best friend, is in a marriage, I mean, it's not impossible, but she – Oh, I wish you knew Elaine, Caroline; she'd be so much better at explaining than I am! She's mature and sensible and funny and sane and doesn't want to sit down sometimes and howl like a dog at the moon. Without Elaine I probably wouldn't be here now; I'd have crash-landed in the Thames years ago. Elaine was there for me, when I was on the outside of orchestras looking in, getting no freelance work at all. When my tax returns were a sick joke, when I felt like a bog-standard horn player, when I knew my entire life was a complete and utter failure, Elaine would pick me up and calm me down. Not that Stephen wouldn't, believe me, it's just that he was at work or something, and, besides, no one person is enough for anybody, that's another thing to remember. Don't expect David to be all you'll ever need; that's a crippling burden to put on anybody. In Elaine's own marriage – Oh, never mind! I just want you to have the best that you can, Caroline, that's all. Life's tough enough for women in our profession without a difficult marriage.'

'Really,' said Caroline, busy inspecting her nails. 'I appreciate everything you say, Mirabel. I'm grateful for your advice. But my married life will be so very different from yours! My husband will be here, in the same orchestra, doing the same tours. We won't suffer the separations that couples like you and Stephen have to cope with. David's promised me all the support in the world – besides, I've never been very ambitious. Once David wins an international cello competition, life will be easier for us. We can both stop working in orchestras once he's as famous as he deserves to be.'

At this point Mirabel gave up, as a lesser person would have done a long time earlier. I could perceive the strain she was under, though Caroline couldn't. Mirabel was longing to say (a) that David was the sort who would be carelessly and congenitally unfaithful, (b) that his actual chances of winning an international competition were pretty stunningly low, (c) that, if he did by any chance or skullduggery happen to win one, his unsufferability would reach such gigantic proportions that not even Caroline could live with him, and (d) that, by pinning her hopes on this paragon of unselfishness, Caroline was missing out on a few people who really did care about her, Warren Wilson being notable among them.

I'd never seen Mirabel so trammelled by delicacy; it was a new and enriching experience, like an earthquake with clenched teeth, a thunderstorm with its hands tied behind its back. Accustomed as I was to seeing her pulverise conductors with a single horn blast, I was awed by a side of her I'd never seen before. Perhaps I even felt a little wistful at what she'd said. Marriage. Stability. Two lonelinesses united. Well, it wouldn't ever happen to me, that was for sure. Which felt, if only momentarily, a bit sad. However, Mirabel's eloquence was to prove wasted in more ways than one, only a couple of weeks afterwards. With my innate talent for being in the right spot at the wrong time, I discovered Caroline in the backstage area of the Royal Festival Hall more usually reserved for cellists.

'Extraordinarily sorry to have disturbed you, I'm sure,' I told her, attempting to withdraw.

She looked up and I saw, to my complete horror, that her eyes were swimming with tears. 'Don't go! Don't leave me!' she begged me, or something to that effect.

I paused in astonishment. 'You would prefer me to stay?'

(Permit me to apologise in advance for the quality of dialogue to come.)

'Don't go, Piotr!' she cried, being a girl of one idea. 'I need to talk to someone so badly!'

My first thought was to fetch William, a man of admirable, even legendary, skills at dealing with the sex. My second thought was that my curiosity would enable me to bear up under the ordeal. In the end, I stayed, sitting down at a safe distance from the girl. No earthly use, of course. She immediately rose and put herself at my feet, upon which I assured her that I was all attention.

'It's David,' she said, as if I hadn't guessed. 'He won't talk to me.'

'Lucky old you,' I muttered, and then, 'Why on earth not?'

'He won't tell me, but I think I've found out.'

'And your theory is – '

'I don't think I'm wrong, Piotr.' (Extra helping of tears here.) 'I think he's with – someone else!'

'You amaze me,' I said languidly. 'I thought his passions were entirely self-directed.'

'I think it's Isabel.'

'Isabel! Impossible!' I scoffed.

'What do you mean, impossible?'

'I am happy to elucidate, dear lady. Imposs, for at least three reasons. One, Isabel's standards are extraordinarily high; her behaviour is abominable, but only with the most attractive people. Two, I'm confident that I would have noticed, seeing as much of David in the section as I'm lamentably forced to do. And three, if she has it in her nature, which I generally doubt, to be in love with anyone, Isabel is in love with William Mellor. I shouldn't have mentioned this last, as it was told to me in strictest confidence, but there it is, you can take it or leave it.'

'William!' gasped the girl, 'but he's so old!'

Here she had touched on one of my pet themes; I became inspired.

'To you, still in your twenties, he may seem old. But one of the great things that life teaches you – do pay attention, Caroline, you're getting a pearl of wisdom here – is that age is an illusion, a trick, that nature plays to make black appear white and vice-versa. Take your David, for instance – please, and as far away as possible. David is quite a beautiful youth, no one could deny it. He's also sheer poison, vain even beyond his claims, silly, superstitious and mentally blunt to the point of feeble-mindedness. "You are old, Father William," you may say, you could even go farther, as he is a grandfather, and easily fifty-five. But said William is not only a noble soul, Caroline, and I do not bandy words like nobility lightly; he is, once you come to study his face, about forty times more beautiful than David is. What shows in William's face, you

109

see, or rather you don't see, but you will, if you reach thirty-five as I have with your eyes open, is character. You can get away without character in the first flush of youth, but at fifty-five, my dear girl, it is character or bugger all. The lines that our lives carve into our face are more than lines, they are school reports. The lines around William's mouth sweep straight, not downwards, signifying courage, and the lines around William's eyes are legacies of so many good-humoured, kindly acts that the heart rejoices to see them. The cut of William's jaw is still unpinched and generous; there are no slashes of frowning bitterness between the eyes, or lines of cynical pessimism demeaning that open brow. All this is why, believe me, you're safer with an older man than with a young one, because he carries his life on his face, and anyone with eyes to see can read it.'

All this was wasted on Caroline, of course. The young don't think, not properly, it's part of their complete lack of charm.

'But David's always looking at Isabel,' she said feebly.

'And so are we all. Even I stare at Isabel, and you cannot be unaware of the fact that looking at women does nothing for me. Isabel, blast her, is a fascinating creature. She's fascinating as a thunderstorm is fascinating, or a waterfall. It's got nothing to do with desire, looking at Isabel. Think of Isabel as a force of nature.'

She was bewildered, but I think convinced. I venture to say, with the wind behind me, I am something of a force of nature myself.

'Then who else – '

'Why does there have to be someone else? What makes you so sure that there is? Of course, David has a roving eye, but I haven't seen anything suspiciously particular in his behaviour towards anyone. He seems, the generous lad, to fancy every woman about equally.'

'But Piotr, I found this letter.'

'Letter? What letter? Let me see.'

She handed it over. An unstylish missive, as one would have

110

expected, in David's angular, rather over-elaborate hand.

My darling, Thinking over what you said last night, I guess maybe you're right and anyway Madame Shushila is doubtful about timing. The last time she wrote (the spirit flow was outstandingly clear) she said 'Great is the darkness flowing from hasty actions' and 'Beware of misdeeds on a Wednesday as they may lead to your undoing.' So perhaps Friday would be a better idea, usual place. As for being hasty, well, I'll leave it till next week to tell C. Don't think she has any idea, so far, so it doesn't make a great deal of difference. Your forever devoted, David.

I handed it back. 'Hmm. This letter, I would have to say, bears out your allegations pretty conclusively, Caroline. Allow me to apologise for doubting you, and for thinking your behaviour even the slightest bit hysterical, as, to be honest, I had somewhat pigeon-holed it.'

'But who is she? What do I do?'

'Two entirely separate questions, dear lady. To address the first, I can only respond, at the risk of rubbing it in, that the correspondent is David's "darling". But as to what you can do, a number of solutions suggest themselves. Firstly, you can remain in tears, to the eventual detriment, as scientists suggest, of your internal organs. Secondly, you can confront David with the evidence, a much more dramatically satisfying alternative, but completely futile, as it won't make it the slightest bit more likely that he will desert his present choice for you. Thirdly, and this I admit would be my recommendation, you break open the champagne, invite your friends around for an orgy and toast David's downfall. I cannot recommend this course of action too highly, as it not only makes him wonder if there's more to you than he'd thought, but also makes him worry that you might have had your own interests to start with. It's the only really dignified route for a rejected person to pursue. Also, I'm in a position to tell you that your winsome charms have not gone unnoticed by men in the orchestra other than David. I know for a fact that Warren

Wilson has a very soft spot for you – also, though his may perhaps be a harder spot, Paul Ellison.'

Useless of course. I might as well not have bothered. Because just as I finished, David came in, and our little duet became a trio.

Caroline, naturally enough, became upset again. She said, Oh David, how could you, or some such drivel.

'You'll excuse me,' I said, edging doorwards.

'What's all this?' demanded David, like a ruffled police officer.

'Don't go!' Caroline begged me.

I paused at the door. 'This is personal, surely?'

'I want you to stay!' she said, illogically. I stayed. I was curious. Need I say more?

David began to look uneasy. 'What's the matter, Caroline? You look as if you've been crying for hours.'

This is a further disadvantage to position A, which I regretted not having drawn to her attention earlier. There are few things which do more to destroy a person's looks than tears, causing, as they do, a loss of eye definition, temporary blotchiness of complexion and a particularly unsightly redness around the nose.

'And so I have! Ever since I found this in your cello case!'

David identified the note but missed the point, as usual. 'What the hell were you doing nosing around my cello case?'

'Borrowing rosin, is that a crime? How dare you deceive me! How long has all this been going on?'

I couldn't resist adding, 'And who, if you'll forgive me for asking, is the lady?'

David looked sourly at me. 'What's it got to do with you anyway?'

'Your friend here has chosen to honour me with her confidence. Besides, I'm bloody curious.'

David turned to Caroline, his unease watered down with some smugness, and said, 'Elinor Jay.'

'God help us,' I said, and meant it.

'Is this some kind of joke?' demanded Caroline, who, having met Elinor, knew the classy, strictly C of E type of worthy she is.

'Damn and blast you,' I simmered. 'You're using that girl for her money. I told her you would. She's been taken for a ride, deceived, tricked, hoodwinked, bamboozled!'

I would have spoken further, but without my thesaurus, I was stymied.

'Elinor!' repeated Caroline, in a daze. It would never have even occurred to Caroline to consider Elinor. Typical of Caroline, I'm afraid, who has no imagination. The truth is, there are a lot less attractive heiresses than Elinor Jay; and money was always going to be David's object. I took it on myself to explain all to Caroline.

'Elinor's always adored David, though how such a decent girl could be cursed with such a fatal preference is beyond me. Hang on, how did you get together? I've scarcely ever seen you speak to her.'

'I used to meet her in the audience bar, if you want to know. After a concert.'

'He met her in the bar. Great holy balls of fire, at the bar after a concert! Don't you see, Caroline, the crucial, the hideous significance of this? How many bars after how many concerts is David, in all human probability, likely to decorate? And how many temptations, over the course of a lifetime, is he likely to meet there? You have had, my child, a fortunate, a heaven-sent escape. All right, he's jilted you, but it could very easily have been divorce, children, alimony! Even you must now admit – '

It was at this point that Caroline rose to her fullest height, trembling, and belted David on the jaw. He reeled, hitting the ground with a satisfyingly solid sort of noise, and commenced wailing. Dialogue-wise, there was a momentary if contented silence, our special correspondent being left entirely without words.

'Oh, I wish I was a man so I could fight you properly!' she cried passionately.

'I don't know,' I encouraged her, 'you're not doing at all badly as it is.'

The girl paid me no further attention. She was busy pulling off her rather vulgar engagement ring and throwing it at the stricken cellist on the floor – missing him, as it happened, but the spirit was still admirable. 'And here's your horrible ring, which I never really liked anyway! Give it to Elinor Jay, with my warmest sympathy, or else just shove it up your ass!' And recognising a decent exit line when she stumbled upon one, the girl stormed offstage right.

You may think what you like – it doesn't make a particle of difference to me either way – but I pride myself on being a prime comfort in times of affliction. I made a good-natured stab at consoling my still-prone section principal.

'You know, I wouldn't do either of those things, David. I could give you the name of a ducky little fellow on Wigmore Street, does a lovely line in second-hand rings – '

And yet, even at the time, I thought something in his expression suggested that he didn't appreciate it.

Bryony and Jane called on Elinor the day after the announcement appeared in the *Daily Telegraph*. It was hard to tell which was the more excited, but as Jane's excitement was largely composed of indignation, it certainly appeared that Bryony was the more surprised. She rushed into the room, kissed Elinor, and looked anxiously into her eyes, as if she had just been given a year to live.

'How do you feel?' she asked.

'Never better,' Elinor assured her. 'I'm so pleased you both called in.'

Jane dispensed with kissing her friend. Her quick gaze took in the changes in the room since the dinner party – the music slopped on the floor, the increased rows of compact discs, the general air of muddle and untidiness – and then fastened on to Elinor. Elinor looked different and, in Jane's opinion, that change too was for the worse. She wore a pair of jeans, along with a silky sort of blouse in a vivid turquoise shade, and her long earrings seemed caught up in her frowsy hair. Anything less like the normal, smoothly ironed Elinor could scarcely be imagined, and Jane greatly feared that the change was not only external. She gave Bryony a meaning glance, as Elinor turned to greet her.

'Nice to see you, Jane. Let me get you both coffee.'

'Oh, well,' said Jane. 'After seeing the announcement, we simply *had* to come.'

'Oh, you read it, did you?' said Elinor, almost gaily. 'I didn't think anyone younger than our mother's generation read the announcements in the *Telegraph*.'

'It's the young cellist that was here that night, wasn't it?' demanded Bryony. 'That beautiful Israeli with the eloquent face.'

'Yes,' replied Elinor from the kitchen, 'you've both met him, so you can't complain that you haven't. Here you are, I hope that's how you like it. I'm glad that you remember him.'

'One could scarcely forget such a stunning young man,' replied Bryony. 'But isn't it all a bit sudden, Elinor? You can't have known him very long.'

'Life is a bit sudden, sometimes, isn't it?' said Elinor with a smile. 'Look at what happened to Mother.'

'That was a bit different,' put in Jane. 'That was unavoidable. Death just happens.'

'So does love,' said Elinor softly. 'As of course you both remember.' And she smiled, thinking of Sidney, and Jane's advice to her at the dinner party. There was a rather uncomfortable silence.

'When's the wedding?' asked Bryony, to fill the gap.

'Not until the orchestra comes back from its Canadian trip in June. We haven't fixed a date yet.'

'Well, there's no rush, is there?' said Bryony nervously. 'He's awfully young, isn't he? He can't be more than twenty-five.'

'Twenty-six,' said Elinor. 'Last November.'

'And you're thirty-five,' interrupted Jane. 'A thirty-five-year-old heiress. Honestly, Elinor, what would your mother have said?'

'I hope she would have wished for my happiness,' said Elinor steadily. 'As I know you both do.'

Bryony looked at Jane.

'Believe me, we do want you to be happy. We're just – as friends – a little concerned that you're going into this with your eyes opened. I mean, I suppose, that you ought to be really sure. You do know him well enough, don't you?'

'Bryony means,' put in Jane, 'that he may really be more interested in your money than in you.'

Bryony gasped. 'I didn't mean that, Jane!'

'Yes, you did,' retorted Elinor. 'You both did. You're here because you believe that, aren't you? It was the first thing you thought of. It's the first thing everybody thinks of! It's why Piotr isn't speaking to me anymore, and why everybody in the orchestra avoids my eyes. Nobody – nobody! – understands David as he deserves. He's not like that – you can believe me – and you must know, after all these years, that I'm not like that myself. Don't you? Do you really believe that I'd be stupid enough to be deceived about such an important thing? Do you really believe I'd rush into marriage as if it was nothing, after all this time on my own?'

'Of course not,' said Bryony miserably. 'We don't mean that at all.'

'But he's dumped other girls,' continued Jane. 'His track record is patchy, to say the least. It is only normal to wonder if, this time, he means what he says. You must agree that he's deceived people before. Why, you told me yourself, not two months ago, that he was engaged to that blonde girl who played the viola. What happened to her?'

'That's exactly what John says,' said Bryony, adding, without irony, 'now if he was a churchgoer, that would be different.'

'Or if you had one thing in common other than this ridiculous orchestra – '

' – which you don't even belong to – '

'Or if he looked the kind of steady type to settle down.'

'The fact is,' said Bryony thoughtfully, 'he's too beautiful to be real. I'm not sure that I met him at all. And all this just seems like a dream, Elinor, and everybody knows, in real life, dreams don't happen. People don't get left a million pounds, out of a wide blue sky, and then be proposed to by gorgeous men who are idiotically talented. It doesn't seem plausible, and just think how hurt you could be. I couldn't bear that, and nor could John.'

'That's all very illogical and silly,' said Jane briskly. 'Of course you met him; we both did. And Elinor was unarguably left a million pounds. The likelihood is that you're being taken for a ride; that's all there is to it. We've been your friends for some years, my girl, long before there was any question of all this money, and I'd just like to know one thing; did David what's-his-name show you the slightest notice before your mother died?'

'That's not the point,' said Elinor, her voice quivering.

'Answer the question,' said Jane irresistibly.

'He didn't know me then.'

Jane looked steadily at her. Elinor flushed.

'There was that other girl that you remember, Caroline. She – '

'You're avoiding the question.'

'I think she's answered the question already,' said Bryony. 'Perhaps we ought to go now, Jane.'

'Elinor, for your mother's sake – '

Elinor turned on Jane with a deadly slowness. 'Get out of my flat,' she said, 'Just get out. You've insulted my judgement, my intelligence and the person I love! You've no right to call yourself a friend of mine.'

Bryony gasped.

'We don't need you, or the rest of the orchestra,' continued Elinor fiercely. 'We don't need anybody except each other. You may think what you like – you may disbelieve me entirely – but we love each other. You've patronised me and introduced me to suitably boring men and looked down on me and pitied me. Well, you don't have to do all that anymore. You can just get out of my life! Your kind of friendship is the kind I don't need. You know the way out – take it.'

And with this Elinor fled into her bedroom. Jane walked to the door majestically, conscious of the drama of her position; Bryony scuttled out behind her, shutting the door so lightly that it seemed to sigh like wind in the trees. And Elinor put her head on her pillow and cried and cried, wondering when David would call, wondering whether love was an illness that could ever be cured.

However, Piotr hadn't given up on Elinor. It was true that, upon the announcement of the engagement, he had ignored Elinor at the pub; and he had certainly been more than usually short with David in orchestra. But his immediate annoyance was outlasted by his concern. His nature was flawed, but disloyalty to his friends was not a part of it. Furthermore, he felt guilty. Had he not approached 'Pym's Delight' that winter's night while waiting for his friend, had he not taken Elinor under his sardonic wing, this midsummer madness might never have happened. She might still have become besotted with David (women, in Piotr's opinion, needing precious little encouragement to become besotted with anything), but it would all have been at a safe distance. Thanks in part to Piotr, the watcher in the balcony had become a player in the game; he blamed himself deeply for that. He waited and watched developments, but in the meantime he laid his plans.

The tour of Canada was short, as Orchestra of London tours went, and, as tours proved much more lucrative than working at home, they went with surprising frequency. The orchestra was to cross the country from the west to the east, over a period of two weeks. There was more time off than usual, although David, who was an entrant in the Budapest cello competition, had early in the tour declared that he intended to spend his spare time practising.

This, to give him credit, he mainly did, eschewing sight-seeing, sauna parties in the hotels, receptions given by local music societies, and most company. His section encouraged him in this, it being their ardent wish that he should win some solo competition and leave them in the peace to which, during the blessed reign of St Felix of the roses, they had become accustomed. But on the last night of the tour, Piotr knocked on David's hotel room door.

'Your esteemed presence is requested,' he observed.

David put his cello down. His practice had been going badly, and he was suspicious of Piotr. Apart from anything else, his spiritualist in Manchester had warned him against 'false friends and those born under the sign of Capricorn', and both descriptions, in David's opinion, fitted Piotr like the paper on the wall.

'I have work to do,' he said testily. 'It's only a month until the competition, and all this wedding business – it is a distraction.'

'I can imagine. But we all know you're bound to win in Budapest.'

'No, no, you cannot say that. The judges may be against my teacher. They may have their own crazy notions of sound.' He was about to add that they might, in whole or in part, have been born under the sign of Capricorn, but decided against it. 'It is not as simple as just playing the best,' he finished gloomily.

'You're probably right,' observed Piotr, seating himself. 'I wasn't good enough to compete internationally when I was your age, so I really don't know. But you sound pretty terrific to us.'

David eyed him darkly. 'What? You like my playing?'

Piotr commended his soul to God and lied like a trooper. 'Well, I'll be honest with you. It took me a long time to admit it to myself, but it was really jealousy. I just couldn't accept the fact that you play better than I do – and better than William, who's an old friend of mine. It was just blindness, pure and simple. But the other day, when you did that modern solo, I was bowled over. This boy is the goods, I thought.'

'You thought what?'

'I thought you were great,' explained Piotr. 'I Saw The Light.'

'What light?'

'I realized I'd been wrong about you all along. You are a genius.'

David brightened. 'When did this happen?'

'During the solo the other day, that frightful modern rubbish. You shone out of that,' said Piotr glibly, 'like the moon out of a blackened sky.'

'It was so good?'

How much more, oh Lord? inquired Piotr of his immortal soul.

'It was electrifying.'

David savoured the word. Electrifying. A good word, that, very descriptive. Elinor may have been right about Piotr. Perhaps there was no harm in him. After all, he had admitted he had been wrong about his genius, and that was not an easy thing for him to do.

'I was quite pleased with the solo,' said David thoughtfully. 'Of course, it was not easy. The bit on the third page – I had such trouble with the fingering. But on the night, yes, I think it was distinguished. Thank you for telling me what you thought about it.'

He prepared to pick up his cello again, but Piotr forestalled him.

'You forget. Your presence is requested.'

'Tell the orchestra that I have no time for parties this trip.'

Piotr registered disappointment. 'William will be sorry.'

'William? What has William to do with it?'

'Nothing that he knows about. But it's his birthday tomorrow and we're holding the surprise party tonight. It'll be very disappointing if you're not there, as section leader. The rest of the cellos are all coming.'

David stood up quickly and put his cello away. 'William. That is different. Of course I must put in an appearance, as you say. It is my duty to my associate principal. I will change, and come down. Where is the party?'

'At the pool. The cake's being brought in by a female gorillagram at eleven.'

'I will be there, but first I must call Elinor. She worries otherwise, thinks I am already dead. Thank you for telling me, Piotr. Yes, right, now where are my swimming things – '

It was well past midnight by the pool. Quite a number of revellers had dispersed, but a hard core were dressed and dancing to a disco tape, and a handful were still grouped in swimsuits by the side of the water. Warren had elected himself in charge of cocktails. His voice was slurred, but his hand, had anyone been alert enough to notice, was completely steady.

'Anyone care for a really fine Harvey Wallbanger?' he inquired.

'I'll split it with you,' suggested Piotr to Isabel.

'Oh, Lord,' said Isabel, exquisite in a black one-piece, 'I've drunk more than enough already.'

Piotr turned to David. 'To the first prize in your competition-thingie. Success to the cello section. Mud in your eye.'

'What about mud?' inquired David, but he accepted rather more than half the drink.

'Where's William gone?' inquired Piotr of Isabel.

'Don't ask me,' she said, tossing back her hair.

'Hey ho, what's this? Have you had a row? Is there a rift within the lute?'

'Oh, forget it!' snapped Isabel.

David looked up with interest.

'Come on, my dear, tell Uncle Piotr. William was here, was a terrific sport about the gorillagramette, seemed to be enjoying the party – then suddenly disappeared. Was it something I said?'

'Don't be absurd.'

'Did he object to your rather revealing swimsuit? What goes on?'

Isabel opened her mouth, then shut it; her lip quivered.

'Leave her alone, Piotr,' commanded David, who had been following this closely. 'She doesn't want to talk about it, I can tell.'

'Not to Piotr anyway!' burst from Isabel, and something glistened on her cheek. 'You hate women, we all know that. You know that you're secretly pleased, just because – oh, forget it!'

'Temper, temper,' said Piotr coolly, watching her run off. 'She's wrong about me, though; I never fail to give credit where it's due. Her complexion is so velvety, isn't it? And her proportions please me. If only she was a man, and had less of a temper . . . Where are you off to, David?'

'I'm going after Isabel,' said David stiffly. 'I consider your behaviour quite impossible. I shall apologise on your behalf.'

'Dashed considerate of you,' said Piotr, waving his glass at David's retreating figure.

Warren came up to him and they clinked glasses. 'We've done our bit,' Warren told him. 'Now it's up to Isabel. I wasn't sure it would work, all that sprinting off stuff.'

'My own humble notion,' said Piotr, with a strange, savage smile. 'David's not the only artist around here, you know.'

'And William?'

'Will's ready.'

'To the Budapest cello competition, then.'

'To Budapest, and Elinor Jay, and poetic justice.'

They finished off the drinks by the side of the lapping pool.

David located Isabel just coming out of the Ladies. She had changed and calmed down, though she still looked subdued. Upon seeing David, she started visibly and moved as though to pass him by.

'Isabel.'

'Yes?'

'If you need someone to talk to – '

'Thank you, but people – '

'I know what you're going to say. People would talk. But look, no one is around, no one is here. I could come to your room with no fear of being seen and we could talk in privacy. Believe me, you would feel better.'

Isabel appeared to weaken. 'It's kind of you.'

'Someone has to make up for Piotr. He can be quite impossible.'

They went up in the lift together, David's hand solicitously on Isabel's shapely shoulder. She collapsed onto the bed, hoping that he was not too tipsy. She could see David out of the corner of her eye, and judged him about as far gone as she'd ever seen him. The punctiliousness of his enunciation bore this out.

'A little whisky or something else from this cabinet?' he inquired. 'Are you comfortable there?'

'Very comfortable; I don't need anything.'

'So what has William done to you? I thought you were in love.'

'I suppose it depends what you mean by love,' she murmured.

'I can't hear you, come closer.'

'He's so jealous, so terribly jealous of everybody. If he knew I was alone in this room with you, he would murder me.'

'I'm not surprised, not at all. It is impossible that he should not have noticed that we are the only two really fine-looking members of the orchestra, you and I.'

Isabel laughed. 'I'm not fine-looking.'

'No, you're beautiful. I use the wrong word. You are stunningly beautiful.'

'My features aren't as good as yours.'

'Well, well, perhaps not. But the way you move, your skin, your shape – William is crazy to risk losing such things.'

'I suppose Elinor's just as jealous about you.'

'Oh, Elinor – how she worries. She worries for my health,

for my playing, for my happiness. But she does not worry about me. She has faith in me, in my faithfulness.'

'I don't think I have it in me to be faithful,' said Isabel with a little sigh. 'I envy women like Elinor, who are made like that. I can't help feeling – fantasizing – about people, at least, about some people. Besides, I think some things are simply fated to happen.'

'You feel that too?'

'About fate? Of course; you can't help it. Fate simply takes over; nobody can be held responsible when that happens.'

'Yes, yes, I know exactly what you mean! My tarot cards say the same. All is fated, predetermined, complete.'

'And is Elinor – fated – for you?'

'Oh, yes,' said David vaguely. 'The cards agree. She is a Virgo with Taurus rising.'

'I wouldn't chance it, if I were you. What if it didn't work out? The risks are tremendous, and it'll only put new pressures on you. Well, it would on me, anyway; I could never stay married. I couldn't manage the faithfulness.'

'Yes, all this is difficult, true, but it is different for me. Great artists require stability in their family life.'

'I always thought artists needed experiences to draw on.'

'What kind of experience do you mean?' asked David, leaning over her. Isabel steeled herself, softening her voice.

'Oh, David, you know I've always wanted you. From the first minute I saw you, during your trial last year I knew that this was certain to happen someday.'

She leaned into David, and a delicious tingling filled him as their lips met. There was a long moment while he pressed her to him, then she pulled away.

'Stop, David, we mustn't.'

Doubly intoxicated, David stroked her arm. 'What did you say? Why not?'

'You're engaged to Elinor – and William – '

'I thought that William is being unkind to you.'

'But what's Elinor done to you? It's not right, David. I'd

feel too guilty.'

'Just let me kiss you again.'

Isabel submitted, and David began to whisper urgently. 'I don't love Elinor, not at all. She is a nice, quiet girl, and she will make a good kind of wife for me, but that's all. I need her for other things.'

'For the cello you deserve, you mean.'

'Oh yes! For the cello – the sound – and also the time to practise. I will never succeed if I am tied to this orchestra's crazy schedule. I need to afford the time to do my talent the justice! And, for that, I need the money, so I must marry. But that does not mean – that does not mean – '

'I understand,' whispered Isabel, as he unbuttoned her blouse.

'What beautiful breasts,' he murmured, cupping them in his hands. 'I always imagined them.'

'Take your jeans off,' she begged him, 'I adore men's thighs.'

'There,' he said, whipping off his jeans and T-shirt. 'They are very good, yes? All my girlfriends like them. So now – '

The knock came just as his lips were sliding down Isabel's neck. She started, pushing David away.

'Isabel,' came a deep voice from outside.

'Oh God, it's William,' she breathed. 'Get dressed – quickly!'

'Pretend you aren't here!' David ordered, but she had already answered, 'William?'

'Of course.'

'I'm – not feeling very well.'

'Open the door, Isabel. I know who's in there with you. Warren spotted him going in.'

'William, my dear friend, I can explain everything,' said David pacifically.

Isabel buttoned up her blouse, and opened the door to admit William. David, always cautious, hurried with his jeans on the far side of the room. He reasoned to himself that he was anxious not to hurt William's feelings – it was not after all his fault if such a girl preferred him to William. Besides, she had practically thrown herself at him, or so he could say. Yes, that would be all right; people would believe that. But all explanation died on his lips when he saw his colleague's expression.

'Get out,' said William wearily.

'My dear friend, you must let me explain. There was nothing, nothing happening that you might be thinking. We were only talking, that is all, about my needing a new cello, for example, and – and – '

There was a flash of genuine fury as William turned to tower over him, a spark of reality that slashed through every layer of deceit and pretence. 'David, I'll give you ten seconds to get out of my sight – ten seconds. After that, I warn you, you take your chance.'

David gathered up his things, and moved to the door. He turned there as if to try again, but a glance at William's face changed his mind. David left them, absolutely shaken, and hurried back to the pool to find Piotr.

'Piotr,' he said solemnly. 'Quickly, quickly. You must call the police, do something! William is going to strangle Isabel!'

Piotr's smooth, otter-like head reared itself up from the poolside chair where he had been dozing.

'Oh, jolly good,' he said sleepily. 'One less woman in the orchestra. Cheers.'

As soon as they were sure David had gone, William slipped his hand under the bed and retrieved the tape recorder.

'Did it work?' she demanded. 'Piotr put another one beneath the table, in case it didn't.'

'It worked all right,' said William grimly.

'Then kiss me.'

'Haven't you had enough of that?'

'I need someone to kiss his kisses off me. Mind, I did think you might have left it another five minutes.'

126

'Longer! I was in agonies as it was!'

'I just thought it could have been more obvious.'

'For someone like Elinor Jay,' said William, tapping the tape recorder, 'half of this would have been enough.'

'You don't seem pleased with me.'

'You were good. You were too good.'

'Oh! William – '

'And what you said about faithfulness – it sticks in my brain.'

William stood up, his shoulders sloping. She was struck by the tiredness in his face. She tried to pull him towards her, but he refused to be comforted.

'I didn't mean it, of course I didn't mean it! Can you really have any doubt of my faithfulness?'

'I haven't the right to doubt it; I haven't the justification. But no, that isn't it, it goes deeper than that. The business sticks in my throat, somehow; or perhaps – perhaps I'm simply too old for these games.'

'It wasn't a game,' said Isabel, more sharply. 'It was justified by the need to help Elinor. It was fully justified. I know it wasn't easy for you, but in such a cause surely – '

'People make their own mistakes, and live by them. And perhaps we manipulated David nearly as much as he manipulated Elinor Jay. Lies and more lies, a glutenous morass of lies! Lying to Margot, lying to our neighbours, lying to our friends. Where does the line finally fall, Isabel? When do we start lying to each other, even to ourselves?'

Isabel looked at the strength of his face, the open conscience of his grief. Oh, he was warm, uncorrupted, intensely, even frighteningly loveable. He was the truest person she'd ever known; and even though she knew their relationship was hurting him, without it part of her would die. He had irretrievably altered her; he had shaken the self-destructive habits of her heart. Unable to operate on any level other than truthfulness, he had taught her heart truthfulness too. She took his hand.

'When it's over,' she told him. 'That's how we'll know.'

He took a long look at her face, serene again, but with that fateful quality upon it that had disquieted him before he knew her. He turned her chin up towards him and kissed her, first delicately and then with more conscious power, caressing the places where David's breath had touched her, kissing her pure again, and all his own. Then her body rose fresh under his possession and they flowed together in a burst of pleasure like a waterfall, as if their love was new, immortal, and untouched by anything that wasn't as sure as truthfulness.

Stories don't really end. They carry on and on, with ramifications and echoes that only become clear over the passage of time and years. They overlap and interweave. Stars of one story only receive walk-on roles in another; and nothing is completely finished until death. But lives are certainly divided into periods, strata, of time. Just the fact that you could hardly bear, now, to go back and live the way you were living just ten years ago proves that. The people you most cared for have slipped in and out of their corners of your heart; your lifestyle has changed; your priorities have changed; even your tastes have slowly, subtly altered. The core of your being is the same, but it's been swirled until it is almost unrecognisable. A surprisingly short period of time will do this, even without many experiences; and Elinor, of late, had experienced more than enough.

The shock of having Piotr appear on her doorstep with the tape would have demolished a weaker character, but there were reserves of strength inside Elinor which enabled her to bear it.

'I wish you could have seen her face afterwards,' Piotr reported. 'Like the Mona Lisa. Resignation, determination, an unearthly serenity. "I think I knew," she told me, "I think, I knew all along." I hardly knew what to say – me, Piotr! I was speechless. She floored me with her dignity. She left the room and I thought, she'll cry alone. That's typical; that's the kind of girl she is. But she didn't go away to cry. She came back with this box, and told me it was for Isabel, with her love. And then she took the ring off her finger and gave that to me, with a look that I can't describe, and asked me to give it to David, adding that she never wished to see or hear from him again. Simple, you see, no messing about. A woman in a thousand. She kissed me at the door and said she hoped we'd always be friends. She said, "I know what you've done for me, and, one day, I'll show my gratitude as you deserve." '

'What was in the box?' asked Warren, after a silence.

'An antique necklace,' said Isabel. 'The most beautiful thing. I don't know how to thank her.'

'I think David suspects that we told her,' said Piotr. 'But he can't prove it.'

'She wasn't at the last concert,' said Warren suddenly. 'Did you notice? Or the one before. It was so strange, not seeing Elinor sitting in the balcony.'

'I'll ring her in a day or so, find out how she's taking it,' said Piotr. 'But something tells me she might just unload her tickets for the rest of the season.'

There's a view that human nature is doomed to repeat itself, but Elinor's life didn't bear out this notion. It's true that she became a subscriber, a month later, to the Royal Sinfonia of London – arch-rival of the Orchestra of London – and appeared, in her self-contained way, at the same box for each concert. However, despite a fleeting interest in one of the clarinetists, she has never, except in passing, met any of the members.

It was during the interval of a Royal Sinfonia concert, however, that she met a charming, forty-year-old divorcé, a City businessman by the name of Russell Palmers, and their engagement was announced just a month later.

Piotr, who still visits her, informs me that she has two little boys and an enormous house in Surrey, as well as a villa in Tuscany. She has made it up with Bryony, although Jane has never forgiven her all her good fortune. It may be that sometimes, spotting a cellist whisking around the corner of the Festival Hall, or noticing a cello recital on Radio Three, or even catching sight of the Orchestra of London on television, she thinks of David, but she has never been seen at the orchestra's concerts since, and the Elinor Jay principal cellist chair is the best-endowed in the Royal Sinfonia.

Her philanthropy does not end there. Gifted young cellists in need of cash for better instruments can apply to the E. W. Jay fund. It is wrongly assumed that the donor is xenophobic, however, because foreign cellists need not apply.

XII

The Frozen Heart

There was a man whom sorrow named his friend,
And he, of his high comrade sorrow dreaming,
Went walking with slow steps along the gleaming
And humming sands, where windy surges wend.

Yeats

Clarence was never an orchestra insider, that wasn't his way. An ardent cricket fan, scuttling away to Lord's or the Oval at every opportunity, he could remind people without blinking how many runs Botham had scored in every test of the '81 Ashes, and who'd got him out in the end. It was known that he was gay; like Piotr, he made no secret of it, but he lacked Piotr's exuberance and sparkle. Piotr was either liked or loathed by everybody; he was the needle jabbed in David's flesh, William's loyal deputy, the mustard in the cello section sandwich – meanwhile, hardly anyone bothered to notice Clarence. He wandered from rehearsal to concert, smiling vaguely at anyone kind enough to greet him, but not imposing his presence anywhere. The very air was not disturbed by Clarence's passing; he seemed to lack the need to be noticed. Recognition, approval, the most basic human hungers, it seemed, were not required. If invited to an orchestra party, whether in London or on a tour, he would appear, politely smiling, at the doorway, speak to a few people then gently disappear. There was no sense of arrogance or superiority in his solitude; it simply seemed that he preferred to be alone.

The role of a second bassoon is one of strong but unobtrusive support, and Clarence was reckoned by bassoonists the finest second bassoon in London. He had a gift for leaning just under his principal's note, never insinuating, never pushing, and the adjustments he made, both in time and pitch, were electrically instantaneous. He made following Gerald, never an easy task, appear simple, but, because he never drew attention to himself, his skill was little remarked. Occasionally a conductor, more astute than most, might praise him, but praise seemed to deliver no particular pleasure. Two pink spots would climb into his pale cheeks, and he would start to busy himself with cleaning his instrument, checking his set of reeds – anything, in fact, to distract him from the notion that a portion of the orchestra might, however briefly, be thinking about him.

The wound which he had suffered, the wound nearly all musicians carry, some lightly, some less lightly, had fallen early on Clarence. He was not to be a first bassoon. This was decreed at the Royal Academy of Music, during his second year. Glory days were not for him; Stravinsky's *Rite of Spring*, the show-stopping solos of *Sheherazade*, these were never to be his province. Bridesmaid status was officially conferred; to the end of time, when the medals were awarded at the end of Shostakovich symphonies, his would be the silver. No one knew, no one guessed, what this cost Clarence, the strength of the dreams he had dreamed growing up in his parent's modest semi in Rickmansworth. The hours he had spent, scales, exercises, concertos; the competitions, local and important, he had won; the very sweat of his brow had been weighed for a moment in the balance and declared inferior stuff. Close, but no cigar. Honourably mentioned. Good, but not brilliant. Clarence? Not at all an unmusical fellow, really, but lacks – character, that's what it is. Poor old Clarence doesn't have the character for solo work. Although Clarence would, in a blind audition, have displayed twice the character of his nearest rival.

As for his reaction, no one even guessed that he thought about it. His small smile, which hid a nature so terrifyingly passionate that only one human had ever realised it, covered everything.

'Clarence? He's doing very well,' his mother had used to say comfortably. 'Lives for his music, always did.'

'The Orchestra of London,' his father would pronounce, quelling his inward feeling that they were a corrupting lot, and had a fair amount to answer for, quelling even a doubt that, had he kept Clarence in India as a child, the music craze might never have happened. 'You'll have heard of Roger Ash. He's their principal conductor, you know. Thinks a lot of Clarence, does Roger Ash.'

His sister, who with sisterly impatience had often tried to take Clarence in hand, blamed his school. 'Honestly, father, it was the school that did for Clarence. Boarding school! If you ask my opinion – '

She invited him for Christmases, criticised his clothes, invaded his home with schemes for redecoration and exclaimed at his bald spot when the orchestra appeared on television.

'Clarence, I've told you before that you have to think more about your appearance! I'm amazed that nobody in the BBC thought to wave a powder puff over your head . . . As for that diabolical tie you chose for the kiddie concert, I thought little Amy would take fright up the chimney. Was it a sixties tie or a seventies tie, anyway? Why don't you give it to the deserving poor?'

Clarence did his best to please his family, but other hungers were long in dissipating. He took pride in his work, he loved his bassoons; but the yearning for glory was a long time in going. As is perhaps common in youth, he had begun by associating fame with happiness; there were times when his second bassoon status felt like a life sentence of defeat.

'What I like about you, boy,' Gerald, who was his age precisely, once confided, 'is that you're so unpretentious. None of this rubbish about wanting to be principal, no catty comments about me to other people! No, you know your place and stick to it, and that's a rare thing in this profession. Wish there were more around like you, boy, and that's no joke. Another round?'

Clarence's forays into matters of the heart – the only escape, or so it seemed to him – were equally doomed. When the loneliness grew too painful he wandered into the seedier sectors of London, or met people at friends' parties got up for the purpose. A romantic, whose favourite composer (though it wasn't something he would speak about) was Puccini, he knew that someday he would meet another person whom he could love. Around some dusty London bookshop, at the crisis of a Test at Lord's, it would happen again, except that this time there would be no false dawn, the long drought would really be ended. This time the one passion of his past would be at once recovered and forgotten, the scab would close over a wound that had bled for far too long. But in the meantime there were only misread expressions, mistaken understandings. In the meantime, off and on, there was only Ralph.

Clarence had met Ralph through a gay friend, who had known Ralph to be in need of lodgings. The friend had not been aware that Ralph was a petty pilferer and former drugs dealer, but Ralph had made the first of these drawbacks abundantly obvious during the period he'd stayed in Clarence's house. Touched and amused by Ralph, and perhaps expecting nothing better, Clarence had put up with the situation until he missed something of genuine importance to him – old cricketing photos, complete with autographs. Then, for the first and last time in his life, Clarence had allowed his fury to get the better of his patience. Ralph had moved out the next day, his belongings to follow. But even this episode left its mark on Clarence's warmheartedness. He could never remember Ralph without a vague guilt that he'd let Ralph down, without hoping that Ralph was doing better without him. Although his heart, which never knew lies, only omissions, told him that there was nothing in Ralph to mourn.

So when Ralph occasionally returned for a short stay, Clarence loaned his parents the things he most cared for, and took him in. To hear footsteps around the house, even pounded footsteps, lightened his heart, bringing back the time, only a few years before when –

Clarence could never talk about that time, the only time when his life had equalled the intensity of his art. Even his family never knew of his loss, the past he could neither verify nor return to. Without music he wouldn't have survived it, because Clarence was a real musician, one of the few whose love of playing had survived everything, the rejections, the travelling, the sated repetition of conductor after conductor and symphony after symphony. Fearful of ridicule, he wouldn't admit to enjoying his work, but there were still times when he adored it. Even to be (only) second bassoon, to have his anointed place in the midst of all this splendour! With Mahler surging through his veins he would sometimes have to bend his face over his instrument in order to hide his emotion.

The world imposes its strictest miseries on people who feel everything with Clarence's intensity. Having spotted Clarence biting his lip to keep from crying during Mahler's Fifth, Gerald would later joke: 'Thought I'd have to catch you on your way down, C. Thought you were going to faint on me, I wouldn't kid you. Feeling all right now?' To which Clarence could only have replied, 'No, worse, far worse. The music, which reached out and plucked me up, has only put me down again' – replies Gerald could have neither forgiven nor understood.

Shortly before the September tour of the Far East, Roger Ash conducted Elgar's *Enigma Variations* in the Festival Hall. It happened that this piece had resonances for Clarence that went far beyond his present trauma – which, though no one knew it at the time, was severe. His little face, with its kind moonlit smile, was more closed-up than ever, his frame seemed to shrink in on itself in undiluted self-effacement.

'Poor little tyke's getting that flu,' was Gerald's verdict, as he waited with Mirabel before the second half of a concert.

'Who, Clarence? He hasn't looked well for ages,' said Mirabel. 'I don't think he'd be doing the Far East tour except that he needs the money. Shame, because I'm really looking forward to it. I'm even stopping off in Aussie-land afterwards to see my family.'

'Yes, should be a good tour, long as Roger Ash doesn't overdo the rehearsing . . . You don't think I ought to get the old boy seen by somebody before we go?'

'What, a doctor? It's not a bad idea. Though you might just make him self-conscious. He's so sensitive.'

'Sensitive! Hell, we're all sensitive,' said Gerald forcefully. 'Fact is, I need him over there. Only second bassoon I'm really comfortable with. He was my second as far back as the Royal Academy, did I ever tell you?'

The *Enigma* began. It was one of Roger's favourite pieces, and he conducted it with unexpected feeling. Privately, he assigned characters of his own to Elgar's variations; all his ex-wives had their slots, which he dispatched with particular vividness . . . His orchestra. His own orchestra. Of course they were a royal pain at times, but there was nothing like it really.

There was David Schaedel – biggest mistake of his career – beside William Mellor, Piotr and Adam Halloran behind. God knows how William landed Isabel . . . Isabel and Caroline together in the back of the violas, best-looking desk in the band. Paul Ellison taking the lead effortlessly at principal oboe. Whip up the violins – Warren Wilson negotiating all those flurries beautifully; first and third horns preparing, Henry first, then Mirabel. Wants watching, does Mirabel, gutsy, sexy sort of character, completely fearless. Be a first horn someday . . . Cue the bassoons, Gerald and Clarence entering on the same heartbeat. What a team they were, the bassoons! What an orchestra, what a motley unworkable collection of egos and beta-blockers, evangelicals and alcoholics, poets and farm-hands, liberals and anarchists! His own particular world-class orchestra.

Suddenly Roger loved them all – even Piotr with his wicked tongue and David Schaedel over-schmalzing his solo. Even Isabel, who'd refused him twice, and Paul Ellison, who (he had reason to suspect) was negotiating backdoor deals with other conductors, from his powerful position on the orchestra board. Inspiration descended upon Roger, the kind of inspiration that favours humans only rarely in a lifetime.

'Yes, he's on form tonight,' ran through ninety minds.

'Not bad, all right, not bad, but not as great as Hochler,' seethed Paul Ellison. 'I'll get Hochler in if it's the last thing I do.'

'One would almost imagine,' considered Piotr, 'that he hadn't conducted it before. That's a gift, you must admit, to make it suddenly fresh, paint just drying on the fresco. It's played too often, far too often, but this time it's different, richer. As if every barrier between us and the music has been suddenly, shockingly torn away.'

'The difficulty in this little solo,' David reckoned, 'is the delayed shift. Very few cellists can delay this shift so long without ruining the delicacy – there. Precisely. Yes, I think that was good, very good. It is a great shame the other cellos must join me at this point, perhaps an error of judgement on Elgar's part. Assuredly the whole variation would be better written as cello solo – '

'I lift up this theme to Isabel,' thought William, during the cello section variation. 'The triplets are Isabel, and the line is the line of Isabel's body, from shoulder to thigh. It's an evocation of beauty and submission and ending – that dying fall at the end. Because nothing holds out against death, not even love – and love itself is nothing but the last defiant gesture of our steadily failing hearts.'

And Clarence, in the centre of the music, heard the slow tidal swell of the threatening lower strings, heard it cupped in Roger's hands, as he'd never heard it before. The clarinet's sustained plea, the tolling of trombone bells, the remorseless tread of the timpani – nevermore, nevermore. What unearthly

137

regrets these vibrations released! There were tears peppering Clarence's cheeks as he prepared for the Finale, unprofessional tears, crying out to a God who, beyond all justice, had taken his love away. He tried to hold them back but the chilling beauty of those bars had stripped him of all resistance.

Such music! It was more than music, like all inspirations, performed with inspiration, by players goaded into inspiration, it was beyond music, beyond poetry, beyond all we can know, with all our human fragility, of courage and loss and defeat. Clarence's silent tears were tears of sudden understanding, inexpressible, untranslatable, outside the perfect sympathy of the music. The second bassoon laid them with reverence at Elgar's feet, and slipped out alone into the transfigured night.

XIII

O My Lady

O lady, consider when I shall have lost you
The moon's fully hands, scattering waste,
The sea's hands, dark from the world's breast,
   The world's decay where the wind's hands have passed,
   And my head, worn out with love, at rest
  In my hands, and my hands full of dust,
    O my lady.

Ted Hughes

The doorbell – a measured announcement like an offstage trumpet – roused Isabel from her preparations. How many times, she wondered, as she put down the lit candle and moved to the door, how many times and still the startled gear-change of the pulse? Spring had eased into summer, into autumn, the day's pace had lengthened then started inexorably to shrink again yet still came the prickling nervousness, that it would end, that it couldn't last, that it was too genuine to last, too crucial. Though she struggled against this fatalism, or else pushed it aside as something too terrible to contemplate. It was enough that it was, that it existed, she thought, no point in thinking beyond, as if worrying could ever help anyway.

He stood in the doorway, hair just blurred by the breeze outside the apartment building, but she preferred his hair untidy, slipped beyond his strict control. He was carrying flowers – long curling purple blooms that flattered the violet tones in her front room – but she gathered him to her, reckless of their safety. It was William who kicked shut the door behind him, who slipped the bouquet onto the top of the television set before warming his arms around her. And they were both momentarily relieved, comforted, as though they hadn't seen each other for months, or might never have seen each other again.

'I always think,' said William, his mouth muffled by her hair, 'that I dreamed all this.'

'And I always think that you won't come back.'

'Sometimes, on the way here, I feel strange, crazy – thinking about all the others.'

'There aren't any others; there never were, not like this. Oh William, I've never felt anything like this.'

He buried his lips in her hair, aware that his heart was echoing her, but forcing his voice not to answer. These days, it was as if, as long as he didn't say it, it wasn't true, and treachery was allowed. He despised himself for this sophistry, but was aware that he used it all the same. Or perhaps he was only thinking as Margot herself would have thought, if they could ever have discussed the issue dispassionately – that for sex alone his behaviour might be tolerable but not this, not this. Not this longing to know as well as possess, not this yearning for complete immersion in some other person's soul. It was how he might have thought himself, had he been in Margot's position, and it didn't make it any easier that he knew it.

'The woman across the hall,' he said, striving for a lighter tone, 'gave me a very odd look just now.'

Isabel remembered her bouquet. 'How gorgeous these are! You must mean Mrs Agnew; she spies on everybody. She noticed last week and asked me who you were; I told her you were an uncle. An uncle from Sussex. I suppose she noticed your ring.'

William's hand fingered his ring uneasily; it was a heavy signet which had been in his family for generations. 'My ring. I hadn't thought about it.'

'Oh, I don't care what she thinks. I only lied for you.'

Disquiet seized him; lie upon lie, deceit piled on deceit! And she was so casual about it, so practised. She was arranging the flowers in a vase with deft, fluid movements. The candle fluttered below her, creaming the soft line of her arms, her black hair clouded over them. He wished suddenly that she was less obviously desirable, if only to enhance his dwindling self-respect. In order to distract his mind, he took refuge in humour.

'Why Sussex exactly?' he inquired.

'I see you as Sussex, I don't know why. Not too near reality, perhaps. More country than home counties, but accessible – oh, accessible! In a village with a duck pond, walking a couple of Irish setters. And no, I don't know why Irish setters either – just a whim.'

'No, it must be Irish setters, no other breed will do. I must have told you how I'd always wanted to keep them.'

'No,' said Isabel. 'You never told me.' And they stared at each other for a moment, shaken.

'Perhaps,' he said, 'I'll retire to some Sussex village and make it come true.'

There was an almost imperceptible pause in her movements with the cutlery. 'You're far too young to retire.'

'Five years,' said William gently. 'Sixty. I could retire at sixty.'

She was always startled when she remembered his age, could never decide whether he carried his years lightly or, to her at least, no longer looked his age. How well he moved! And her body still hummed from his embrace, readying, tuning itself. It was all foreplay, the tone of his voice, the feel of his hands and the meal she had prepared for him. She pushed the thought of retirement – desertion – away. Absolutely anything could happen over five years; and Isabel had always specialised in living in the present.

William slipped past her in order to make himself a drink; his hand on her bare arm unfocussed her mind. 'The cello section,' he told her from the kitchen, 'is in complete shambles.'

'What, more than usual?'

'I think even more than usual. Old Eugene is very unhappy; he feels devalued where he is and he's quietly overdoing the drinking. Piotr's unstable, moody – more to the point, he's slacking off. I've warned him, officially and unofficially, but you know Piotr, he won't take anything seriously. Instead he needles Adam Halloran beside him and David in front of him, while not performing as well as usual. It's crazy; he's just giving Adam ammunition. I told you that Adam's been mounting an increasingly vicious campaign to get Piotr demoted from his position.'

'Surely nobody listens to Adam.'

'David does. David listens to anyone who consistently admires his cello playing. Not only that, but Paul Ellison listens to him, and Paul's position on the board gives him power.'

'Paul's got enough fish to fry as it is,' said Isabel. 'There's his on-and-off affair with Nancy and all his schemes about conductors – not to mention his family and his silly boring planes and other things.'

'Meaning you,' he teased, sitting down beside her on the sofa.

'Not at all; he's given up on me. He knows by now.'

The unspoken truth behind this – that everyone knew, that the rapacious orchestral grapevine had completely encircled them – hovered in the air. It was the grapevine, greedily entwining around his private life, that kept William from sleep at nights. It seemed unlikely, impossible that so public a business could be kept indefinitely from Margot's ears, that the miasma of rumour would not, eventually, waft as far as Ealing. By unspoken consent, however, they refused to mention her.

'Warren doesn't seem very happy about us,' said William, at length.

Isabel's eyes softened. 'Warren. He proposed to me, did I ever tell you? On Victoria Station, completely surrounded by harried commuters and announcements of derailments at Clapham. Ages ago – nearly ten years ago it must have been. Oh, we were young! I remember thinking how young he was, but really, I was hardly more experienced myself . . . We keep a certain corner of our hearts, don't you think, for people who once adored us?'

'I wouldn't know,' said William, with a smile. 'I haven't such a quantity of them, personally.'

'Not even before you married?'

'I can hardly remember.'

Isabel turned his hand over and kissed it; the blunt strength of his hands had always aroused her. 'I don't suppose you noticed. I found it difficult enough to get your attention myself.'

'Oh, I'd noticed you; who could have failed to notice you? I was simply better at resisting.'

'You're still better at it,' she said acutely. 'You're resisting now.'

Perhaps he loved her for her acuteness, just as she loved his scruples, the perpetual tang of conquest. I'm lost, he thought, almost with relief; there's no recovery possible. It had chosen to hit him late, very late, probably too late, but it had come; the maddening, perfect, ignoble and overriding feeling of his life. It was wrong; it was terrible; it was against every reasoning of his heart, but it was there and he could no more root it out than he could die.

He unbuttoned the top buttons of her blouse and slid his fingers over the cream-laced riches inside. At the first warm breath on her skin she felt herself sinking, surrendering, her blood abruptly charged with greater fervour. There was surreal magic in his hands and lips on her body, power, purpose, imagination. He had pulled her onto the carpet; he was harnessing her impulsive rhythm to his own; he was orchestrating her responses, his confident instinct composing her internal music. First there was always the shock that he had succumbed, thought Isabel, but then almost anything could happen. And after the arched moments of oblivion, once the last tremulous pulse had reabsorbed itself into her heart's normal rhythm, she felt an uprushing tenderness.

'It really is better,' she told him.

'What's that?' William inquired softly.

'It really is different – better – when you're in love with the person. I never believed that before – well, before you.'

'Perhaps I'm just better,' he said quizzically, because what she was telling him meant too much, touched him too deeply.

'That could, of course, also be it,' she admitted, recognising what he couldn't bear. 'I still dream, though.'

'You've got the reality. What can you be dreaming about now?'

'I sometimes dream that you're still here in the morning,' she said, sitting up and hugging her knees to her. 'I dream that I wake up and find you're still here, curled up asleep beside me, wearing rather old-fashioned pyjamas.'

'Sorry, I won't wear pyjamas, not even in dreams.'

'I suppose it's that fuzzy domesticity that gives them the appeal,' she said sadly. 'That, and the fact that it couldn't happen, that you couldn't ever stay.'

'Isabel – '

The phone rang. The girl sighed, and rose to answer it. She recognised the imperious sarcasm of Piotr – Piotr, who so resented William's feeling for her that he could, by this time, hardly be civil to her in orchestra. A part of Isabel accepted that he felt aggrieved, even, however crazily, displaced – but her pride rose rebellious against it all the same.

'I *do* trust I'm not interrupting anything tumultuous,' said Piotr nastily. 'Can you reach out a long arm and drag Will to the phone? I know he's there; he told me he would be. And a good think he did tell me, as it happens.'

'Piotr,' said Isabel coolly, holding out the receiver towards him. William was already up, half-dressed.

'Piotr,' he said. 'What's wrong?'

'Margot called me. Wanted to find out where the rest of the

orchestra was playing tonight, because the office is closed and she needed to talk to you. I couldn't remember where the hell you told her the orchestra's supposed to be, but I told her, leave it to me, old scout, not to worry, I could singlehandedly haul the six prostitutes off you, or as near as makes no difference.'

'Did she say what had happened?' asked William, gripping the receiver.

'Women,' said Piotr, after considering, 'are an irritating breed. I think she told me very nearly everything that was wrong, with that solitary exception. I am a recently qualified authority on your car's leak, and could score highly in an examination, whether written or oral, on your dyslexic grandson – in point of fact, on either of your grandsons. Howsoever, all I can immediately recall of the crisis at hand is that it has something to do with her nurse. Yes, I'm convinced that the nurse came into it somehow, though whether she proposed elopement with the milkman, bugging the serious fraud office, or infringing the laws of copyright is beyond me. Depends very much what sort of milkman you've got, I suppose.'

There was nothing to be done with Piotr when he was in skittish mood, thought William. 'Thanks,' he said. 'I'll call right away.'

'Not if you'll be guided by me, you won't. Even Margot must know that now would be plumb spang in the middle of the second half of this non-existent concert. Leave it half an hour, is my advice. Just make sure by then that you're a plausible distance from home. You've been bloody lucky, though, if you think about it. If she'd chosen to call someone other than the undersigned who knows what she might not have heard.'

'Yes,' said William quietly. 'Thanks. I'll see you tomorrow.'

He hung up the phone, thoughtful. Of course it had been a risk, just one more risk out of so many. And naturally Margot would have chosen to call Piotr; he amused Margot; he amused everybody. Amusing people was how he survived. And yet, had Piotr been out – surely she wouldn't have called anyone else! Margot knew the rest of the orchestra only as names, names on a programme, lists of touring parties and disembodied voices on the telephone. She wouldn't have called a name on the orchestra register, he thought, though without conviction. Piotr's words had only been a revenge, a tweak at Isabel, whom he'd never trusted before, and certainly didn't trust now.

'So you have to go,' said Isabel. She felt cheated, although he couldn't have stayed very much longer in any case. The fact that she had no right to feel cheated changed nothing.

'It's the nurse, something's gone wrong.'

'Do you have time to eat anything?'

He caught the look in her face, and changed his mind. 'I have half an hour,' he said formally, 'thank you.'

If he couldn't be there in the morning, he thought, at least he could allow her a few of those intoxicating domesticities that some part of her longed for. Bad enough surely to betray Margot, without also betraying Isabel; bad enough to be betraying himself. She turned into the kitchen, leaving him alone.

And he ought to be alone, he thought, with a wave of self-disgust. If he'd been alone, no one could have blamed him. Piotr would be powerless then to skewer his conscience with his well-timed sarcasm, and Margot's cheerfulness would cease to reproach him. He hadn't meant it to happen, he thought; all he'd tried to do in the first place was to help Isabel. It had started as well-meaning, even fatherly, friendliness – how was he to suppose that someone like Isabel would ever choose him? That would have been the wildest conceit, in a man of his age and habits, and, at first imagination, he'd accepted it as such. It wasn't until she'd made her preferences perfectly plain that he blamed his own behaviour. She had been rebounding from Clive, vulnerable, reaching – and he'd used her just as all the rest tried to use her. He had behaved like Paul Ellison, like Roger Ash; he'd seen his opportunity, and seized it. It was that first night on tour that had been reprehensible. She had been hurting, he had used her hurt – but beyond that night he too had been doomed, captured by the imprint of her body on his, by the weakened powers of resistance, the pent-up desires of years. After the first death, there is no other.

He followed her into the kitchen. She had left the main light off; the glow from the street lamp slivered in through the window. Isabel was standing at the window, her back to him, brushing the tears out of her eyes. He turned her gently around, conscious of the little kick of electricity between them, but fighting his awareness of it. Time for the truth; she deserved that at least; perhaps, in the end, the truth was all that he could give her.

'There's something I have to tell you,' he said seriously, and she thought his voice had never sounded so raw and beautiful. 'I don't know why, but I feel the time's come to admit it to you, to myself.'

She squared her shoulders beneath his hands: Clive, she thought, it's Clive again, and Joel and all the others. This time, when he leaves, he's going for good. Piotr's won and I've lost; I've lost all I really care about. But when she raised up her eyes she read something different, different and overpowering and suddenly it didn't matter that he had to leave, didn't matter that it had – but for Piotr, who despised her – so nearly been the evening that spelled disaster for them. However it ended, it didn't matter, not now she had the reassurance she'd always longed for.

Oh, end the world now, thought Isabel, lifted beyond reason by the only gift he'd previously denied her; this is all I wanted, only this moment, only this.

XIV

Mirabel's Will

Think where man's glory most begins and ends,
And say my glory was I had such friends.

                                                Yeats

There was absolutely no reason, of course, why I should have
been surprised by Mirabel's legacy. I could not recall the time
before which she termed me, with a fervent, public loyalty,
her 'best friend' – It was that kind of exaggerated, naive
appellation which only sounded unembarrassing in Mirabel's
still-Australian accent. I had no reason to suppose that the
fierceness of her partiality – and Mirabel's partialities were
invariably fierce; she had once stabbed a lover with his own
nail-clippers – would fail to be reflected in her will. In fact, I
should really, I suppose, have been surprised had Mirabel
elected to leave me out altogether. But what she left me
proved to be so odd, so outrageous, so Mirabelesque – but I'd
really better tell the story from the beginning.

She was in an accident, of course – a long, lingering affair
was never Mirabel's style. No, she had to depart with éclat:
phone lines buzzing from continent to continent ('I say, have
you heard the awful news about Mirabel?') Nothing else
would have been remotely in character.

'A heart attack,' she had told me firmly, when we discussed
it. 'I shall have a fatal heart attack. A-type personality.
Obsessive behaviour patterns. Competitive lifestyle. Runs,
indeed scampers, in the family. A heart attack can only be a
matter of time.'

'Doesn't seem to upset you much.'

'Why should it? Oh, I expect it will hurt like the devil but then, you see, it will be over – no nerves, no agonizing, no boring, drawn-out suffering. Much the best method, my dear Elaine, I heartily recommend it.'

'From your long experience.'

'From my in-depth consideration,' she assured me a little huffily. If Mirabel had a fault, and I could have named you dozens, it was a tendency to take herself, that personal, dramatic creature, a touch too seriously.

And yet her heart never failed her, not that she had given it much chance. Her heart went with the plane, down, mercilessly down, head first into the black South China Sea.

It took me weeks to admit that it had happened, weeks to accept – if such an enormity can ever be accepted – that she was gone, that she would never be swinging in from her latest tour, laden with trinkets for my girls, or, more rarely, for me. She had been gone so often, you understand, that her very absences had become part of the rhythm of my life. It never failed to thrill me, like the country mouse, when she called me up from Brussels or Singapore or wherever the orchestra had taken her, to tell me, over a line never quite as crackling as I expected, about the latest trauma to befall her.

And there was no shortage of traumas. Mirabel loathed boredom, so, even if dying young was the penalty, the orchestra world in some ways suited her. She played third French horn in the Orchestra of London, a group which appeared, as far as I could tell, to spend half its time scrambling from one corner of the globe to another, in a constant, desperate quest for solvency, audiences and CD sales.

When she was at home and unengaged in recordings or concerts, she tended to drop into our house for attention and sympathy, never failing to be irritated if we were, by remote chance, out or entertaining other company. Which was not to say that Mirabel had no home of her own. She was married to a research chemist of exemplary character, looks, patience and generosity. In fact, so ridiculously admirable was Stephen, and so energetically was Mirabel in the habit of enumerating his perfections, that some people took an irrational dislike to the fellow.

I didn't dislike him; I admired him, for his lean looks, exquisite manners, his unselfish support of Mirabel. But I never felt close to him the way you might expect that I would, never failed to marvel that Mirabel – that impulsive, generous, vital creature – should have been attracted by such opposite characteristics. Stephen's inner strength was impressive, but perhaps a little forbidding; when he smiled he looked wonderfully handsome, but then, he rarely smiled. I think I was always a little afraid of him, a little nervous of retaining what Mirabel impatiently assured me was his good opinion. His scientific career was also intimidating; somehow the image of Stephen serenely manipulating chemical molecules and test-tubes seemed to lift him out of the realm of normal mortals and into a different sphere altogether. Perhaps it would have been different had I been good at science in school – but then, Mirabel too had been appalling at it and her natural egotism still denied her the option of admitting Stephen to be her superior. The only people whose superiority Mirabel acknowledged were better horn players than herself, and, by her own admission, there were precious few of these.

I found myself, after the first few days of stupefied misery, remembering whole conversations I'd had with Mirabel, remembering her, in fact, as vividly as if she had appeared, Banquo-like, and seated herself at my kitchen table. I remembered the first time I'd been asked to Mirabel's house – an honour, because Stephen loathed guests. We were already intimate, we had become intimate within the first ten minutes; it was that breathless, that headlong, with Mirabel. Risky, was how it felt to my British notions, like falling in love, risky and exhilarating at the same time. As if the blood had been shaken out of its ordinary course in the veins; a new and strange sense of being propelled into being fully alive.

'What was it you said your husband does?' she had demanded.

'He teaches physical education at a public school.'

Her eyes clouded, but then she laughed. 'Could have been a politician,' she comforted me. Politicians manipulated people, was her point, and Mirabel had an inbuilt horror of being manipulated. Power played such a large part in her life – conductors, principal horn players, orchestra managers – her whole life seethed with intrigue and power ploys which at once fascinated and repelled her. But she was also a snob – she would have been the first to admit it – and she definitely considered that I, her publicly appointed best friend, deserved a more impressive spouse than poor Rodney could ever be. She had visualised, I could tell, a Stephen-clone, a Shakespearean lecturer or concert pianist, as my consort. And who's to say that she wasn't right, in a way, at least in so far as I felt myself that I could have waited longer and done better. But I was not long married when I first met Mirabel, and the thrill of possessing my own home had yet to fade.

At any rate, she soon invited Rodney and me over for a dinner which I knew, even before it happened, would be a disaster, one of those disasters that haunts you afterwards, as if everything might have been different if it hadn't happened. Stephen was still, Rodney uneasy, Mirabel, as if flogged into action by their unhelpfulness, alternately kittenish, tigerish, Labourite, Conservative, Green. She displayed all her claws, examined them, manicured them. She flirted with her husband, with mine, with me. Finally she lapsed into sulkiness, a child deprived, unfairly, of happiness. I realize now that I often thought of her as my child. I judged her wilfulness as I judge the behaviour of my children; and I loved her the way you love a child who is yours, completely, furiously, endlessly. I remember that Stephen and I were dutifully discussing Chopin – we both play piano, me badly, Stephen well – when Mirabel slammed her hand on the table so hard that I winced, as if it had been my own hand.

'This is all so stupid!' she cried out fiercely. 'Can't you see how stupid this is? It's not enough, not nearly enough. *There has to be more than this*, don't you see? Otherwise it makes no sense at all.'

I glared, not at Mirabel but at Stephen. I always felt as though Stephen should have been able to control Mirabel but didn't trouble to. This was unfair, of course, but it was how I felt. Most of our feelings are unfair, when you come to think of it; we imagine that we give people the benefit of the doubt, but in practice we rarely do. We tolerate each other, which is exactly what tormented Mirabel. Toleration wasn't nearly enough to suit Mirabel, with her temperamental opposition to peacefulness.

'For God's sake,' muttered Rodney, 'she must be drunk.' He was annoyed at me, for putting him in such a position, I suppose. Stephen calmly sipped his wine. As early as that first evening I suspected that her outbursts relieved him of his own burdens, as if she gave voice to all that in him remained unexpressed.

'Of course there's more than this,' he reasoned. 'Poetry and nature and music, all kinds of things. But quiet evenings with friends are not to be sneered at, Mirabel. Life doesn't always have to be gunshot and fireworks. Care for some more wine, Elaine?'

'Thank you,' I responded, although I hadn't intended to drink any more. The simplicity of his explanation soothed me. I felt closer to Mirabel too, as if all I had needed was an interpreter all along. But Rodney, excluded, only felt that Mirabel had been intolerably rude.

'Nice kind of friend for you to choose!' he moaned on our way home. 'What a maniac, slamming tables and getting plastered. Feminist, too. Did you hear how she put her husband in his place over politics?'

I suppose to Rodney's old-fashioned notions Mirabel might even in those days have ranked as a feminist, though she was far too idealistic for any sisterhood to claim her. I don't believe

I ever heard her express a really feminist idea. All she wanted was an equal chance, the chance her talent had won her in the orchestra; it made her fume when other women weren't given the same chance. Eight years ago, however, I was even less feminist than Mirabel. Rodney ruled our house, economically, politically, temperamentally, fundamentally. I didn't mind, because the girls loved me best. It was as simple, and unfair, as that.

I did attempt to mollify Rodney on the drive back, but he was absolute in his opinions, as absolute as Mirabel herself. From that evening he distrusted and detested her, while she felt precisely as cordial towards him. The difference was that, while Mirabel used to mock Rodney to me, Rodney could hardly mention Mirabel's name without working himself into a complete fury.

He felt threatened, I can see now, or perhaps he saw further than any of us were inclined to give him credit for. He recognised that, with Mirabel, a new unit had entered the smooth equation of our marriage. And perhaps he guessed, in some almost drowned intuitive way, what would be the end of it.

There was a period, as I suppose there always is in grieving, when Mirabel's absence seemed like a suicide, a complete betrayal. I went through a sequence of irrationality, snapping the girls' heads off, screaming at my piano pupils, being hardly able to speak to Rodney. His hatred of her – and hatred was not too strong a word – seemed to divide him from me still further once she was no longer there. Or perhaps his hatred, instinctive as an animal's, had become too strong to be dissipated by anything as obvious as death. Perhaps, dislodged, it had to travel somewhere, and I was the nearest stopping point. And it's possible that I wanted him to hate me too, once Mirabel had gone, possible that it felt, in some obscure way, like justice, like loyalty.

I fought against it, for the girls' sake. Laura was fractious at school, Tina increasingly shrank into herself, Clarissa became fretful and demanding. I knew this was because I was cutting myself off from them, because my grief had become cancerous, invading every segment of my life. I knew I was unbalanced, that the death of a friend isn't allowed to do this to a person. The Samaritan I called had been almost incredulous, that someone with a husband and three children could be so numbed, so slanted, by the death of a friend. When I had tried to describe Mirabel as my 'best friend', the way she had always described me, my throat jerked shut and I couldn't form the words. I sat choking for a moment, then put the phone down. Later I realised that not being able to admit it was another betrayal, of Mirabel, of myself, of how she had mattered to me.

The only person who understood was Stephen. He had a miraculous inability to feel jealous. The intensity which Rodney so mistrusted in my understanding with Mirabel did not disturb Stephen in the slightest – or perhaps he just knew Mirabel better than Rodney knew me. Rodney's feeling, unexpressed but all the uglier for that, was that there is something fishy about a female companionship as all-encompassing as ours; Stephen admired it. Although (or perhaps because) he was incapable himself of so much openness, so much honesty, he thought it marvellous what women could do to support each other.

I remembered how tough Mirabel had been when I needed her to be. I had been thought to have cancer, and had twice put off the exploratory operation. It was the sort of selfish behaviour that Mirabel and I were always ridiculing – being unable to face the possibility of knowing the worst. I knew it was wrong, I knew better, but I couldn't help myself. I thought, 'We're all dying anyway. What good would it do to know for sure?' I thought, 'Rodney couldn't cope with it; the girls couldn't cope with it. It's braver not to know.' The first time I feigned flu, the second time a virus. Mirabel came to visit me the day before the third time.

'Get up,' she said, 'We're going for a walk. Do we have to take Clarissa?'

'You know we do,' I snapped, resenting her tone, resenting the way Clarissa pulled at me, the fat three-year-old passivity of her bones.

'Well, come on then.' Patience not being Mirabel's strong point, I hurried to get Clarissa ready, hearing Mirabel's keys jangling in her pocket in the hall. It was Mirabel, I realised, who should have given birth to three children, who should have suffered them softening down her swift edges, her defences, her remorseless certainties. If I had cancer, I would leave Mirabel my children – it would make it more bearable dying, knowing that I had influenced her so completely . . . I smiled at the thought, at the very notion of Mirabel's clever angular fingers struggling to button up Clarissa's little blue coat, of Mirabel's horn practice – arpeggio after arpeggio, punctuated by swearing – being broken up by Laura's bullying and Tina's wails. Better her than Rodney, I found myself thinking, illogically, unfairly, even untruthfully, because Rodney was a good and loving father, the kind of father who would always make an effort to do the right thing, unimaginative, well-meaning, dull.

'I'm coming with you tomorrow,' announced Mirabel, once we were out in the open air.

'Coming where?' I asked stupidly.

'To the hospital, remember? You're going to hospital.'

'I'm not going,' I told her.

'Of course you are.'

'Look, Mirabel, we've been through all this. It's my life, right? Hands off my life.'

'What do you mean?' she inquired, using that genuinely puzzled tone which meant that the contents of an entire conversation had slipped her mind.

'You're hopeless, you know that? How can I have a relationship with someone with a memory like a sieve?'

'There's nothing wrong with my memory,' she assured me irritably.

'Let me spell it out for you again. I'm going to live my own life, regardless of your opinions. I'm not going to leave Rodney – '

'You should,' she interrupted, chewing her lower lip. 'Should have left him years ago.'

'– and I'm not going to be ordered about, either. By you or him or anybody else.'

'Right-ho,' she said, looking up. 'That's a start, anyway.'

'Just listen, will you? You tell me to do this, he moans at me to do that – I'm like somebody's football, chucked about by every neighbourhood child. I'm my own person; and what I do is my own business. What do you think of that?'

'I think you'd better get down to that bloody hospital. Do you want to die?'

Seen off one ground, Mirabel could always find another. I remember thinking how illogical she could be, but still she shook me. 'Of – course not.'

'Just checking. Because I know your church buddies all suppose it'll be miles better on the other side – Really, I never know what lunatic notions those Baptists will shove into you next.'

I was too accustomed to hearing her slander my church to pay much attention to this. Anyway, her roughness wasn't intended to be taken seriously; it was code, code for what not even Mirabel could bear to put into words.

'It's too late,' I told her miserably. Mirabel took this literally, seized on it. She was a fund of statistics, some correct and some imagined, all of which she swore to have culled from *The Times* or *The Economist*.

'No, it isn't. I'll bet it isn't even cancer. I read that eight out of ten women who are sent to have cultures removed from their breasts don't even have cancer. And half the ones they do find are curable, as long as the stupid sods don't wait too long to have it checked out. How can you live thinking you might be dying and the clock running out on the bomb like the end of a James Bond film? Look at little Clarissa. Do you want her growing up forgetting what you looked like? Think of me. Think of – '

'Rodney.'

' – how much I need you to be here. You're the person I come to when I feel low. You're the one who keeps up my courage before auditions and solos. You abysmal toad, what am I to do without you?'

'Flop your auditions,' I told her callously.

'And if it's bad news,' she said, turning to face me, 'if it's bad news, I'll be there for you, Elaine. Forever and ever, to the end of time. It'll take death to separate me from you, and afterwards – afterwards I'll be the leading angel singing you to your rest. Hamlet, end of. Seriously. I mean that.'

The notion of Mirabel, who was as solid and rocklike as Rodney to look at, as an angelic chorister made me smile, but the odd part is, I found that I could go to the hospital after all. And, luck or no luck – statistics or no statistics – I didn't have cancer.

It wasn't long after that incident that I remember Stephen saying, 'I wish I was better at needing people, better at knowing what they need me to be.' I thought, that's the first step, isn't it, when men realize they're missing something, and that what they're missing is what they've been looking for all their lives. And I realized, catching Mirabel's smouldering glance towards Stephen, that she had everything, everything I wanted, a real career, a real marriage – everything I wasn't ever going to have.

It had been a gradual realization, I see now. When I first knew Mirabel, I'd felt sorry for her. Sorry that she felt so driven to succeed in an unhelpful field (horn sections are to this day bastions of male chauvinism), sorry that she seemed so limply uninterested in the joys of motherhood. I didn't even envy her Stephen back then, because he seemed so remote, so intellectual. However, as her career had progressed, so that it wasn't unrewarded auditions and blocked doors I had to console her for so much as exhausting foreign tours and

157

jealous, difficult colleagues, I became aware that her life – in a wildly different way, of course – was as rewarding as mine. More rewarding, in that she received payment for it, and more rewarding, in that her confidence and personality and expertise were being stretched and stretched.

The longer I knew Mirabel the more I regretted not having tried for university, the more I regretted having voluntarily cornered myself into early and complete motherhood. It amazed me, sometimes, that she still called me up, wanting comfort, consolation, understanding. It amazed me that she still wanted to know everything I felt, the trivia of Laura's banged ego and Clarissa's banged knee, when what she was doing was so much more creative and intriguing. Oh, I knew enough to know how unglamorous her glamorous life really was – how insecure, even terrifying. But still it drew me with its unpredictability. She was a soap opera to which I was addicted. She was what gave life its uninhibited zest.

Suddenly she was none of these things, gone beyond prospect of forgiveness. No wonder I felt lonesome. I even caught myself, childlike, staring up at the stars and wondering if some angelic, curiously sylphlike Mirabel was gazing tenderly back at me, even though, God knows, church teaching suggests otherwise.

About the second week after the funeral, I received a phone call from Stephen. His voice sounded worn-down, creaky from disuse.

'Are you free tomorrow?' he inquired, after asking me how I was doing and receiving a completely inept reply.

'After taking the girls to school,' I temporised, aware that childless people constantly underestimate the time children involve. 'And before taking them to hockey and ballet afterwards.'

'The solicitor has asked for you to be present for the reading.'

'The reading,' I repeated stupidly.

'Her will.'

'Good Lord. Did she actually organise a will?'

'It's Brace and Pinkett, 130 High Street, at ten-thirty. Can you come by then?'

'Yes, of course. Stephen – '

I wanted to say I was thinking of him, that I felt hollowed out inside, that I knew at least something of how terrible he must be feeling. Mirabel could have said something, something forceful and eloquent, slangy and telling. However, I, all too typically, failed. He was waiting courteously at the end of the line.

'Nothing. I'll see you tomorrow then.'

'Thank you,' he replied. 'Goodbye.'

Rodney, who felt with some justice that Mirabel had pulled a fast one by dying, was conspicuously unconcerned about my business with her solicitors. He made his usual moan about the state of the carpet, which I promised to clean as well as vacuum, then set off for work. I didn't tell the girls, but perhaps they guessed that something unusual was happening, because Clarissa was especially clingy when I deposited her at playgroup. Mirabel had been Clarissa's first death, not being able to remember the death of my father, and I think she still believed that my friend was coming back eventually, from a tour somewhat wider in scope than usual.

Stephen greeted me at the door of the solicitors. His eyes were puffed, dark-edged, but I preferred his looks slightly marred, made more human. He didn't embrace me, but he held my hand for a long time, as if it was he who needed comforting.

I had expected a stereotypical lawyer, a shrivelled, laconic specimen, but Mirabel had chosen otherwise. Mr Turner was exuberantly youthful, pink and overweight. He was by turns over-solemn and over-cheery, an actor uncertain of his part.

'Mrs Brown, come in. So pleased you could come. Mr Felton, sit wherever you like. A tragic circumstance, a terrible thing, this. I've never come across anything quite like it. She was with an orchestra, I understand.'

I undertook to spare Stephen the necessity of response.

'Not exactly. She'd finished the tour, but was flying on to Australia to see her family before coming back. Most of the orchestra came back a day earlier.'

'Engine failure, was it?'

'They think there was probably a fire. But there weren't any witnesses at night over the sea.'

'I should think not. No. Well this is really most unfortunate for both of you. I only met Mrs Felton twice, but she made a deep impression of – vitality upon me. If you take my meaning, ha ha.'

'Vital,' I agreed, 'was the word.' The solicitor's unctuous determination gave me nerve, as did Stephen's depression. Mr Turner seemed loath to get to the point, so I looked at my watch.

'The will,' he said, grasping my feeling, 'is rather unusual, in some respects. There are a number of small legatees, sentimental presents, that sort of thing, and obviously the Australian contingent could not be expected to be here today. But the crucial things are that you, Mr Felton, according to the insurance, completely own your house, contents, your wife's jewels, shares and musical instruments, while you, Mrs Brown, are awarded the entire amount of monies residing in your friend's accounts, the whole amounting to thirty-two thousand pounds.'

'That can't be right,' I interposed, dazed. 'Mirabel's money must be Stephen's, by law.'

'I can assure you that the will in that particular is completely valid,' replied Mr Turner, trying not to dimple.

'What do you mean, in that particular?' inquired Stephen, silencing me with a gesture. 'Of course, Mirabel had a right to do what she liked with her money. It was her money, not mine, anyway,' he told me. 'Mainly inherited.'

Mr Turner seemed pleased to have been asked that question.

'I mean that the will's codicil is not legally enforceable, and I told Mrs Felton so when she drafted it. It amounts to no more than a wish, in terms of the law.'

'What on earth are you talking about?' demanded Stephen.

'Let me see, it's at the very end of the codicil, after the part about her chamber music collection going to her cousin in Australia,' said Mr Turner, putting on little gold-framed spectacles in a doomed attempt to resemble my notion of a lawyer. 'Here we have it. "And lastly, I bequeath my husband Stephen to the above-named Elaine Brown. I trust her to look after him for me." She further added something about your present husband, Mrs Brown, which I thought it more prudent to delete from the last will and testament before it was signed.'

I burst out laughing – I'm afraid, rather hysterically. 'I'm sorry, Stephen, but the idea of bequeathing a husband – only Mirabel would have dared!'

'That part of the will is completely non-binding, not to say eccentric,' agreed Mr Turner looking hopefully at us over his spectacles as if he expected us to rush into each other's arms like the last reel of an MGM classic. 'I told Mrs Felton so when she brought it for my approval. But I couldn't talk her out of including it in the codicil.'

Stephen tried to smile, but it was a thin and nervy effort. 'Talking Mirabel out of anything was never easy,' he said.

There were various other formalities; then Stephen and I found ourselves once more outside the office.

'I'm not taking the money,' I said at once. 'It would have been yours anyway, if she hadn't made a will.'

'That's absurd; she did make a will. And, I think we both know why she left you that money.'

'So I could afford to leave Rodney, if I want to.'

'Well, to give you the chance to choose.'

'Perhaps she was a feminist after all,' I said, thinking of Rodney.

'No, she just wanted women to have opportunities,' he said,

taking me literally, the way Mirabel herself might have done.

'I'm sorry I laughed. I just can't take it all in,' I said suddenly. 'I have to go home, think it over. I'll – I'll call you, Stephen.'

We both felt too awkward to shake hands again. I watched him move off, pulling his shoulders back the way Mirabel had always scolded him into doing. He looked like a child who had suffered a beating and was trying to pretend that it hadn't hurt. I did love him, I see that now; I always had loved him, for Mirabel's sake. But there are many different kinds of love, and I wasn't going to make another, different, mistake with a man. I took a deep breath and drove home.

As I drove, I thought again – as I had thought so many times – about the last conversation I'd had with Mirabel. She'd called me from Hong Kong, two days before she died.

'What time is it there?'

'Eleven. Is it really urgent, Mirabel? I've got an awful day tomorrow.'

'Of course it's bloody urgent. Did I wake the kidlets?'

I cocked an ear. 'Don't think so. What's going on?'

'Have you left Rodney yet?'

'Be serious, Mirabel. I'm really tired.'

'Do so, without loss of time. He's not your soulmate.'

'I haven't got a soulmate. Most people haven't.'

'That's odd. The principal cellist has. In droves.'

'Mirabel – '

'I'm coming to the point, my cherub. In a roundabout way.'

It was only then that I spotted the panic in her voice; I suppose I'd been too sleepy before. And, you must admit, all she had done so far was wake me up out of a dreamless sleep and needle me about my marriage. I remember feeling protective of Rodney, snoring inelegantly in the next room, poor Rodney, who never to the end knew what had hit him.

'Mirabel, are you all right?'

'Not particularly. Neurotic is, I think the *mot juste*.'

'Why neurotic?' I demanded.

162

'Because I've been raped.'

'What?'

'Raped. Sexually assaulted. With a black eye they can see in Singapore.'

'Who in the world would do such a thing?'

'The principal bloody conductor, Roger Ash.'

'What!'

'Oh, you must remember Roger Ash, Elaine. I've told you about him. The slippery, scheming, selfish, slimy egomaniac.'

I couldn't believe I'd heard her right. Roger Ash was by then tolerably famous. It was as if Mirabel had said she'd been raped by Jeffrey Archer. I recalled her penchant for exaggeration.

'When you say raped – '

'I mean raped. I said no way and then it happened.'

'There has to be more to it than that,' I urged her, looking in my English fashion for a commonsense solution. It was the wrong thing to say. There was a silence at her end, which meant, I knew, that she was weeping. I never saw Mirabel cry any other way than with silent tears crashing down her face, mouth clamped as tight as an oyster shell. Men more often cry like this, and perhaps there was a lot of masculinity in Mirabel, the original Australian tough cookie. Real Australians don't cry, that kind of thing.

'Tell me about it,' I coaxed her, but it was quite a long time before she could, and even then I had to piece together a story from fragments. Orchestra party, everyone having quite a lot to drink. Wound up dancing in the hotel disco with the brass section in the small hours of morning. Ash shows up, sozzled and angry about something, insists on speaking to her on some important private matter. Mirabel irritated; Ash insistent. Allows herself to be led into deserted conference room next door. Raped.

'You shouldn't have gone with him,' I told her, having grasped the story.

'Of course I shouldn't. Do you think I'm a idiot?'

'Yes, you are an idiot; you were too plastered to judge properly! Anyway, I told you not to drink too much. Your whole orchestra drinks too much.'

'Are you trying to blame me for what he did to me?' she screamed down the phone, over every continent.

I was silent. I had been trying to blame her, of course. To make it more bearable. To make the thought of her pain tolerable to me. I felt ashamed.

'I'm sorry. It's simply too shocking for me to want to believe it. I can't stand the thought of you so far away and feeling so terrible. You shouldn't have called me, Mirabel, I'm far too weak to be any use.'

'You're one of the few reasons to go on living,' she told me resonantly, and then, suddenly, I was there for her, as she'd once been for me. I talked for half an hour, about guilt and innocence, despair, self-forgiveness, about being kind to herself. 'A steaming bath,' I remember telling her, 'read something stupid, some women's magazine. Put on the telly and watch whatever it is Hong Kong TV puts on first thing in the morning. Sleep it off. If you can separate yourself from the circumstance, you can cope with it . . . At least you're still alive,' I told her. 'Some women die.'

'I ache so much I wouldn't mind dying,' she said sleepily.

'It's not your time,' I urged, remembering her dramatic impulses. 'Promise me.'

'I promise.'

'You could always sue.'

Her voice snapped back into energy. 'The principal conductor! I'd never work again.'

'Kick him in the balls.'

I heard her smile. 'That didn't work.'

'Next time.'

'Next time,' she echoed and drifted away from me forever.

At least there would never be a next time for him, I thought when I spotted Roger Ash's dashed-off signature on the official orchestra condolence card. I glanced at Stephen, who was leaning over the CD player in his living-room. Something he would never know. The last – and worst – of the secrets we had helped each other to bear. And it struck me again how, in some ways, we share ourselves more deeply with other women than with our husbands; not that we don't love men better, but they're always different, a different species, nearly a different culture, and, as such, more separate from us. 'They complete us,' Mirabel once told me, 'but we can't travel on parallel courses with them, side by side. With men there's always a collision, isn't there, sometimes good, sometimes not so good. Somehow that's always bothered me.' It seemed to me that only now, without her, was I beginning to figure out what exactly she'd meant, about that as well as other things. As if, although separated, we were still growing closer. Perhaps the time when I ceased to feel that would feel like another death.

I was visiting Stephen two weeks after the reading of the will; the money was meanwhile winging its way to me via an endless series of legal procedures. Stephen had avoided me since that day – no, to be just, we had avoided each other. Seeing his back in the supermarket, looking completely, helplessly out of place, I had dodged into another aisle. And once, driving the girls to ballet, I had passed him emerging from the train station in the rain. Embarrassment filled me at the thought of what he might be thinking of me – an embarrassment compounded of money and sex and guilt plus the trauma of our divided griefs.

Also, the situation with Rodney had got worse. I hadn't even told him about the codicil, but the money aggrieved him extraordinarily. He felt as if Mirabel had doubted his earning capacity (which she had, if secretly), as if the foundation of his masculinity had been queried. He tried to persuade me to invest it for the girls' college years – so long off! – but I resisted. It was my money, mine and still, obscurely, Mirabel's. I wanted to make up my own mind about it; I trusted to time to clarify my feelings. I woke up remembering the money and fell asleep comforted by the recollection of Mirabel's confidence in me. I grew calmer with the girls, calmer altogether. It was if the money – more than the money, what lay behind it – had drugged me, loosened the cord around my neck. Perhaps the knowledge of potential freedom, I thought, would gradually make everything easier to bear.

I didn't know why Stephen wanted to see me. He had sent me a little note, courteous to the point of blandness, saying that he would be obliged if I could manage to drop by one evening. Cordial regards.

I had tried to imagine Mirabel sending anyone cordial regards and had failed, had wondered for the thousandth time about the dynamics of their marriage. Yet I'd found myself nervous while waiting for Stephen to answer the door, fluttery inside, as if I knew already that something irrevocable was likely to happen on the other side of it.

Stephen looked self-possessed, shook hands politely, then guided me into the house I'd known so well.

'I've got the trinkets for your children ready,' he told me. 'In that box there. Would you like a drink?'

'A little one,' I agreed, pleased to feel that we could speak normally, act in a mature and adult fashion, however young and hopeless I felt inside. I wanted to ascertain Stephen's state of mind; that was my duty to Mirabel. Inside my own – inside my own mind there was a sudden swelling of certainty, as if stepping into what I still thought of as Mirabel's house had imposed her truths inside me.

'How are you bearing up at work?' I called to him as he disappeared into the kitchen.

He returned with an unopened bottle of old claret.

'Not too badly,' he responded, smiling at me. I recalled how handsome he looked when he smiled, but it didn't have the effect on me that I remembered.

'You're feeling better,' I told him.

'Resigned, I think,' he said, after a small deliberation. 'Calmer.'

'Yes, me too.'

'She would have wanted you to get over it.'

'After a sufficiency of trauma,' I reminded him. 'She would have insisted on that, as being only her due.'

I was pleased with myself for having coaxed him to laugh.

'How well you knew her.'

'Better than life,' I agreed. 'And, you know, I think I've made up my mind what to do with the money.'

'What! You're actually leaving Rodney?'

'With the girls, yes. Yes, I must. He'd never let me do what I have to do. But you don't have to worry. I'm not going to marry again, Stephen – you or anybody. I'm going to get a degree and start where I should have started all those years ago. I'm actually going to be independent for the first time in my life – I'm going to force myself to became the person I once lacked the nerve to be.'

He grabbed my hands, inspired. 'If you need any help – '

'Oh, you'll still see me,' I assured him. 'You were left to me, remember? To look after. That was the greatest trust of all.'

Stephen started pouring out the claret. The colour was wonderful, a golden iridescent crimson shade, the colour of leaves before they break and fall, the colour of certainty, forgiveness. I felt peaceful, more peaceful than I had felt since I was quite young, and powerful, like the roaring engines of ten thousand separate planes. I could hear Rodney's objections, the girls' bewilderment, my own struggles – oh, I under-estimated nothing, I could sense the comfortable meaningless-ness of my life collapsing at my feet, but I felt strong enough to bear it all, to cope with everything. I didn't sense the fragility of these feelings; I felt immortal, like a child, like Mirabel. God had willed me my freedom back.

'It isn't enough, it isn't enough. There has to be more than this!' I heard myself repeating, and the voice was my own, although the words were Mirabel's. Stephen, who missed nothing, caught both voices – they seemed to shake him into remembrance. Bach rose gently out of the CD speakers as he just brushed his wine glass against mine.

'There will be,' he told me. 'Good luck, Elaine. I hope it works out for you; I know how much her heart was in it.'

'Thank you,' I said, and wondered if I would ever have the words to express what I felt for him, the power, pain and pity braided so fiercely together that they almost choked one other . . . But then, Stephen never seemed to require foot-notes. Perhaps that was the real secret of Mirabel's fascination with him.

'To my best friend,' I said, lifting up my glass.

'And mine,' echoed Stephen quietly, and when I saw that he was crying, I reached out and held him like a child. Grieving for the first time felt uncomplicated, a simple, basic thing – missing somebody, comforting each other. A poem Mirabel had once sent me came back to me:

> Failing to find me at first keep encouraged,
> Missing me one place search another,
> I stop somewhere waiting for you.

XV

The Unravelling

And if I laugh at any mortal thing,
'Tis that I may not weep.

Byron

(from Piotr's private files)

The orchestra took Mirabel's death hard. She was one of those people who, without having held a position for very long, had always made her presence felt. A curious business this, because some members of the orchestra – Clarence, say – could have disappeared for weeks at a stretch without anyone's noticing, while the gap in the horn section gaped like an open wound. Isabel wept openly after Roger's announcement, and I don't think I've ever seen the orchestra mood so sombre.

Henry, the tough-as-nails principal horn, was unable to play decently for days afterwards. He went around pugnacious with his chin stuck out, daring anyone to complain. His eyes looked swollen too, as if he'd spent a long time rubbing at them, and he was notably quarrelsome in the pub. Some people maintain that he never completely got over it, certainly his temper seemed to worsen. And there were those crabbing gossips who suggested that there was more than comradeship between them. But this was crazy, because Mirabel was one of the boys in the horn section, and, besides, never looked at anyone except her husband.

Her integrity – I suppose her integrity was what I remember best about her. All her famous disputes arose from her inability to play in a way she couldn't believe in, and most of her troubles in the orchestra – and she wasn't universally liked, no one is – arose from her devastating honesty. Adam Halloran could never forgive her dismissal of his (Neanderthal) cello playing, for example; and Isabel used to call her the human sieve on account of her utter inability to keep secrets. Yet there was a warmth, a direct sincerity, about her that was as appealing as it is rare. She was an original, a Shakespeare fanatic, an uncompromising musician, devoted to being the best. Built to last, it was hard to believe she hadn't lasted. Her death diminished us in surprising ways, opening up unsuspected tendernesses, of which Henry's ferocity was only one symptom. The loss of Mirabel, while it didn't kick off a difficult period for the orchestra, gave it new momentum. The boat, already rocking, started to capsize.

Warren, who had recently devoted himself pretty comprehensively to Caroline, proposed marriage to her. This caused no very massive surprise, Caroline being the sort who was always going to be signed up by somebody or other, and it didn't take her long to agree. Her infatuation with David was completely over, and she seemed suddenly less young and silly, which was something of a mercy, at least.

Having said that, I can't say that Warren seemed very happy about the engagement. I suspected that he had chosen Caroline as consolation for losing all chance of Isabel, but was still repining. He missed Mirabel too – she used to chaff him, about his little violin-putting-away ritual, for example, and about his Giotto mania, as an older sister might. He was not the sort to make a song and dance about it, but I saw that he was feeling it.

If he'd known the truth about William and Isabel, I suppose he might have resisted teaming up with Caroline, but no one was aware of that at the time but me. William hadn't told me anything at first – too loyal, I suppose – but after a while, I didn't need telling. His face, always expressive, gave me every clue I needed, if Isabel's brittle emotionalism hadn't told the tale already. It had always been bound to happen, given time, and the nature of the profession. It was more than Mirabel's death, the condescension with which David treated him on first desk, or the Elinor Jay affair that finished William. His heart, his conscience, was to blame as much as orchestral tensions. Though it cannot be stressed too much to those who protest that office politics are the same everywhere, that orchestras are different.

Where else is one forced to sit, hour after hour, not two feet away from despised rivals, playing the same part, having jarring idiosyncrasies driven daily down one's throat? Where else are adults forced to be silent for hours at a time, in self-disciplined agony? Where else are sensitive and artistic souls placed at the mercy of egotistical conductors, who bend their musical wills, where these stubbornly persist, to service their particular whims? And where else, other than in a dramatic company, is one forced on the road for long stretches of time, herded into coaches, planes and hotels like so many cattle, dead in the end to everything except the passage of work and time? Outsiders wonder that we are driven to affairs, to alcohol, even to suicide. The astonishment I feel is that a handful in every orchestra escape all these fates, escape even disillusion and despair. The amazement really is that some of us survive intact, year after fractious year, both as individuals and, more rarely, family members.

But enough of my opinions. What happened was this: I met William in town on my way to get a bow rehaired, and persuaded him to have a drink with me. I didn't like his looks —not that he wasn't as good-looking as usual, in his world-weary, aristocratic fashion, but he looked drained. He first resisted the notion of a drink and then succumbed.

'Now, old bean,' I said, having imbibed a pint of the brightest and the best. 'Get it off your chest. Tell me all.'

'About what?' he inquired, putting down his cider.

'About what's worrying you. About why you persist in going around the place looking like the boy, who, as you recall, stood on the burning deck, whence all but he had fled.'

I was rewarded by a smile, but I've seen juicier. A thought struck me. 'Had a row with Isabel?'

'No.'

'Margot any worse?'

'No, that is, no worse than usual. The doctors believe her case has stabilised, at least for the time being.'

But the way in which he spoke of his wife gave me an idea. You could say, if you like, that I Saw All.

'William,' I said earnestly, 'I see all. Margot suspects, is that it? Some bloody idiot's told her.'

It's no use holding out against Genius, as Tolstoy's friends could probably have told him. William gave in.

'She suspects, yes,' he admitted. 'I don't think she's been told, exactly.'

'Then how do you know she suspects?'

'Little things. For example, she checked up on me the other day, when I said we had an extra rehearsal for the Walton.'

'But we did have an extra rehearsal!'

'Of course; and that's what the girls in the office told her. But the fact is, she called to find out if there really was. She's never done that before. Plus, she's asked me questions.'

'What kind of questions?'

'Questions about women in the orchestra, the secretaries in the office. She's never displayed any interest in anyone in the orchestra before, not since her illness, anyway. For years she's been – self-absorbed, I suppose, worried about her condition. Now it's improved, perhaps she's got more time to wonder.'

'So you told her about them, including Isabel.'

'Well, I could hardly omit Isabel. I said – I said she was a flirt, and had numerous lovers. Margot seemed to lose interest in her then – which isn't odd, you know, because Isabel really isn't what you might call my type at all. She's so dynamic and dramatic and passionate. I always preferred – used to prefer – gentler, more sensible kinds of girls. Margot was like that. Still is, when she's not fretting about her health.'

'You know, I don't think I've ever heard you speak about her before.'

'No, well, you don't, do you, not when someone's got a

172

terrible illness like that. I think people are afraid to ask about her, in case she's dying. Not that they do die, usually. It's not that kind of disorder, on the whole.'

I pushed him farther. 'Did you used to love her?'

'I don't know. I used to think I did. I was very contented with her, in an undemonstrative sort of way. Perhaps I took her for granted, and Sam too. And yet she never made me feel the way Isabel does – hungry for her, desperate. It's like an illness, this feeling, it grips me by the throat. I can't be happy unless I see her; I feel impatient when we're apart. It's an adolescent fever – it's demanding and ridiculous and wonder-ful and the breath of my life. If it was only lust, some animalistic thing, I could bear it, but it's worse than that. Though it probably started because she is beautiful, it's changed into something much more drastic. I love her now in spite of that. If she got leprosy, I would still want her.'

I exploded – jealousy perhaps, who knows? 'Oh God, I saw this coming. I saw this a mile off. I told her a year ago that she would destroy you, the vain little bitch.'

'Piotr,' said William gently. 'There's nothing she could have done differently. There were no other options. If you blame Isabel, you must blame me equally – more, in fact, because I always saw more clearly.'

'Don't worry, I blame you as well! You were old enough to see what kind of creature she is, fanciful, self-obsessed, deceitful. You saw how easily she manipulated David into her bed – why can't you see that she's fooled you just as clearly? Without your interference she'd have had Paul Ellison too – no taste worth mentioning, or morals either. And you think she's been faithful to you? I don't. Mind, I've got no proof, but she's devious enough to hide things, wily enough to get away with it. How do you know she hasn't invited plenty of people to her flat after you've gone home to look after Margot? And what about all the times you haven't been able to get round to her place? Do you really imagine a stunning girl like Isabel, single and not yet thirty-five, is going to be faithful to somebody's grandfather indefinitely?'

I think anybody but William would have struck me, but the man's not normal, never was. He only stood up, breathing harder, as if he was finishing a race.

'Goodbye, Piotr,' he said, like a more dignified Othello giving Iago the raspberry. I willed him to turn around, to come back, I longed to apologise for making such unjustifiable accusations against Isabel. But I couldn't; I felt too upset, too miserable, and too angry at her for making him miserable. I wanted to smash something, but, imagining that this might be frowned upon by the worthy pub's proprietors, I merely kicked over a stool and left.

(from Isabel's diaries)

I ran into him first in the corridor outside the orchestra office – literally ran into him, because I was chatting to Caroline over my shoulder. 'Oh! Sorry,' I said, immediately, without seeing who it was, and then blushed, blushed deeper than I can remember blushing in ages.

'It is I who should be sorry,' he said courteously, giving me the irresistible impression of having removed a non-existent hat. 'I hope you are well.'

'Very well, thank you,' I replied, and moved on, cursing myself for not having inspected the orchestra schedules to see who was conducting that week. Mind you, I hardly ever do, one conductor – Roger of course excepted – being pretty much the same as the next one.

To say that I'd forgotten Hochler would be inaccurate. I had frequently, during the months since he was last with us, compared him favourably with whoever was carving that week, but I'd closed out of my consciousness the peculiar way he'd made me feel. Since then, after all, so much had happened; Clive had dumped me; William had picked me up; I was actually in love, in tormenting, agonizing, improbable love. I felt as if I was being ripped open by love, by the sadness in William's eyes and the ache he seemed to leave inside my body. I felt hardly alive – and at the same time I was living at a pitch of intensity which, like a violin string, could be tightened no further without breaking. I felt stretched to snapping point, suspended, terrified. The crisis was coming – who should know clearer than I? – and I could do nothing about it. There was even part of me that wanted it to come, that could take no more.

And into this morass stepped Mr Hochler, Karl Hochler, or, to give him Piotr's nickname, The Eyes of the Living Dead. He looked exactly as I remembered: pinstripes still immaculate, hair parade-perfect, bearing exquisite, eyes – the same. Still searching into me, liquid, brown, drooping at the corners. Still fascinating. I tore my mind away from the thought of him, swerved into the instrument room, just in time to hear William say: 'Don't mention it again, Piotr. God knows I've said plenty of things to you that I've regretted as well.'

And yet, William's manner wasn't as warm as it usually was, and Piotr, who is more sensitive than he pretends, must have been aware of it. However, he threw me a brief, hostile glance, and left us alone together. I immediately drew William up against the door and kissed him impetuously. You couldn't say that he was unresponsive, only that I could sense a lack of freedom, as if he was afraid of someone's pushing the door open against us.

'Is anything wrong?' I whispered.

'No, nothing in particular,' he said, but I knew he was lying. That he lied so badly was a great comfort to me; all the other men I'd known had lied so well.

'Come to me later and talk,' I begged him.

'I can't come tonight,' he said patiently. 'You know I can't. What could I use as an excuse?'

'Anything, it doesn't matter. Pretend there are cello auditions.'

'In an evening? My dear, we must be more careful. My wife has become suspicious.'

I felt as if a great weight had rolled from my shoulders. If that was all! Not that it was nothing, of course; it was unlucky, bad news. But he hadn't ceased to want me; I hadn't lost him. Nothing disastrous had happened.

'But she doesn't know anyone in the orchestra. How could she have found out anything?'

'There was a phone call,' he said, with some reluctance.

My first thought was Piotr, but a clearer head dispelled the notion. Piotr might have done it, but he would have told me; he would have spared me nothing.

'Some neighbour of yours,' he continued, 'perhaps the one I've spoken to.'

'What, Mrs Agnew! How could she dare!'

'Whoever it was said nothing that wasn't true. She didn't even name names.'

'What did she say?'

'Very little. She said that men were all alike, as she'd had reason to know, and that I'd been paying numerous visits to a single girl who was no better than she should be. When Margot asked who was speaking, she rang off.'

'Surely your wife didn't believe her!'

'Well, she claims that she didn't believe her, but I don't think she knows what to believe; I don't know what her intuition may have told her. There was the little note you once sent to me . . . Besides, I may not have acted well enough; you know I'm not a good actor. You can imagine how hard it is on me. Isabel, my darling, I don't know how much more I can take of this.'

You read, don't you, of people's hearts stopping, but hearts don't stop. Mine gave a jerk, like a train coming too briskly into a station, and then carried on beating, faster, perhaps, but otherwise the same as before.

'You don't mean that,' I said.

'I do mean it, and not only for Margot's sake. I'm thinking of you.'

'But I love you!' I cried, forgetting the need to be quiet. He pulled me to him, his familiar warmth cocooning my pain.

'Shh,' he said, 'you know how strongly I feel about you, but listen. You're still young, Isabel, still very desirable, but in terms of marrying and having a family you're not quite as young as all that – '

'But I don't want a family! I don't care about marriage!'

'Now you may not,' he admitted, still holding me, 'but that will probably change. And, if it does, and you find that your – attachment to me has prevented you from having what most women find they want, you'll feel cheated. And you'll be right to feel cheated. I'll have cheated you.'

'I know we'll never be able to marry; I've accepted that!'

'Now you may accept the situation, but for how much longer? Already you make demands upon my time that I can't meet; that may be the reason Margot's begun to doubt me. Will you want less of my free time in the future? Won't the frustrations of secrecy become even stronger? Of course, the orchestra guesses what's happening, though no one can prove anything. But how many years of pretence can you take, Isabel, before it's too much for you?'

I wrenched myself free. 'You mean, how many years can you take! I don't mind; I don't want to give you up; I can't get by without you! Oh, tell me the truth! You don't want me anymore, is that it?'

'No,' he admitted, in a low voice. 'I do want you. I want you now, this moment. I could take you here, on the floor, and still not be satisfied. I'm – addicted to wanting you. But it's an illness, Isabel; it's obsessive. It's turning me inside out: the guilt, the fever, my insatiability. Perhaps I thought I could be freed by giving way to it, but I know better now. Surrender doesn't work; escape is the only answer. So, you're only half right. I don't want to be parted from you; I *need* to be parted from you, for your sake, for my sake, for the sake of my marriage. For both our sakes, I'm asking you to let me go.'

'How can I? How can I give up the only thing that matters to me?'

'You're so dramatic!' he exclaimed, smiling. 'As if you had no friends, no career, no prospect of ever falling in love again! Look in the mirror, Isabel – then look at me. How long would it be before my age would start to disgust you? Do you think I could bear that, to see your eyes turning towards men of your own age? Anything but that! No, we should finish it now, while there's still some shred of dignity about it. We love each other, and some part of ourselves will probably always love each other. But part of me cares for my wife too, for the peace of mind that comes with living the truth. Perhaps, as we grow older, that comes to matter more.'

How could I struggle against him? Yet every fibre of me did struggle, every selfish particle. I recognised some truths in what he'd said – not about disgust, that was absurd – but about the perceptions of other people, dignity, his yearning for peace. What had his face signalled all year other than a mind at war with itself? I may have made him happy, but I'd given him no comfort, no ease. He had healed me, but I had ruined him, exactly as Piotr had predicted. It was I who needed him; I'd taken his peace away. Yet the very idea of living without him opened up a vast void before me, a complete howling wasteland. His face wavered in front of me, and I spun out the door like a crazed thing, scarcely seeing where I was going.

I still don't know how I got through the rehearsal. I took some pills – tranquillizers, the usual – but they didn't work. My desk-partner, Caroline, gave me some very curious looks, but I didn't want to confide in her. Ahead of me diagonally was the first desk of cellos; David and William. William, I noticed, played very badly – I was pleased to see it; it gave me an almost vindictive satisfaction. Yet his eyes had that bruised look, the wounded eagle look that always pulled my heart. As for Hochler, I'd forgotten he was there; I'd forgotten everything but William.

In the canteen I noticed Piotr and William in the corner, wrapped in intense conversation. Warren came up to me, not knowing how much I longed to be left by myself.

' – so I hope you're able to come,' he was saying, his eyes never leaving my face.

I had to be reminded what he was talking about, so

completely had the two in the corner captured my attention.

'Oh! Your wedding, of course!' I said, turning what I hoped was a bright face towards him. 'I wouldn't miss it for anything. Caroline's already shown me her dress; she looks divine in it.'

Warren sat down beside me and took possession of my hand under the table.

'I don't care about Caroline the way I did about you,' he told me in a low voice. 'But perhaps we suit each other better; she wants to settle down, have a family, that kind of thing. Mind you, she's not overfond of poetry either. Do you remember a poem I once sent you?'

'Something about Troy,' I said vaguely, trying to keep my composure. It wasn't Warren's fault, but he could hardly have picked a worse time to remind me of my careless youth.

'I have a notion,' he went on, smiling, 'that married people shouldn't go about giving poetry to old flames. So this is the last poem I'll ever give you . . . I ought also to tell you that I've never told Caroline about – about the first tour I did with this orchestra. Or about once proposing to you.'

'On Victoria Station,' I reminded him, quick tears rising up. Why should remembering make me cry? 'Don't worry, Warren. I wouldn't ever tell her. I know – I'm sure you'll make her very happy. I'm sorry . . . I'm not in very good shape today, excuse me.'

His hand tightened on mine. 'Why, Isabel! What's wrong?'

It really wasn't my lucky day. At that moment Mr Hochler, having collected his coffee, passed by, accompanied by David Schaedel and Paul Ellison. There was no chance of collecting myself in time. I jerked up from my seat, spilling tears and the rest of my coffee over the table. I fled the canteen somehow, going straight to the orchestra office, where I told Susan that I had flu and would have to miss the rest of the rehearsal. If she didn't believe me, at least she had the decency not to show it.

I didn't uncurl Warren's note until I'd got home. It said:

Others because you did not keep
That deep-sworn vow have been friends of mine,
Yet always when I look death in the face,
When I clamber to the heights of sleep,
Or when I grow excited with wine,
Suddenly, I meet your face.

I read it twice before I knew what he meant me to know, and
then it all seemed too much, and I really did cry until I was
exhausted.

Warren phoned me immediately after the rehearsal. As soon as
I heard his voice I knew that someone had told him, in fact,
that the entire orchestra knew. Piotr, probably, was the
culprit, gleeful at his victory over womankind. However, I
was almost too tired to care.

'I'll be all right,' I told him. 'I'm coming into work
tomorrow night . . . No, I know I could get away with not
coming, but it's like falling off a horse, isn't it, you need to
climb back on . . . Thank you, Warren, you're very sweet,
and I do appreciate it . . . See you tomorrow.'

I suppose, looking back on it, if I'd been less proud, I
wouldn't have gone back to work for a few days and the rest
would not have happened. If I'd been less determined to prove
that William meant nothing to me, I'd have stuck with the
virus fiction as long as I plausibly could. But, holed up in my
silent flat, I began to feel nervous about what people might be
saying about me; I determined to go and put a brave face on it.

I attended the rehearsal the next evening, drugged
sufficiently to be equal to pretty much anything. I saw William
in the canteen and steeled myself to behave normally to him.

'Hello, darling,' I said, squeezing his arm in passing. He
turned a haggard face towards me, and I saw from the sharp-
swivelled heads of Lucy and Caroline in front that my
conjectures had been well-founded.

As for William, I'd done my best to feel as he had suggested.
I'd repeated his age to myself, recalling each eye line, every

symptom of maturity that he possessed. And all that happened was that I wanted him harder. His body – this must be a function of love – had become my notion of perfection, even the blemishes (like most big men, he ran to a touch of midriff fleshiness) adding to the sum of his excellences – the rippled shoulders, the wide strong thighs, the warmth and power of those hands which never failed to thrill me.

I passed him in the queue, wanting him more than I ever had, tasting the brutality of that hunger, that defeat. But I behaved well; the first shock over, I had my control back.

Clarence sat opposite me, hugging his coffee to his scrawny chest. I felt sorry for him; he looked so thin and ill. Come to think of it, he hadn't looked right for a long time. He was Piotr's opposite in the orchestra; solitary, devoted to his bassoon, his books, and the English cricket team. I was surprised when he spoke to me; he didn't usually speak to anybody.

'Believe me, I'm sorry, Isabel,' he told me. 'I went through something similar myself once, and I know how hard it is.'

'You poor thing,' I said, turning hot bright furious/sympathetic eyes on him. He took the hint and shrivelled back inside his tortoise shell. I felt sorry after that, but I knew that my balance was too precarious, my head too light, to help anybody. I wanted a weapon to hold pity at bay, and it flew to my hand, as weapons do, immediately after rehearsal.

It came in the form of Hochler, of course. He stopped to watch Caroline scribbling in the latest bowings passed down from on high.

'Isabel,' he said, and when I looked up I felt my fragile grip slipping. Caroline glanced up too, her suspicious little brain whirring.

'Well? Are you ready?'

I can't describe the manner in which he said these words, almost the first he'd ever directed to me. It was at once matter-of-fact and tantalizing, serious and amused. He was assuming – everything. That we'd been properly introduced, that he wasn't a conductor (off bounds, believe me), that there'd always been something between us (had there been?). I could hardly deny that there was a chemistry, but that's common enough, in all conscience. Conducting is a sexual experience; the conductor's giving every member of the orchestra a ride, a subtly different ride, carrying them through the most passionate, expressive, emotional outlet known to man. He's caressing their melodies and letting them lead him through their solos; he's in control, playing on them, feeling their yielding to his every movement. When a real conductor lifts you up, you surrender everything to him, technique, brain, feelings. Hochler had stepped off the podium, but his eyes were still conducting me. Was I ready? I was. I rose; he took my unresisting elbow and guided me off the stage, Caroline staring stupidly after us.

'I think you said,' he observed, 'that you were free for a drink.'

Perhaps I still had some notion of extricating myself, but at that point we were passing William and Piotr, who were putting their cellos away. I turned to Hochler with the prettiest laugh I could summon up. 'I'll be with you in a moment,' I told him, and slipped into the Ladies to collect myself.

Hochler didn't say anything startling until we were seated – a restaurant, not a pub, because he said he hadn't eaten all day. We were far enough away from the Festival Hall that I didn't suppose we would be seen by anyone in the orchestra, which suited me fine. I couldn't remember the last time I'd been out with anyone except William, and obviously that mainly happened when we were away on tours, most recently in the Far East. It felt strange and reckless to be sitting with Hochler, who, however, exuded the most strait-laced respectability. I tried to calculate his age, which must have been nearer forty than fifty. His wedding ring was heavy, richly patterned, darkest gold. It seemed to weigh down his hand, which had a delicacy about it.

'Tell me,' I said, after he had ordered. 'To settle a bet. Do you get your suits in Savile Row?'

He smiled. 'No, they are handmade instead in Italy. I have a second home in Milan.'

I had guessed the second home, I remembered. The wife, a couple of clever, spoiled children, a weakness for sports cars, good wine, something like that.

'Why did you ask me to come with you?'

'Because you were unhappy,' he told me. I'd expected some rubbish about my beauty, I suppose, though in all honesty I don't think I'd ever felt less beautiful. In the Ladies my face had looked bone-coloured, the skin stretched sharply over its frame, the eyes cavernous, as black as my hair. Unhappy. Had it been so obvious? I asked him and he answered simply, 'Only to me.'

He paused a moment before he inquired, 'Is he one of the cellists?'

'The second cellist,' I answered without surprise. He had seen the way my eyes had been drawn, the way William's back, erect as a martyr's, had burned itself into my vision. 'William Mellor.'

'The older man,' he commented. 'He does not play well.'

I flushed. 'He usually plays better than that.'

'He is married.' A statement, not a question.

'His wife's been an invalid for some time.'

'And so, he falls in love with the most beautiful woman in the orchestra, naturally. And she, tired no doubt of importuning young men and meaningless relationships, falls in love with him. Then, after a time, his conscience torments him – his playing suffers – his wife spots the clues – and it is over, finished. The game begins again, but they are both too wounded to play. The loneliness is worse than before, and the pain more lingering. Yes? This is how it was?'

'Who told you?'

He shrugged. 'No one. It is an old story, one of the oldest. You must recall, I have conducted so many orchestras. And you must know from your own observation that there can be only three ends to such affairs: separation, marriage or death. In other words, in your case, it was always doomed – though perhaps all the sweeter for that autumnal feel. I sometimes think lovemaking goes best when both are aware that it cannot last.'

I felt winded, half-insulted at being so easily dismissed, half-stunned by the virtuosity of his deductions. Self-conscious too, at his instantaneous intimacy, his casual reference to sex. I had met a lot of Germans, plenty of them musicians, and I could imagine none of them behaving with such insouciance.

'You make it sound so – simple,' I told him impulsively. 'But it isn't, it really isn't. The feelings are so mixed, so inconclusive. One moment I'd do anything to hurt him, as he's hurt me; but when I see how much he's suffering, I'd give years of my life to comfort him. I forgive him – and I can't forgive him. I accept that he's doing it for me, and I think he's a selfish bastard, who's only used me until he's tired of me, like all the rest. Oh, I could tear his eyes out, at this moment, and then kneel down and kiss his feet. Just sitting here without him makes me feel frantic, and yet – '

'You mean, I think,' he said slowly, looking at me, really looking into me, for the first time since we'd been alone, 'that you feel also, inexplicably, drawn to me.' And I did mean that, exactly that.

'This is crazy,' I breathed.

'Then we will be crazy together. But first I must eat something. It has been all day, I tell you; I have had *Till Eulenspiegel* on my brain all day with no calories. And you must not make me too jealous with talk of this William! A little jealousy will be good, put me on my mettle, but too much and I will be forced to seduce you on the floor. That will upset our neighbours, as well as the restaurant managers, so that we should not do . . . Ah, my starter has come, excellent. I will amuse you much better after a good meal.'

'Would you care for another glass of wine?' the waiter asked me.

'Yes,' I heard myself saying. 'Another of the same.' Because

I didn't want to wake up from the wine, and find him gone, and myself alone, alone again, the way I could never bear to be.

'Had a pleasant evening?' Piotr inquired waspishly the next morning. I ignored him, of course, but the girls in the dressing room were not so easily disposed of.

'Did you go back to his hotel?' Lucy wanted to know. 'Was he brilliant? I'm sure he was brilliant, you lucky swine. You were very mean to take him up on it, when everyone knows I've been after him for ages.'

'He was brilliant,' I assured her. 'Keep at it, is my advice.'

'Pig,' said Lucy, without malice.

Caroline snorted disapprovingly, and it occurred to me that, now, everything Caroline heard might just as well be said to Warren. I said to her, in a lowered voice, 'I'm just teasing Lucy, you know. Though we did have a very pleasant meal in this French place.'

Nancy needled me as well. 'You certainly don't believe in wasting time, do you? You know, I was almost beginning to feel sorry for you, a couple of days ago. Shouldn't have wasted my sympathy, should I? Or is this just a scheme to make William take you back?'

Everyone looked at me then, while pretending not to.

'William?' I said, puzzled. 'William who?'

I have reason to believe that this stupid quip, which convulsed the room, made its way back to William. I felt a stab of compunction when I saw him filing onstage for the concert, his face, white as his dress shirt, looking in any direction but mine . . . Which was, incidentally, a shrewd move, because I was dressed, if not to kill, at least to seriously injure anyone who beheld me. In honour of the occasion I had wheeled out my Jane Russell special. Black silk cut low in the back and exquisitely fitted, it has been known to drive strong men mad, which was exactly my purpose in wearing it.

Oh, I was well above myself. A scalding night spent with

Karl Hochler – a demon between the sheets – had propelled me into the second phrase of grieving. I had moved seamlessly from desolation to bravado, with only half an hour's sleep in between. I was living on borrowed adrenalin, whipped-up sexual drive, dream-like fantasies. I had been tantalized, tied up, and made love to in every position I'd previously attempted and several I hadn't actually imagined before. I could hardly recognise myself as the girl who had kissed William in the instrument room the previous day. My body might be aching, but my mind was higher than a kite. Everything that happened to me seemed instead to be happening to some other Isabel, some darkly beautiful, enchantingly vivacious creature whom I'd almost forgotten I could impersonate. That was how Hochler made me feel – inspired, transported. He walked onto the stage, wrapped in his own impersonation – the German banker, correct in every particular, every shirtpleat in place, shoes gleaming with military precision. Only the uncanny intensity of his eyes gave him away.

The concert did nothing to bring me earthwards. I floated with a delicious feeling of weightless surrender. Karl wheedled an effortless *Till* out of the orchestra, and then an exquisite Mozart piano concerto, the phrases arched, the dynamics finely graded. When he looked at me, there was a stoked-up power that made what I'd previously noticed seem tame, but there was more than that to make me feel caught in the middle of a waterfall. There was William before me, steadily, doggedly playing, William's silver head and broad shoulders in his tailcoat, towering over David beside him. And I knew, even at the peak of my anger at William, that I wasn't in love with Hochler, that I could never love anybody but William, that he had curled himself quietly into the middle of my heart.

('Don't wear any underwear for the concert,' Hochler had told me. 'And come to me in the interval.')

I slipped into his room when no one was around, and he had me up against the wall before I could greet him. I'd never met a man so sexually imaginative, or with such undeviating stamina . . . I found out later that I was partly to blame, myself and William too. The dress was a provocation, and the way I looked for William while he was conducting drove Karl distracted. It was as if he was trying to beat William out of my brain, and perhaps, if it had been less recent, less anguished, it might have even worked, but the time was too near, the wounds too fresh. We were recalled back to reality by Susan's discreet knock on the door and her gentle: 'Five minutes if you please, Mr Hochler.'

'Don't look at him again,' he whispered in my ear, but he smiled, half-mocking himself as usual. 'Otherwise, after the concert I will kill him. I have taken a great dislike to your William.'

I pulled myself up, a little breathless. 'Conductors can be horrible!'

'Naturally. We are too accustomed to having our own way.'

I straightened my hair in his mirror. 'You know you're ruining my reputation.'

'And you are making mine,' he said, humorously. 'Wait for me after the concert. I will probably have to shake some hands, sponsors, the usual bores.'

I changed quickly after the concert and dawdled by the exit, reading notice boards and speaking to friends. Warren passed by with Caroline, giving me a very odd look; Lucy glanced enviously at me. Karl had just left the green room when William appeared, pushing a woman in a wheelchair.

My first thought was, how old she looks! How much older than William! But she wasn't older, a second glance proved that. She was about forty-five and had probably once been pretty, small and round-faced, with curly hair. However, her face now looked merely puffy, her body and feet bloated, hands quivering helplessly on her lap. Her hands were terrifying; I could hardly whip my eyes off them.

Not that she seemed to ask for pity. She was talking

animatedly to William about the concert, and, spotting Hochler down the hall, immediately asked to meet him. Karl had come to claim me by this time, and the worst-case scenario was forced to happen. William's eyes met mine, he flushed like a boy and forced words to his lips.

'Mr Hochler, my wife Margot. Margot, this is Mr Hochler, also Isabel Bonner, one of the violists.'

Margot's eyes rested on me briefly. 'Hello,' she said vaguely and then, more freely, 'Mr Hochler, what a marvellous concert! I've not been well enough to come for many years, but I'm so pleased I did. It was wonderful, especially the Strauss.'

Karl was equal to the situation, of course; it was part of his job to be equal to it. He captured her old/young hand and spoke gently and charmingly to her of German symphonic structure and the orchestra's wonderful string sections, laying particular stress upon the cellos. Her face grew pink with pleasure under his caressing charm – oh, he could make love to anybody, in his fashion; it was his particular genius.

I saw William's lip curl; he could no more pretend to like Karl than he could pretend anything else. I loved him suddenly, for his honesty, his conscience, his honour, for everything I'd been punishing him for before. He stood with his hands resting lightly on the back of his wife's wheelchair, and I was saying goodbye to him in my heart, goodbye, goodbye, you were too good for me; it was all a mistake, goodbye. There were tears in my eyes as I hooked my arm through Karl's, playing the impatient tart, pulling him away from his invalid admirer. ('We really must go, darling, or we'll be late.') I sensed William flinch, felt his hands tighten on the chrome metal. Karl was not displeased by this demonstration; he made our excuses, curling his arm around my waist, and led me away, while I smiled up at him, laughing, laughing.

XVI

Escape

For ever, brother, hail and farewell.

Catullus

Of course, you understand, I still think about him, wonder
how he's getting on. But I've never felt that it would be right
to ask. I rang him up once, pretended I'd found something that
he'd left behind – but he hadn't of course, moved out, bag and
baggage. I'm sure he guessed the truth but he was very polite,
charming. They are very polite, aren't they? Asians, I mean,
not that I usually thought of him as Asian, particularly. I just
thought of him as Rob, as himself. And perhaps that's as good
a definition of friendship as you can get, do you think, when
someone transcends categories like that, and simply is – the
way a tree is, or a house is, or a book is that you've read before
and know that you'll want to read again.

We were friends for years, a long time it seems to me now,
but of course the orchestra schedule rolls on the same every
year and in fact it was less than three years. We met through
my neighbours at the back; to be honest, we met because I
went to complain about the noise.

I don't want you to imagine me as one of those complaining
sort of characters; in fact, I can't say I'm very good at
complaining in general, but they had some kind of barbecue
going on all summer and it wore me down somehow, so in the
end I went down the next road and knocked on their door. I
realised that I was so frightened I was nearly shaking, my heart
hammered at my ribs so hard. Perhaps I was afraid of being
thought racist, which I'm really not, except that I don't care

for the French, never did, but they're not exactly a race, are they? I mean, I didn't mind the participants so much as the level of noise, plus the feeling of being excluded, that too. Maybe it made me feel lonelier, watching this huge extended family – great protecting wings of it – overflowing into the garden behind mine. I can accept that. Yes, part of it was probably jealousy, because all I've got is my parents in Rickmansworth and a sister that never did approve of me.

Anyway, I stood at the door with my heart flailing, but determined to say something if only (I told myself this) for old Mrs Bradley across the road, who had mentioned how badly she'd been sleeping Sundays, what with all the noise from that garden. Robert opened the door and the first thing I noticed was that he looked as unhappy as I did. He wasn't tipsy or laughing or running up and down the garden with the kids like the others; there was a quality of inwardness about him that I recognised like a Masonic handshake.

'My name's Clarence. I live at the back,' I said stupidly.

'Oh. Come in,' said Robert, and I couldn't think of anything else to do, so I did.

'Would you like a Heineken?' he asked, and I nodded. There was a fatefulness about it, an inevitability; I felt as if choice had been taken away from me. Mind you, I've always believed in fate, without having any time for spiritualism or Ouija boards. I was simply born knowing instinctively that some things are fated, that there is absolutely nothing to be done about them. Simplistic, my sister calls it, but there it is; and we're all too old to change now.

The house surprised me. It was the same type as my house, post-war, stubbly semi-detached, but inside it felt alive in a way mine didn't. There were hangings, crazy patterns, on the walls, and the colours were warm and crowded and cosy. The furniture didn't match – I'd never seen a three-piece-suite with three different styles before – but it didn't seem to matter. There was Indian music going on in the house, which clashed vilely with the pop music from the garden, but I suppose only a professional musician would have carped about it. We get fussy, I expect you've noticed, about our own little fields of expertise; we lift our delicate noses in the air. I've always been determined not to do this; I can't seem to rail at the masses who ignore our opera houses and eschew our concerts. We've failed, that's all; up and down the country we've failed. We ply our élitist trade to our élitist clientèle; meanwhile, the youngsters turn their backs on us and Beethoven both. This is the direction the entire world is taking. Why should we expect anything better?

At any rate, Robert didn't steer me towards the garden, for which I was grateful. He sat on one part of the suite and indicated for me to sit on the other. I felt instantly comfortable with him, untroubled by the silence, or comparative silence, between us. We sipped our lagers and listened to the far-off whoops of the children, the pop album, and, overlying these, the raga's undulating serenity from the next room.

'It's more peaceful here,' said Robert, as if we had been interrupted while arguing some closely-reasoned point. 'Out there, believe me, you cannot hear yourself think. It is "Uncle Rob, throw the ball to me" and "Uncle Rob, give me a piggyback." Not that they are not fine children, you understand, it is only that they get over-excited with all the people. There are times, do you not agree, when all a man wants is a little beer and conversation in a quiet room.'

I was struck by this. 'The exact same thing happened to me the last time I went to Somerset to see my sister. She has two children, both of them lively and curious and clever, but they wouldn't leave me alone. I began to feel positively haunted after a day or so; I felt the most tremendous longing to escape.'

Robert didn't smile, as perhaps I'd hoped he would. 'But don't you want to escape all the time?' he demanded.

I was about to laugh, and then I realized that it was no joke. I did want to escape; it was my first wish. Most of my dreams represented some form of escape; music itself was – or started out being – a kind of escape. I longed to escape, from my boring semi, my over-read cricket boots, my over-played bassoon, from the used-up faces and bone-dry feelings of most of my colleagues in the orchestra. There was nothing in my life that I wouldn't change, had change been offered me. Robert had looked into my eyes and read escape, and he wasn't wrong. I began to wonder if he was an alien, a mind-reader. (I'd read a good deal of science fiction in my time. The genuine article, J. G. Ballard, that kind of thing.) Perhaps my shock, my relief, was also written in my eyes. Robert didn't wait for the answer; he knew it already.

'My name is Robert,' he said, as if my admission changed nothing. 'I don't like Clarence very much.'

'I don't either,' I admitted.

'We will think of something better,' he said, and this time he did smile, a blazingly beautiful smile that re-scalped the cheekbones of his face. It was a thin, angular face, too narrow for his gangling, twenty-year-old body, but when his lips curved it became entrancing. Just then a small boy of about nine scampered in, stopping blankly upon seeing a stranger.

'Say hello to your neighbour,' said Robert. 'This is my favourite nephew, Jamie. Jamie, this is Nathaniel, who, I'm sure, is some kind of artist. Are you a writer, Nathaniel?'

'No,' I said, conscious of the boy's clear-eyed scrutiny. 'I'm a musician. I play the bassoon in the Orchestra of London.'

The boy tugged on his uncle's sleeve. 'Is he an artist or a musician, Uncle Robert?'

'He is both,' said Robert judiciously. 'You can be both, you know. If you play the bassoon artistically, you become an artist. Have you heard a bassoon played, Jamie?'

The boy shook his head.

'Maybe you'll get lucky. Maybe, once Nathaniel goes home, he'll play a few bassoon sounds out his back window into the garden.'

Jamie dimpled, well pleased with the notion. 'Outside into the garden where the whole world can hear?'

'Perhaps.'

'I'd like that,' said Jamie definitely.

'Even if you had to turn off your album?'

The boy pursed up his lips, in a clear imitation of some

adult, I wondered which. 'I don't know. Tara always gets mad if we turn it off.'

'Go and ask her,' suggested Robert, and the boy disappeared.

A wild, pungent smell, spinach and almonds, chapatis and spices, drifted into the room from the kitchen. The association made me smile.

'Reminds me of my childhood,' I murmured. 'I grew up in India, have I told you? Decades ago.'

Robert put down his glass. 'You will stay to dinner and tell me about it,' he said, and I found my half-hearted protests drowned out by children's laughter.

Well, that was the beginning: one of the world's great complaints, you must admit. I was won over by the entire family, though to this day their names sometimes elude me. There were cousins of cousins and aunts of aunts and, in the middle of it all, Robert, smiling his sad, endless smile at me. I stayed late, and felt no need to get tipsy, unless I was tipsy from happiness. After the children had gone to bed (where? in a three-bedroom home just like mine, I couldn't see how they fitted) the adults stayed out in the garden, the singing accents of the family rising into the silver birches. That was when I learned that Robert was a recently trained electrician, and looking for a room to rent.

'Take one of my rooms,' I suggested, without thinking.

'You don't take lodgers, do you?' inquired Auntie George, who was no one's aunt, as far as I could discover. She was a huge, domineering woman, retired from running a hardware business, with a striking presence, a natural habit of command.

'I haven't any at the moment,' I responded, 'but I always used to have someone in the house. For security, mainly.' Until I discovered the pilfering that Ralph was doing on the side, I added, silently. Until his disloyalty became too hurtful to bear. I smiled at Robert.

'I'm probably twenty years older than you are,' I said. 'I suppose you might get bored living with me. But the house is in good condition and the room's quite pleasant. You could have a look at it, if you like.'

Never again, I'd vowed, after Ralph's whirlwind departure had left the house vibrating like a badly-tuned string, never again would I look for long-term companionship. It was safer living alone, safer physically, safer emotionally. I had decided I was a loner, and, in my heart, I knew I was a loner still. But Robert was different; Robert was a blood-brother. We carried the same defeats in our eyes.

'You should take it,' said Auntie George firmly. 'Just behind the house, perfect. You could come for dinner, or cook for yourself if you wanted. Unless of course it is too expensive.'

I tried to recall how much Ralph had paid, but either it was too long ago or the pain had shut it out.

'Come have a look,' I said. 'We can discuss terms if you decide you like the place.'

So we left together. I remember feeling defensive about the house as I led Robert around. There was nothing unusual about it, I thought gloomily, nothing of more than passing interest. The colour scheme had been elected by my predecessor, a crisp series of browns and beiges, practical to the point of dullness. It was also tidy, too tidy, the finicky tidiness of bachelorhood; even the kitchen, in grey laminate, was primly tidy, as if no one had actually cooked in it for a long time.

Robert wandered incuriously from room to room. He had a quality of drifting, the art of moving noiselessly, seamlessly, from place to place. I recalled the tramp of Ralph's number eleven boots with distaste. Why had I ever put up with Ralph? Kindheartedness, I suppose, or the remorselessness of pity. I felt no pity for Robert; my identification was too keen for that. I felt as if I'd found a wounded wild animal and carried it into the house – honoured, nervous, almost unbearably affectionate.

'Is this the room you give to lodgers?' asked Robert, upstairs.

'It was the room the last lodger chose,' I told him. 'But the cream one's lighter, faces the front. I'd prefer it, if I were you.'

Robert inspected the front bedroom.

'Of course,' he said. 'This is the very room.'

I can still taste the flavour of that moment, that happiness.

There's nothing duller, I'm sure you'll agree, than the description of someone else's contentment. This is particularly true of me, because I'm such a dull fellow. My longing for glory's mainly gone. I used to think success was another word for happiness, but now I know there isn't another word. Centre stage, applause, what the world terms success: these have lost their appeal for me, because, in case you never noticed, it never makes for happiness. How many times have we played for a famous conductor or accompanied an eminent soloist, and wondered at the emptiness in their faces? The music, the acclaim may lift them, but they seem to start from the very depths in the first place. It's the lifestyle, people say, sagely. It's the jet-setting conductor with his third wife, the soloist afraid to say no in case his recording contracts go up the spout. And I'm not saying it isn't partly these pressures. I just think the reasons lie deeper: I think that musical stars are stars not only because they're stunningly gifted but because they're hungry for approval, because something's missing inside themselves. The soloists without this hunger, however well they may play, never seem to go the distance; happiness seduces them, and they falter and fall along the side of the mountain. Only the ones at the top are never satisfied. Believe me, that's the main reason they're there.

But my own notions of happiness don't vary much from anyone else's. Someone to come home to, a few friends I can trust, a walk in the country, a pub lunch. Perhaps it's more an absence than a presence. Not feeling exhausted or nervous or irritable. Not feeling alone. Before Robert came, I had a few good friends, but I always felt alone. After he came, I recognised the depth of loneliness I'd grown accustomed to. He completed me, can you understand that? He took the burdens off my shoulders, rubbed the lines of worry off my brow. We went to visit the family, took little Jamie to the art galleries. We slipped into Cambridge or the Cotswolds for a weekend's punting or just a wander. We went to see cricket matches when England was playing India – he supported India, but my heart was by then so divided I longed for both sides to lose.

The house felt different when he lived in it, something more intangible than the miasma of last night's chicken tikka or the dark red and gold that infiltrated the furnishings. The very air had a freshness that he carried with him; I used to wake up looking forward to the day, even if it only consisted of a rehearsal and concert in the Festival Hall, conducted by some East European youngster who was simply clueless about Elgar. Even before we became lovers, and that took a while too, I felt completed. I was in love not just with Rob, but with India, with its foods, its textures, its shivering, wavering accents, the warm-breaded alienness which was what I'd always known. It was an indescribable sensation, probably even more so for me, with my childhood roots in the place. It was a return to the womb, there was such rightness, such certainty, about it.

I used to stare at myself in the mirror and wonder if it showed. Not that I much enjoy looking at my reflection – it always surprises me how thin I look, with my scholar's hunch, salt-and-pepper hair and colourless, deep-set eyes. But perhaps it did show, because I remember someone remarking that I looked younger; maybe that was why I kept checking the mirror in the first place. In case it was true, and youth was as catching as happiness.

I know you, Warren, there's a primness about you; you'll tell me it wasn't meant to last. From some puritan depth of consciousness you don't believe we're meant to be happy, certainly not when living with another man. And perhaps you're right. But I'm a romantic, I go on believing in love and truthfulness and the inevitability of fate; I went on believing it even after he left me, and I can't stop believing it now. Nothing changes; nothing that matters is really limited by anything as puny as time. That rug your wife Caroline admires – one of his cousins gave it to us. And the colourful fabrics in the sitting room; Robert picked those out for me. The house is a shell now, compared to what it was; I cook the food the way he taught me but it never tastes the same. And yet I'm happier in my shell than I was before he came; the resonance of contentment lingers, just as the fragrance your mother used to wear haunts her old handkerchiefs.

I have no complaint. I can't accuse him of unkindness or thoughtlessness. He never lied, not to me, that is; I know he knew how. It was late one winter's night, while the fire was dying; I'd just mixed the whiskies, and we sat, as we had in the beginning, in that other house at the bottom of the garden, in different sections of a three-piece suite. There was music in the background; the *Enigma Variations*, one of Rob's particular favourites. I remember the woodwind lines weaving into each other, endlessly weaving, just as I began to realize that our own counterpoint was almost finished.

'I have to go, Nathaniel,' he told me, and his voice, always soft, was by then so gentle that it was almost part of the music. 'You know I have to go, don't you?'

And I suppose I had known, not recognisably, but in those parts of ourselves where the secrets lie buried. It had been three years; the time limit was up. Eternity starts here. I buried my head in my arms like a child, and felt his narrow arms around my shoulders.

'I am to be married,' he said. 'I don't really want it, my dear friend, but I know it must be.'

'You won't be able to be with a woman,' I said, but I said it weakly, because I sensed he could, that he was complete in a way that I was not.

He shrugged. 'I've done it before,' he said. 'Of course, she is not a blood-brother, this girl, but she's clever and kind. She'll be a good mother to my children. It was always known that we would marry.'

'It's barbaric to marry someone you don't love,' I said automatically, but even as I said it I knew I didn't believe it. Lots of people – in every kind of society – contract marriages for reasons other than love, for money or security or family pressures or for no better reason than because it was 'time', as if there was some kind of time limit on singleness, as if when the music stopped you were obliged to marry the partner of the moment. This had always seemed comical to me, and yet – yet, even these days, more unions last than not. Most people are different from me. For most people, most marriages mostly work.

There was no need for him to answer; he knew these truths as well as I did. We'd never been able to lie to each other, not even with silence. He shrugged.

'Believe me, I have thought it over, exhaustively I have done so. There is no other way. The balance of my life is so delicate – but you know this too. You may think – you may even say – that I've deserted you, but you'll know differently. You'll know I had no choice, that our paths lie separately. We have rebelled against much, between us, but not against human destiny. Mortals have no answer to that.'

My mind was confused. I thought of the differences between Eastern and Western notions of marriage, of his affection for little Jamie, of the urge all humans have to leave something of themselves behind them. But in the end all that registered was the inevitability of it, and, again, he'd chosen my weakest point, perhaps our strongest bond, our shared fatalism. I tried to accept that he was right – I knew in my heart he was right, but to accept it, that was too much for me. For his sake, I didn't weep; instead I grasped his shoulders hard, too hard; he winced but didn't shake free. I told him to be happy; I told him that nothing could break the bond between us, as if the fierceness with which I said it made it true. Then I went upstairs to my room, muffled my face in the bed and cried.

The light downstairs stayed on long after that; it was still on, hours later, as I slipped into sleep.

I couldn't get out of going to the wedding, though I flirted with the idea of inventing a tour abroad. The children stuck to me like glue, but I didn't mind; I was their Uncle Nathaniel – everyone was given honorific uncleship in that family. I felt that they had a right to part of me, and perhaps their sticky little hands gave me some kind of comfort. The ceremony was long, alien and involved; and while it was going on I watched Robert's still face and felt him slipping away from me, bit by bit, until I had to bite my lip to keep the tears back. The bride was a tiny creature, all red and gold, very serious-looking. She moved through the ceremony dazed; perhaps she was – Auntie George knew more about drugs than most addicts did. Once it was over they had an open-style reception and I tried to get her to talk to me. Her English was poor, but she had a charming smile; I imagined their slim-boned, exquisitely warm-skinned children. Robert clasped my hand – his sweat felt heavy, like blood – and, when I looked up, I saw his eyes were wet but the chin clamped tight. Fatalism, resignation, were in the lines of his face, but the tears were Western tears; I'd taught them to him, the tears were for me. He said nothing; I said nothing. We had finally slipped completely beyond words.

There isn't much more, Warren, you've been very good, very patient. I don't know why I had to tell someone. You know, I never told anyone before? It's true; neither of us did. Mind you, Auntie George knew; no flies on that woman. But I don't believe anyone else guessed. I was Uncle Nathaniel, wasn't I, and he was Uncle Rob. People believed we'd lived together solely for convenience – my security, my bassoons, his low rent. Of course, I still see him occasionally. On summer nights, when the wind is right and the family is staying, I can hear his laughter from the garden behind mine. And the family still invite me around, to hear how many GCSEs Jamie's taking, that kind of thing. Rob has children too, they look very like I imagined they would. A while back, I met him and the boys at a match at the Oval, two scrawny little creatures with eyes like wells, Robert slightly more solid-looking than I remembered. It was a clear, windy day, the sun lashing the seats until they hurt to sit on.

'You remember your Uncle Nathaniel,' he told the boys, his eyes flying to mine. They did remember me, I think; I am their only white uncle, so I suppose I linger in the memory. The smaller one kissed me; the elder attempted to look grave and statesmanlike.

'You are alone,' said Robert; it was not a question.

'I'm always alone,' I replied, with a smile.

'Yes, yes, you do not change.'

'You mean I don't escape,' I told him. 'You saw that from the beginning.'

'Of course not. You prefer to suffer,' and the smile hadn't altered, no, it lashed down, too, as if he was still twenty, and my heart still untampered with. I shook my head in answer to a question left unasked, and said I had to go. The younger one waved his Indian flag at me, and the way his lips curved sliced into my heart. I believe the match was a draw, but I can't be sure I remember.

'I will call you,' Robert told me. 'We'll go for a pint.'

But, of course, he never called. I knew he never would. But sometimes all the knowing, all the maturity, all the acceptance in the world is no help to me. Sometimes when I hear his voice over the back of the garden I feel I can bear it no longer, that I have to move, get away, clean away, start again. Then I know that it's more than Rob I have to escape from, and that from love and loss there is no escape. And the smell of spices drifts over the fence like the death of childhood, and deep in the night the biryani ashes swim on currents of air.

XVII

Orchestral Voices

I am too pure for you or anyone
Your body
Hurts me as the world hurts God. I am a lantern —

My head a moon
Of Japanese paper, my gold beaten skin
Infinitely delicate and infinitely expensive.

Does not my heat astound you. And my light.

Sylvia Plath

'I must admit, it felt extremely odd to be playing an audition at my advanced age,' said William wryly.

John McDaniel smiled and handed him his coffee.

'Nobody could possibly have guessed your age from your playing.'

They were backstage at the Barbican, following a rehearsal of the Royal Sinfonia. John McDaniel, their principal cellist, had just heard William play, without accompaniment, most of the Haydn D major Concerto, along with a solid chunk of Bach. Alongside him had been the leader and his co-principal cellist, who had since departed. The backstage of the Barbican had a strange, hollow ring to it; few players remained; and the bar staff was reduced to one fat humorous soul dispensing occasional drinks. A couple of Royal Sinfonia drivers were trundling double bass cases from the backstage to a travelling van; otherwise they were alone.

William accepted the coffee. 'I suppose my technical ability was probably greater when I was young – you're probably looking for a younger player anyway.'

'Believe me, you sounded marvellous. Few youngsters, even these days, could do better.'

'There's no need to be kind,' said William suddenly. 'I can live with the truth, John.'

'And I'm telling you the truth. If I had my way, you'd have the job in my section tomorrow.'

William breathed, really breathed, for the first time in an hour. He hadn't completely lost it; he was still good enough. The escape route – narrow though it might be – remained open. Yet still he awaited the qualifications, the conditions, the polite, even cordial, let-down.

'I just don't understand *why*,' pursued John. 'That's all. We're all puzzled about why. Why take a job at a reduced salary? Why shift from associate principal in one section to fifth in another? Why are you here at all, William? – playing an audition, as you put it yourself, at our sort of age? Why submit yourself to such a thing, for such little conceivable gain? That's my only reservation, to be honest. I can't think of a reason good enough. If you're tired of being at the front, you could move down your own section, although, God knows, your playing's certainly up to your present position. I won't be satisfied, and nor will Tony, until we know your reason.'

'I'd rather not say,' said William quietly.

'Personal, is it?'

'Extremely personal.'

'And nothing to do with a certain viola player in your orchestra?'

William stood up, white to the nostrils. 'If you knew, how dared you ask me?'

John rose to detain him.

'Forgive me, Will; I just needed to be sure. Not your health then, not your wife's condition, nothing to give us a moment's pause in appointment. Naturally, there have been rumours about Isabel, rumours we had to look into when you put in your application. But I don't want to force you to tell me anything, although I personally feel that your attempt to get out of such a situation does you credit. Your assurance that Isabel is the reason is all I needed, and I apologise again for having to ask for it.'

William reseated himself, burying his head in his hands. John watched him sympathetically, wondering whether to risk a comforting hand. So often overt condolence only made things worse. Yet even in his present position, William managed to convey reservoirs of resolution and strength – which was less surprising, of course, when you remembered his wife's long illness. Even before this business, Will had been accustomed to bearing burdens. Though rumour had it that Isabel's behaviour with Karl Hochler, since the split, had been beyond crediting.

'Listen, I'll do what I can,' he said at last, rising. 'As I hinted, Tony was very impressed, and there's a lot to be said for a calm, experienced person in the centre of a section. I'll call you about when your trial period will be, once we've heard all the others. But you should be proud of how you played, Will, very proud.'

'Thank you,' said William, and the look in his eyes touched John McDaniel deeply. 'I appreciate that.'

They shook hands; then he shouldered his cello and walked away.

Isabel moved through the days drugged like a sleepwalker. When Hochler was in town she felt sore with love, aching with it like a rider too long in the saddle; when he was away she was prowling and hungry, lean as one of his whips, and as dangerous. She mixed alcohol with valium to disastrous effect, picked fights with Caroline without excuse, and was frighteningly rude to Warren when he cornered her outside the EMI studios one night after a recording session.

'Never better,' she snapped. 'Get out of my way.'

'People are saying,' he said with determination, 'that Hochler is ruining you. And he is, Isabel. Anyone can see that.

He's draining your lifeblood. If it was physically possible for you to look terrible, you'd look terrible.'

'I don't recall asking for your opinion!'

Warren grabbed her arms, his voice low, intense. 'Aren't things bad enough as it is? Isn't it bad enough without Mirabel? Don't you think I know I've made a mistake in marrying Caroline? Do you want to bloody kill me?'

'Let go of me,' said Isabel contemptuously. 'I didn't ask you to marry her, did I? I didn't shoot down Mirabel's plane! Leave me out of your troubles; I've enough of my own.'

'But your troubles aren't necessary, Isabel! You could throw away your stupid drugs, lay off the alcohol, and tell Hochler to take a running jump. You're destroying yourself; and, what's worse, because everyone's got a right to self-destruction, you're destroying other people. William – even Hochler. Everyone knows how Hochler's wife's been carrying on, since she heard about it. We're all spiralling down after you. And it doesn't have to happen! William looks – '

'You take his cause,' said Isabel, coming to a halt, 'yet he's the one I chose, over you, over everybody!'

'Oh, we're brothers all right,' Warren assured her, 'though he either doesn't know or doesn't care. I don't blame William, Isabel, I blame you.'

She turned away, suddenly tired, tired of fighting, tired of losing. 'Oh, everybody blames me. I'm used to it. Being alive is being guilty.'

'Then come with me instead,' said Warren strongly, and for one breathless moment she almost thought it possible, glimpsing the slim, eager poet she had captured a decade ago. 'Come back to me. I'll heal you, Isabel.'

'You must be drunk,' she told him, leaning against a wall. 'You've not been married two months!'

'I love you; I'll always love you. I told you that on Victoria Station.'

'If you were William,' said Isabel suddenly, 'what would you do?'

'Will's too honourable to bear it; the amazing thing is that he coped as long as he did. Can't you just be satisfied with driving him crazy?'

'What would you do?'

'I'm not like William.'

'What would you do?'

'Oh, I would die,' he told her quietly. 'But I'm not as strong as William.'

'Then die!' she whispered, tears dissolving down her face. And then she ran off, too swiftly for him to follow her.

'You're very silent this evening,' said Hochler in the restaurant. 'I hope this doesn't mean you are not eating again.'

'I don't feel terribly hungry,' Isabel admitted.

'Your dress is beautiful. I love dresses low over the shoulders.'

'I heard – from someone – ' she said, and as abruptly halted.

He put down his fork in mock irritation. 'You've not been thinking about that cellist again!'

'No, nothing to do with him. About your wife.'

'Ah. Giselle.'

'I heard that she was upset.'

'I regret very much having to tell you that your information is deficient. Giselle is not upset; she is incandescent! I fear, you will observe, that it is not the first time she has heard such things about my visits to foreign orchestras. But you need not trouble; she will never divorce me. There are, you will observe, the property, the children. No, do not concern yourself; Giselle will soon be calm again, or as calm, perhaps I should say, as Giselle ever is.'

And she wondered, watching his expert handling of the steak, whether she herself would ever be calm again. Perhaps this is what losing one's mind is like, she thought; everything reduced to the physical: eating, not eating, making love, not making love. The very effort of thought was too much, because all thought led back to William, to William's darkened eyes and bowed shoulders, to William's face averted from her as she departed with Karl. Only sleep, sex and sleep, drove his face from her consciousness, because, in her present drugged state, she couldn't recall her dreams. But she sometimes stood in her kitchen window, remembering his hands warm on her shoulders, until tears turned her coffee to salt.

Hochler watched her. Normally, by this time, he would have put down the shutters on the affair; he almost wondered at himself, that he had not done so. Her looks were subtly marred, but somehow that excited him; the shifting alterations in her face, her mood, kept him interested. There was peculiarly the feeling, with Isabel, of living life very near the edge, and that was sensually inspiring too.

William himself, though Karl pretended otherwise, lent spice to the affair. When Hochler played his little games with Isabel – pain games, usually – it was amusing to see William's arms stiffen; and when he moved away with her, arm secure about her waist, Karl knew that his image was branded onto William's soul, though the man always contrived to be looking elsewhere. And when he conducted, there was the dual intensity: of spurring William, beyond his will, into superior playing, of controlling every gesture of his rival – as well as managing to skewer Isabel's sensibilities with a glance. Rarely, thought Hochler, had he conducted so well, achieved quite such scintillating reviews, and Paul Ellison, the chairman of the board, had been emphatic in his encouragement.

As for his wife, it was a bore, naturally, but Giselle could be got round, some emerald perhaps, or a bigger boat: something could always be done. Really, the steak here was quite excellent; and he had just thought of something imaginative they might try after dinner.

'They never speak,' said Caroline to Nancy. 'That's the oddest part. I mean, literally, never. Not even if they meet in a doorway, or stand beside each other in the lift. There's the

206

oddest feeling – an electrical feeling – but they don't acknowledge each other.'

'He looks ill.'

'As to that, I never saw what she saw in him. He's so much older!'

'If you like older men,' said Nancy judiciously, 'he's not at all bad-looking, but, as it happens, I don't. Now Paul – '

'Oh, Paul Ellison's very attractive,' agreed Caroline quickly, in order to forestall Nancy's competitive how-many-orgasms-Paul-gave-her-last-night routine. 'But I don't see anything different about William. I don't think he's changed since. It's Isabel who's altered; you wouldn't think there was anything particularly pretty about her, now she's lost so much weight. I do think men prefer a bit of flesh, basically.'

'Up to a point,' allowed Nancy, who was noticeably slimmer than Caroline. 'But not too much. I always thought her face beautiful, but she looks all cheekbones now, like a cat.'

'She doesn't eat, is why. Just the pills. I think she lives on pills, on pills and drink.'

'I still don't understand why he left her in the first place.'

'No, and I don't understand why she was fussed that he left her, but she never talks to me now. Just smiles if I ask her anything, if she hears me at all.'

'Weird,' agreed Nancy, scanning the menu. 'Do you want any dessert? I don't.'

'There was a call while you were out,' said Tracey to Roger Ash, upon his return from lunch. 'Funny accent, too. Antonio Torelli, conductor, composer. Let me see; here it is: wanted to have a little informal chat regarding working with the orchestra again.'

'Not bloody poss.,' said Roger, with a shudder. 'He's been blacklisted by the band. Kayoed, nixed, rubbed-out, destroyed, cement-overshoed, and slashed to buttermilk. If there was a list blacker than the blacklist he'd be on it.'

'Does that mean no?' inquired Tracey. Roger looked at her, considering. There were times when he wondered if even the other sterling qualities Tracey possessed were sufficient to justify keeping her on as his secretary.

'Yes, batgirl, that means no. Start with an N, followed as shortly as possibly by an O, and you'll have the whole shebang in no time. I'll dictate a letter to you about it tomorrow. Any other messages?'

'No,' said Tracey vaguely. 'I mean yes, just one. Paul Ellison called to say he'd be stopping by to see you before the orchestra board meeting.'

'Hmm,' said Roger. 'Thanks very much, Tracey. Fore-warned is forearmed.'

'Four arms?'

'Oh, never mind,' said Roger Ash. 'That reminds me, as soon as I unload Paul, trot along for some Special Dictation, all right?'

Tracey giggled. 'All right.'

She made a little cross against Torelli's name in the conductor's list, where, for some reason, it still resided. Upon mature consideration, however, she added a second cross, because Roger had been so very firm about it, though it wound up looking rather like kisses. Then her mind wandered to the Special Dictation, and to whether Roger would prefer her in her nurse's outfit or not. She hoped he'd gone off the doggy position; it wasn't that she minded exactly, but it was very expensive in terms of stockings, and, after all, nice stockings were nice stockings and didn't come cheap.

(from Piotr's private files)

I was born, in case I neglected to mention it, in the late if unlamented USSR, to a couple of itinerant poets. There were times, and this was one of them, when I wished I was an i. poet myself, and out of this orchestral mess. Not that I write poetry personally – I specialise in more amusing vices – but I have a notion that there is a great comic novel in me somewhere, along with a conviction that someday it will pour out, in one limpid bubbling stream. I'm aware that most of the Great Russians were stronger in tragic vein, but, in my opinion, there was more than enough tragedy around me already.

There was Clarence, still distressed by something he wouldn't speak about, and Warren, trapped into a marriage and already regretting it. There was our beloved cello leader, his temper growing rattier with every failed solo competition, and Halloran, buttering himself over David's boots. There was general sorrow over Mirabel, particularly in the ranks of the brass, and rumours of vicious splits within the orchestra board. There was the demonic Hochler, appearing, even when not conducting us, in order to spirit Isabel away. And then there was the girl herself – My feelings towards her were as mixed as they'd ever been: she was magnificent, diabolical, unfeeling, passive, beyond saving. A conviction grew in me, possibly inspired by wishful thinking, that she had never cared about William, but my communication of this, by way of being helpful, led to the first actual rift of our long friendship.

He turned from me with unshakeable dignity.

'I only meant,' I added hastily, 'that she isn't the sort with particularly retentive feelings. Flighty is perhaps the word. Buzzing, first hither, then thither. Why, since she joined the orchestra, perhaps ten years ago, she's buzzed from person to person, some in the orchestra, some outside of it – I can't for the life of me recall her alone, actually alone, for more than half a day! It's as if she can't bear it.'

'Of course she can't bear it!' he said, turning on me at last. 'Has it taken you so long to understand?'

'But, can't you see, the actual people don't matter! Any more than the fellows I used to pick up outside RADA mattered! She probably can't even remember their names. It's compulsive, Will – sex and power, that's all it is, except for the

209

impulse of the moment. Impulses and whims! I don't believe she's actually cared about anyone in all her life.'

He stared at me. 'You can look at her, as she now is, and say that?'

'Of course,' I said, impatient for him to understand, to free himself.

'Then you're a fool,' he told me quietly.

There was no apology, no retraction, from either of us. I stubbornly stuck to my opinion, coloured as it may have been by pique or jealousy or both. Will made no sign that he remembered the conversation. The coolness between us wore away, but wasn't forgotten. I felt that I'd disappointed him; and I knew he was deluded about Isabel. Not long after this, too, I found that I had something else to think about.

William, walking home, suddenly decided to turn into the open parish church. There was nothing beautiful about it, but the October day was drizzling and chilly, and suddenly reaching his destination seemed more than he could cope with. Margot, brandishing the duster from her wheelchair, making him tea, emerging triumphant over her shaking hands; Margot, valiant, admirable – supplanted. And yet he'd loved her once; it surely couldn't be impossible to learn to love her again. He felt weak, lonely beyond anything he could remember; and the brotherly affection that satisfied Margot could no longer suffice him. His heart, grown accustomed to spicier food, was starving; his hands, once sure of riches, felt empty.

Perhaps he should tell her everything, make a clean start, now it was over. Honesty, which had been the centre point of his existence, still held its attraction for him, but was not irresistible. Honesty pointed out that it would be, in this case, only a transference of misery, a short-lived relief for his conscience, purchased at the expense of Margot's own comfort. No, it was his burden and he had to bear it; even Piotr's idle patience seemed exhausted. If he won the Royal

Sinfonia post, he thought, he would still tell Margot nothing. There was David, Adam Halloran, the divisions within the section: these supplied excuse enough.

He wondered what it would feel like to leave, after so many years. Orchestras have different souls, separate characters; no orchestra's atmosphere was like another's. So many friends to leave behind, so many years, not all of them painful . . . But orchestras were juggernauts, crashing ever onwards despite any victims they might leave beside the roadside. People would be sorry, they'd say they'd keep in touch, but then they would forget, as he had in his own time forgotten. He could expect nothing more; he would have pulled up his own life by the roots and transplanted it in alien soil. Then there was Piotr; how odd it would be not to have Piotr by his side! And never, or hardly ever, to see Isabel again – perhaps, bad as things were, that sacrifice was too much to be asked to bear . . . Through a wash of tears he saw a stained-glass St George, sword just poised above the dragon's throat. Before he could hope to leave, he had his own dragons to conquer, if only he had courage enough. God willing he had courage enough!

'Anything I can do for you?' inquired an elderly lady, too brightly.

William started, and rose.

'Nothing, thank you.'

'Services start at ten of a Sunday,' she called after him.

'You're very kind,' William told her desperately, and strode out into driving rain.

XVIII

Dance Till you Drop

I have a faint cold fear thrills through my veins
That almost freezes up the heat of life.

Shakespeare

'Yes? Piotr here. Who is it?'

'It's me, Charles.'

It was a small voice, tinny in timbre, with a faintly south London intonation.

'Charles?' Piotr repeated, searching his memory for various Charles he had known. Surely his ex-colleague Charles hadn't used to have a London accent?

'Charles Corrigan. We met at Mike Smith's party, last winter.'

'Good Lord, yes. Charles, of course. Well, how are things?'

Piotr remembered Charles well enough, now that the whine had registered. A lean, nervous-looking fellow, with a white-green, snooker player's complexion. Not much going for him, poor sod. Piotr had 'loaned' him some money, never expecting to have it returned, nor had it been. Doubtless he'd been pigeon-holed as a prize mug in Charles' book. He steeled himself to refuse the request, when it came. He remembered feeling sorry for Charles, but enough was enough.

'Well, I was evicted from where I was staying.'

'Sorry to hear that. Clapham, wasn't it?'

'Yes, but then I found a squat in Hackney. That's still all right, as far as it goes.'

'Are you still looking for a job?'

'I don't know. Maybe.'

212

Piotr felt a flash of impatience. Maybe! The world was too full of wonders to waste time and energy on some poor sap who didn't have enough gumption to even try for a job. He couldn't remember what Charles had done for a living – electrics, possibly, or plumbing. Surely a plumber could always plumb? This was one boy who wasn't getting a bean out of Piotr.

'Any particular reason for wanting to talk to me? To be honest, I'm rather busy at the moment.'

'Yes, that is, I'm sure you are. I was just trying to get up enough courage.'

Piotr forestalled him. 'I'm really sorry, but I'm not able to lend you any more money at the moment. I've just bought a new bow, for a start, and my mortgage – '

'I'm afraid you don't understand,' said Charles sadly. 'It's nothing to do with money. I won't be needing much money now.'

Piotr felt chilled. 'What do you mean? Just get to the point.'

'I am trying to, Piotr, but you make it very difficult. I – I'm not very well.'

'If you've got AIDS, bloody say so,' said Piotr brutally.

'I do,' he whispered, expelling a sigh.

'What?'

'I do have AIDS. The doctor said I was to tell you – you and the others.'

Piotr felt fury, unreasoning fury, flood into him. He had met Charles, been kind to him, slept with him, and lent the puny little bastard money. In return, he – Piotr, that scintillating, manipulative, quicksilver original – might, in a few short years, be dead. The idea seemed so contemptible, so incredible, that his brain refused to accept the possibility. It only admitted fury, white-hot, uncompromising, limitless.

'Get off my phone,' he breathed.

'I'm ever so sorry, Piotr. But it's even worse for me; I've actually got it now. The doctor said I should let people know, that's all. That's all I can do. Isn't it? Isn't it?'

Piotr, not trusting his voice not to tremble, unable to bear another moment of the other's bleating, slammed down the phone. He sat staring at it as if it had bitten him. Dizziness, nausea, rushed over him. He ran to the other side of the kitchen and hung over the sink; nothing happened; so he poured out far too much Listerine and spun it round his mouth in an effort to clear the sick feeling. His mind still refused to take in what had happened, refused to accept it, more, couldn't accept it. To accept it would be annihilation. It was annihilation. For Christ's sake, he said out loud, keep calm, keep calm.

Piotr leaned blackly against the kitchen cabinets. He had to think this through. He might be positive; he might be negative. He might die, or not die. He might choose to know, or not to know. Life, which up to that moment had seemed a thing of outrageous and endless complexity (William and Isabel, Paul and Roger's little games, how to get rid of David Schaedel, everything), had narrowed into this unutterably unspeakable simplicity. And the morning sun was still shimmering through the kitchen window, that disloyal sun which would go on rising until the end of time, whether he was there personally to salute it or not. For the first time in his life he felt lost, vulnerable, exposed. For the first time he felt mortal, as if he might, in the end, be the same as everyone else. When the colossal arrogance of this realisation struck him he began to laugh, and after a moment he discovered he was weeping.

'Anything up?' William asked him that afternoon, as he'd asked him so many times before.

'God, no. Had a bit of a late night, that's all.'

'You've gone in for too many of those recently. You're losing weight, you know, and I'm not even sure your playing isn't suffering.'

'Crap! I weigh exactly what I've always weighed, any fool can see that.'

William put his hand on his shoulder. 'I'm only telling you

for your own good. You're going at life too hard. All these parties, these distractions. You'll pay the price with your health, one of these days. We all work too hard to cope with so many other things as well. I wouldn't have said anything if I wasn't worried about you.'

'And you're not alone there,' replied Piotr under his breath.

'What's that?'

'Nothing. I just don't feel like being lectured, Will. Not in the mood, sorry.'

'Are you playing Tuesday?'

'I don't remember. What's on Tuesday? If it's Tuesday, it must be Mahler, right?'

'Tuesday. The memorial service for Mirabel, you remember.'

'Oh God, I'd forgotten about all that.'

'I'd wondered if that was what was bothering you. Do you still mean to play?'

'I said I'd play, so I'll play,' said Piotr grimly. 'Though, come to think of it, will you do me a favour when I hand in my dinner pail? No milk-and-water Nimrods, nothing peaceful and precious and reconciled. Something with a bit of blood and guts to it – Janáček, Shostakovich, Benjamin Britten, something like that.'

'No one would have the nerve,' said Will affectionately, 'to send you off with anything peaceful, Piotr. But you'd better let someone younger know your intentions. I won't be around to see you out.'

'Wouldn't be too bloody sure about that,' muttered Piotr.

As the days passed, Piotr's moods flickered strangely. At times he felt, with all his famed insouciance, that, having led a charmed life until now, he was immune to the possibility of illness and death. At other times, however, a creeping heaviness seemed to settle inside his bones. The evidence then, especially late at night, seemed overwhelming, and he found himself wondering bleakly about the afterlife, and whether his wiles and lies would come back to haunt him. He mused, in morbidly sentimental vein, about leaving the orchestra, and returning to Russia for the last days of his life; he agonized over whether to tell the truth to his trusting mother. Will's face, tortured as it had been so recently over Isabel, rose up before him, and he grieved in spirit for the additional blow that was to fall on his friend.

Tears of self-pity welled up in his eyes as he considered the wonderful novel he had failed to write, the major cellist that, given a bit of luck and considerably more dedication and talent, he might have been. The love affairs that he had pursued, if they could be so dignified – these he recalled with all their intensity of misery and desire, until his hunger for life felt too ravenous to be borne. But daybreak never failed to resurrect his old optimism and energy. The very notion of his being ill then seemed absurd, a combination of an overactive imagination and feverish night-time fears. His behaviour was a bit manic in those days, lurching from moodiness to mischief without intervals of coolness in between. One night in the pub, he had a sudden yearning to confide in Warren.

'Playing in the service for Mirabel, tomorrow?' he asked casually.

'Yes, of course,' said Warren. 'She was always kind to me. Used to kid me – about various things. I miss her.'

'The new guy's all right, though.'

'Oh, Jack's all right. I didn't say he wasn't. It's just been one of those years, hasn't it?'

'What do you mean?'

'Well, what don't I mean? Mirabel was the worst, of course, but there's all that awful business between Isabel and William, and before then David upsetting Elinor and all the politics on the board and something's certainly gone wrong with Clarence, though he won't say what. The orchestra feels as if it's falling to pieces. And I've – well, I've been having these dreams.'

'Don't tell me. Black cats and creatures that fly by night, walls without doors and configurations of tea leaves. I get enough of this from my peerless leader, Warren. Nobody in their senses believes in dreams.'

'I don't know that I believe them, exactly, but I remember them. Caroline says it's simply morbid, but I can't forget them.'

'Well, what do you dream about, then?' asked Piotr languidly.

'About death, mainly.'

Piotr looked up, startled. 'Whose death?'

'A violinist's. I can never see his face, but his hair is grey. He's in a hotel room – somewhere – playing Mozart to himself. And somehow I know that he's – failed – something or someone that mattered to him. And his fingers get whiter and whiter and slower and slower and I know that something inside him is dying. I can feel his heart swelling up and bursting as if it was inside of me.'

'Much,' said Piotr, thoughtfully, 'as I hate to agree with Caroline – and it grieves me to the very soul – I have to admit that this is morbid. Morbid, indeed, would seem to understate the case.'

'But don't you see,' said Warren, twisting his beer mug, 'there's more than that, but I'm no good at putting it into words. It's as if he's holding out hope – the hope of a good death, of a death that redeems something. It may sound completely fanciful, but I think he's lifting up his soul, reclaiming it even, having suffered enough. There's something beautiful about that – that spirit of renunciation.'

'It interests me that you can see anything beautiful about death.'

'Does it? Caroline thinks I'm obsessed by it.'

'Well, it's not the kind of thing Caroline would think about,' said Piotr impatiently. 'You said, "a good death". What do you mean by that? Do you mean a hero's death, a noble death, or can any of us have one?'

'I don't know; how should I know? There's another dream I have sometimes, about drifting out into the sea, the waves crashing past me, that kind of thing. Oblivion, I suppose, nothing more dramatic or goal-oriented than that. I – long for it, even.'

Piotr looked at him curiously. 'You're not awfully happy with Caroline, are you?'

'Oh, yes,' said Warren, the lid slamming down over his face. 'We're very happy. She's excited at the moment, thinks she might be pregnant.'

'No joke? What about Isabel?'

'Oh, Isabel's unhappiness has got nothing to do with me. She knows what I think of her behaviour since – since William's had nothing more to do with her.'

'But you're still in love with her,' snapped Piotr. 'I don't know why you don't admit it. I've known you long enough.'

'Because I'm married to Caroline,' said Warren quietly. 'I don't expect you to understand.'

'You mean because I'm a bloody queer I can't understand anything?' demanded Piotr dangerously.

Warren stared at him, shocked. 'You're in such an odd mood tonight! I only meant that you're not married yourself; that's all I meant! How'd you get such a chip on your shoulder?'

'Sorry,' said Piotr, gulping down his beer. 'I've drunk too much, that's all. I didn't mean to snap at you. You're a good person, Warren; you can't help it if you're miserable, any more than I can . . . Yes, oh I admit it, admit it freely. I, the great, the effervescent, the inimitable Piotr, am miserable. That's a turn-up for the books, isn't it? Shall I get up and do Russian dances on the table? That's what people expect of me, after all. Shall I sit here making lewd comments on passers-by, or attempt to pick up the rather beautiful boy on the far side of the room? No, no, I shall resist; my dancing days are over. Yeats put his finger where it hurts, didn't he?

"Not to have lived is best, ancient writers say;
   Never to have drawn the breath of life, never
      to have looked into the eye of day;
   The second-best's a gay goodnight and quickly turn away."

That'll just do me, won't it, my poetic friend. A gay goodnight and quickly turn away!'

'You're not well,' said Warren, looking at him with a new attention. 'You look awful, Piotr. Your eyes have a funny light in them and you're terribly pale. Is it because of the service tomorrow, or has something else happened?'

Piotr made his decision.

'My behaviour may be slightly over the odds,' he admitted, 'but you will scarcely blame me when I inform you, regretfully, that I, Piotr, the indomitable, the irreplaceable, am going to die.'

'We're all going to die,' Warren said sharply, reaching over to take the beer from him. 'Don't drink any more, Piotr. You've had quite enough already. I wouldn't have let you drive if I'd realised.'

His smile looked strange to Warren.

'I wish I was drunk, but I'm not; I can't seem to get drunk anymore, which is an irredeemable pity. Listen carefully, old fresco. This is what I need to tell you; that is, I need to tell somebody, and I know I can trust you. I had a phone call the other day, from a fellow I picked up once, back when I used to do that kind of stupid thing all the time. He called to tell me that he is good-natured enough to die before me, and pick out the cloud on which I hope to curl my wings and pluck my harpstrings. It's all up with me, the dancing's over. It's only a matter of which year, which cloud, which variety of harp – pink, blue, or mauve.'

'Oh, no,' said Warren, his face crumpling. 'Not you too!'

Piotr recaptured his glass, well pleased with his friend's distress. 'Nice to know someone'll miss me when I'm gone. This reaction is peculiarly gratifying. Tragically, I have little hope of it being universal. Roger Ash and David Schaedel, to name but two, are highly unlikely to shed bitter tears in this eminently suitable fashion. In fact, I wouldn't put it much past his lordship to break out the champagne.'

'But do you know beyond a doubt that you've got it?'

'If you mean, have I been tested, the answer is in the negative. I refuse to test. The consequences of knowing for sure are more than I can bear.'

'But you may be perfectly all right!'

'The thought, you may be assured, has not escaped me. Indeed it's my principal consolation. Without same, the undersigned would, as of even date, have been unable to keep going at all.'

Warren hesitated. 'What about – other people – who ought to be warned?'

'They have been. Does that give me enough points to count, at least potentially, as a good death?'

'Oh, Piotr,' said Warren and gripped his hand until it hurt. 'We can't lose you as well!'

Then Piotr's heart constricted and he could jest no more.

David entered the church with a self-important mien the next morning. He wandered over to where the rest of the cellists were unpacking their instruments in preparation for the memorial service to begin. They looked like strangers wearing ordinary dark suits, and none of them, he thought complacently, looked anywhere near as handsome as he did. William in particular looked older than he used to; he was very quiet, too, although, thank goodness, he'd never been as noisy as some members of the section. David's eye alighted critically on Piotr, who was chewing his pencil while wrestling with the *Guardian* crossword.

'Piotr,' said David sententiously. 'It doesn't look correct for you to be playing games while the people are coming in.'

'Just a sec; I've nearly finished,' muttered Piotr, finger drumming restlessly against the page.

'William, tell him that I am right about this matter,' ordered David. 'It's our duty to show proper respect for the dead.'

'Put it away, Piotr,' said William. Piotr looked up irritably, pushing his too-long hair out of his face.

'Are you accusing me of lack of respect?'

'Of course not,' said William. 'Just finish the crossword afterwards.'

Piotr stormed around the corner with his paper, a dark line intersecting his pallid brow. David looked after him with disfavour.

'This attitude is very bad, reflects badly on the entire section. Piotr was always moody, but now he is ill-tempered. I think we will have to get rid of him.'

'I wouldn't miss him,' said Adam Halloran eagerly, memories of past slights rankling. 'Besides, he's not even such a good player anymore.'

'How could he be?' demanded David rhetorically. 'He never practises. Day after day he leaves his cello in the van.'

'Plus he doesn't care about the section,' added Halloran. 'He behaves just as he pleases.'

'Still, I have to admit that I have heard worse cellists,' David admitted. 'Technically, he is not a bad player.'

'Yes, well, you're quite right, of course, but he just isn't pulling his weight. And his personality – '

'He does pull his weight,' said William, growing alarmed by the turn of the conversation. 'He's just not interested in solo work, like you, David. You can't fire a fine player for going through a bad patch. Also, he was certainly fond of Mirabel, in his fashion, and I'm sure he meant no disrespect to her memory.'

'What did your spiritualist once tell you about him?' persisted Halloran. 'There was something, wasn't there, about people born under Capricorn – '

David clapped his hand to his forehead. 'I knew there was something I meant to tell you! Something amazing!'

Piotr had by this time returned, bearing his cello. He raised a sardonic eyebrow in David's direction.

'What ho! The oracle has spoken!'

'I can't think how I forgot to tell you, Adam. We must be watchful and careful – '

'Absolutely,' said Adam fervently.

'We must keep tabs on all people unfortunate enough to be born under Capricorn, or possessing dark to middling eyes,' continued Piotr.

'No, nothing about eyes,' said David irritably. 'Listen. Madame Shushila sent me this: "After the first death comes the second death, after the second death comes the third." '

Even Adam was momentarily silenced.

'It doesn't make sense to me,' said William. 'There are any number of deaths, especially in countries where people are starving. It's completely meaningless.'

'No, it applies to the orchestra,' said David, 'obviously. The first death, Mirabel. The rest – the rest is what we must beware.'

Piotr burst out into hysterical laughter. 'I'll volunteer!'

William looked at him sharply. 'Do shut up, Piotr. It really is bad form to shriek with laughter at a memorial service.'

'All right, all right, but I do volunteer. Anything to make one – just one – of Madame Shutyouup's warnings bear fruit. Did she give you any clues, Dave old boy? Anything about Colonel Mustard employing a wrench in the drawing room?'

'Piotr,' said William in a low voice, 'if you can't control yourself, I'll take you outside myself!'

Piotr stared long into William's eyes; but it was William who looked away at last.

'Hang on, team, it's time,' said Halloran self-importantly. 'Here's the vicar. I suppose that must be Mirabel's family in the front row.'

A dark man had just led an elderly couple and a young, small-boned, graceful woman into the main row.

'Is that her sister?' Caroline asked Isabel.

'Don't think she had a sister,' replied Isabel listlessly.

The vicar began with a short welcome, then the orchestra plunged into Elgar's Nimrod. At its conclusion, the principal horn walked up to the podium to give the eulogy.

Henry's face looked flushed and he started somewhat

jerkily, but once he was under way he spoke well and eloquently. In Piotr's ears his voice buzzed strangely, some words loud, some almost indistinguishable. 'Ready friendship, good nature . . . character and determination . . . musicianship . . . meant a great deal – ' Then it was drowned out in Piotr's brain – the second death, the second death. Those words accused him. He knew, in that moment, that he was dying, infected, cursed. He would let down Will, cause grief and misery to his friends, his mother. Lucky old Mirabel, to get a clean, clear death! His arms felt heavy on his cello; his throat dry and constricted. Suddenly he became aware that the buzzing had paused, that Henry was in trouble on the rostrum. The man tried to continue, but the words wouldn't come. His face was suffused with redness, he shuffled his notes miserably. The second death, the second death; congratulate me gentlemen; we have a volunteer. Suddenly Piotr could bear it no longer.

Henry looked down, startled, at a commotion in the cellos – Piotr had put down his instrument and bolted. His sudden departure shocked a good many people, but it gave Henry just the jolt he needed. 'We miss her now, we've missed her since, and we'll go on missing her,' he said simply. 'That's all I've got down here to say, but, let me tell you, I mean it. We all mean it. Thank you for your kind attention.'

And he climbed back into his place in the orchestra, blowing his nose, to the traditional orchestral applause of shuffling feet. Few people noticed Warren Wilson quietly creeping out of the back of the first violins as the orchestra prepared to play the Albinoni.

David leaned over to William. 'It seems that you were right about Piotr,' he said. 'I never realized that he was so very fond of that Australian horn player. Perhaps he will be better once all this is over. To be honest, I find his sarcastic attitude very difficult to cope with at times.'

But William hardly heard him. He didn't believe that the service alone could have affected his friend so strongly. There

223

was something wrong with Piotr, something deeply wrong; and he'd been too self-absorbed to notice it. William leaned into the Albinoni, its sinuous baroque lines so expressive of restrained regret, a pain too exquisite for words. And as he played he wondered how much longer it would take his pain to die too.

(from Piotr's private files)

I took the opportunity, a week after the memorial service, of paying an overdue visit to Elinor no-longer-Jay in her new home. I felt a pang as I arrived, when I thought how unlikely it was that I would ever live in such a secluded, pleasant spot: the house was huge, bought with the lucre of her husband's investments, and located in the leafiest glade of Surrey's stockbroker belt. Elinor was pregnant, and looked very well; pregnancy seemed to have taken years off her. I pondered the likelihood of the young sprig being raised an anarchist, and decided that there was hope, as long as he or she eluded the clutches of the champagne socialists of which Surrey is so sadly full. Elinor meanwhile asked after David, but casually, as after an errant brother for whom, in the teeth of all reason, she retained a fondness.

'Has he found anybody else?'

'If you mean,' I replied, attacking an admirably crafted homemade pâté, 'has he found another female, I would have to admit, more than few. But if you are inquiring as to another positive engagement, it seems that none of them is rich enough to suit him. Despite our best hopes, he failed to win the Budapest cello competition, but he did scrape into the quarter-finals, which has assured him entry into next year's Tchaikovsky. Despite soloistic politics, splashy playing and judges born (like my humble self) under the sign of Capricorn, he might yet win something one of these days and put the rest of us out of our misery.'

'Capricorn?' inquired Elinor, completely at sea.

'The same. Didn't you know that he has a phobia, induced by his Mancunian witch, against all Capricorns?'

'Good heavens.'

'Or you might go still further and exclaim, gadzooks. Elinor, this pâté is quite superb.'

'Thank you. It was a spin-off from a cookery course I took locally, in order to get to know some other people in the area.'

'The harmless delights of the bourgeoisie! Such a shame that it will have to end, when anarchy triumphs.'

'And when will that be?'

'You must ask Madame Pickadateandsticktoit,' said Piotr reprovingly. 'World anarchists only ever say that the Time is Nigh – as, it must be said, it has occasionally felt to be of late.'

'Do you mean, in the orchestra? William implied it's been through a hard time. The horn-player's plane crash must have been quite a shock, of course.'

Piotr stared at her. 'What, has Will been here?'

'No, he hasn't. I met him after a Royal Sinfonia concert last week.'

'The Royal Sinfonia? Who was massacring the cello concerto?'

'Nobody. They had a young Russian pianist, very gifted. He played – '

'One moment, my dear Elinor, I pray. Let me get this straight in my addled brain. William attended a concert of our fiercest rivals, without even the pettifogging excuse of a cello soloist. Why, is the word that springs to the lips, or, if French, pourquoi?'

'Oh, John got him a ticket, I think.'

'John McDaniel got him a ticket? The principal cellist of the Royal complete-ballsup Sinfonia procured him a ticket?'

Elinor looked at him, sudden realizing. 'Didn't you know that William has applied for fifth cello in the Royal Sinfonia?'

'No I bloody didn't!'

'Well, I do think he might have told you,' said Elinor in puzzlement. 'It seems very odd.'

Odd! I wanted to shriek at her. Our associate principal to stoop to a hacker's position in a rival chaingang? My best friend to dare to hide his possible desertion from me? My brain whizzed like a hamster's wheel. What wouldn't people think, about the orchestra, about William, about Isabel – Isabel! If the girl could feel anything, she would feel this. She was the propelling force, must have been. Her wild, miserable behaviour had conjured up this nightmare of finality and loss.

'How well,' I said urgently, 'how well does John McDaniel know William?'

'I really haven't any notion. I only saw William talking to him backstage at a couple of concerts. I had the impression – no more than that – that they were old friends, but musicians can be so different from most people; they seem to have fewer barriers, somehow. I can't say I know John either, although we do endow his post. I – I've rather fought shy of getting to know any of the orchestra personally since – '

'Yes, of course,' I said quickly. I stood up without knowing what I was doing and strode uselessly around the room.

'I wouldn't have said,' continued Elinor thoughtfully, 'that William looked very well. Worn out, I thought he looked, as if something was preying on his mind. Perhaps his wife's got worse again.'

Well, I exerted myself to be whimsically amusing after this blow, but I doubt whether I succeeded in deceiving Elinor. She took hold of my hand as I was leaving.

'You will take care, won't you? I worry about you,' she said, and I gave her a hug, the cold shadow of my illness creeping back into my bones. A good death, I thought, hanging onto the notion of Warren's, a good death. Show me a grenade and I'd fall on it.

I confronted William as he entered the Royal Festival Hall that night, shouldering his cello as if it was his cross and he had to bear it.

'Fifth cello!' I taunted him. 'Fifth cello in that chorus of whimpering wino wimps! I thought she was joking!'

'Who?' he wanted to know.

'Elinor Jay.'

'Elinor. Of course. No, she wasn't joking.'

I danced in front of him like an angry imp. 'You must be crazy; you've gone around the twist, it's the only answer!'

'I need a change,' he told me, as we mounted the stairs. It sounded rehearsed, and probably was. 'The cello section – David, Adam, Eugene . . . you know the pressures. I'm tired of being a buffer state between David and the rest of you. You know how often we've said – '

'A lower position, a lower salary, a less prestigious London orchestra – And have you thought how bad it makes this orchestra look?'

'I have thought,' said William, 'about everything.'

'It's Isabel, isn't it? You're still in love with Isabel.'

William moved his head blindly, as if I had struck him.

'I may not get the job,' he continued patiently. 'A younger man; they might well prefer a younger man. The leader's nephew is in for it, and an excellent young player he is, by all accounts.'

'You're bonkers. A propaganda coup like stealing our second cellist to play as their number five and they're going to prefer some kid fresh out of the egg?'

'I'm simply looking at possibilities. I'm fifty-five years old, and not as technical a player as I used to be.'

'Rubbish. Tosh. Balls. You can't tell me anything that will alter my opinion of why you're doing this.'

'You haven't heard, have you?' he asked me softly, at the very top of the stairs.

'Heard what?'

'The new appointment – principal guest conductor. It was Paul Ellison's idea, and the committee voted yes last Wednesday. The board is apparently keen, too.'

'Not – Hochler?' I breathed.

'Of course; and you really can't blame them. He's got everything, talent, record contracts – charisma. He's a superb conductor, you can't deny it. The orchestra's lucky to sign him.'

I can't describe the desolation, the resignation with which William said this. I twisted my scarf so hard my hand hurt. 'Will,' I said, and stopped. He was better left alone; didn't he have enough on his plate? Besides, I couldn't bear the reproach in his eyes if he knew about my illness. But I needed him; I needed him beside me, to make a good death. My panic was so terrific that I lost control.

'Will, I need you here,' I said wildly.

'Don't be absurd.'

'I do, I do – I can't tell you why.'

'This whole orchestra needs me like a hole in the head.'

'Isabel needs you,' I said, too desperate to pretend that she didn't any longer. 'Don't you see what she's doing? You've released her every self-destructive urge. Not only that, but she's pulling Warren Wilson down with her. Let go of me, Will, you're hurting.'

'Say that again,' he said, gripping me harder.

'Are you blind? Isabel doesn't give a tinker's damn about Hochler. Think of him as an animated vibrator. She's never been in love with anyone in her life, except for you. She told Warren so herself. Ask Warren – ask anyone! Anyone less modest than you would have realized it months ago. You've splintered her silly crooked heart. If you reached out one finger, she'd be crying in your arms.'

'I can't do that,' said William, unsteadily, releasing my shoulders after a long moment. 'That's why I have to leave.'

I was frightened by his behaviour, by the empty look in his eyes. After a second death –

'It's cursed,' he said suddenly. 'The whole orchestra's cursed.'

'Too many Capricorns,' I agreed, reaching hopelessly for the humorous. But William had already gone, and my bones felt middled by the December cold.

*

I ran into Clarence before the concert that evening, the good fellow looking chirpier than he'd looked in ages.

'What's up, Clarence?' I quipped. 'Santa Claus come early? England selectors changed their mind about your hero? Or have you persuaded Roger to let you off the Mahler?'

Clarence smiled so broadly his funny little monkey face looked very nearly human. 'None of those things, Piotr.'

'All right, I give up. Tell me.'

'I just found out . . .' he said and then hesitated. 'Something's been really worrying me, that's all, and I just found out it wasn't true.'

Poor little queen, I thought affectionately. Probably exactly the same thing as me, only he's speared the happy ending. I patted him on the shoulder as if he was an England selector and had done The Right Thing by Our Boys.

'Go on,' I said tolerantly. 'Had the test, have you?'

'No,' he said. 'I've been incredibly stupid, Piotr.'

'We all have at times,' I consoled him. 'Even I, the great Piotr – '

'Someone's been blackmailing me, and I've been giving in to them.'

'Good Lord,' I said, startled.

'Fellow I knew, years ago, down in Clapham. I – was fond of him once, or thought I was – we – '

'We'll take that bit as read,' I said, partly to save him embarrassment and partly because, to be honest, Clarence's affairs bore me. I mean, he always seems to begin where Romeo left off. 'Did he threaten to tell your family that you're gay, something like that?'

'Oh, they know already,' said Clarence. 'It was worse than that, Piotr. He called me saying he'd got AIDS and needed money for special private treatments and that I'm the only person who could help him – and anyway I must have given it to him in the first place, so I was for it too.'

His pale eyes were shining, though with anger or relief was

229

hard to tell. 'And you . . .' I prompted him.

'Oh, I paid and paid and worried and worried and then I heard from a friend that Charles had done this to several other people as well and he didn't actually have AIDS at all. It was all a con, to trick money out of people. So I just called him and told him he'd got the last penny he was getting out of me, ever. But I couldn't really be angry at him, you see, because I felt so overjoyed about it. I was – '

'Hang on, hang on, my bonnie laddie,' I said casually, but you can imagine – imagine! – how my heart was flailing at me. 'What did you say this guy's name was? Charlie?'

'Charles. Charles Corrigan. Have you ever met him?'

'No, not the bloke I was thinking of,' I said, possibly overdoing the casual bit because my blood was singing an immortal song and there wasn't a bone in my body that wasn't warm crackling and hot as Guy Fawkes and New Year's and the complete and unabridged history of the Fourth of July.

XIX
The New Year

Go is my wish;
Then I shall go,
But in the light of going
Minutes are mine
I could devote to other things.
Stop has no minutes,
But I go or die.

Dylan Thomas

(from Isabel's diaries)

The new year always attacks before I'm ready for it, and this year was no exception. There was snow the week before Christmas, light, fragile stuff that was blown helplessly around the cement jungle of the Barbican complex. It settled briefly on the trees around my flat, just outlining the shapes as a child might, carefully spinning a magic marker along the edges; but the wind stayed cold, ice cold, and it was slicing still more viciously by the time I arrived at work.

I met Warren in the Festival Hall artists' car park. 'Happy New Year,' he greeted me, his eyes hungry. They seem hungrier since his marriage, unless I, still starving, can only see starvation everywhere. At the artists' bar Paul reached over and put his arm around me. 'Time for a New Year kiss,' he proposed, but I wriggled free. Karl was out of town (latest fax: 'Want to come to Osaka and be crazy with me?'), but I would have to be pretty desperate to turn to Paul Ellison again.

Then I noticed a crowd of people around William, heard

David saying, 'In this case the picture we had recently taken of the cello section will soon be out of date. Perhaps the next one we should do in street clothes, more fashion-conscious. I feel myself – ' I was about to twist away when Piotr grabbed my arm. He pulled me away from the group and into the men's changing room. My elbow pinching, I snapped, 'Let me go! What's this for?' and then I saw the expression on his face.

'He's leaving,' he said, watching me, unblinking as a cat, tail scalping the air from side to side. 'He's taking a job with the Royal Sinfonia.'

I sank down into a chair. 'Leaving!' I whispered.

'Next month. The Royal bloody Sinfonia. Cello five, if you please. Cello five!' He leaned forward, so angry that the veins stood out ugly on his neck. 'This is your doing, Isabel. You took him, you squeezed him dry and you sent him on his way. You did it, you and Hochler, you closed the door. If you – '

I hadn't cried in ages, hadn't been able to cry, thanks to the pills that even Karl didn't know about and the fear that even I pretended wasn't there. But I wept then, great gulping tears that washed away half my make-up and all my pretending.

Piotr distrusts women, most women; and there's a part of him which distrusts me in particular, but his nature wasn't tough enough to resist this. First he shoved a handkerchief in my hand, too hard, his muscles clenched, then he pounded back and forth across the room like a panther in a cage, finally he put a thin, awkward arm around my shoulders.

'You do love him, don't you,' he said, so softly that perhaps I wasn't suppose to hear. 'I always wondered.'

'I'm going to die,' I said, in amazement. 'It's as simple as that. Seeing him – even when he can't bear to look at me – it's all I've got left. If I can't have that, I have nothing. The difference between that and death is nothing; there is no difference.'

'Forgive me,' he said, his voice harsh with feeling, 'for not understanding sooner.'

'You have to help me!' I cried impulsively, clinging to him

as if he was all I had to lean on. Which was perhaps true, because Warren was already slipping away from me, down the long road that has no turnings.

'No,' said Piotr, gathering strength, 'no, it's the other way around; you have to help me, Isabel. You're our only chance, the only person who can persuade him to change his mind.'

'Me? Oh, I'm no use at all. He won't speak to me, hasn't spoken to me since – Oh I'm not strong enough for this! I'm on these pills, I've been seeing someone for depression; I can't bear it; I can't!'

'You have to,' said Piotr calmly. 'It's that or nothing, for both of us. Dry your eyes, take my other hankie. Greater love hath no man than to give up his second hankie . . . Look, we've made mistakes, both of us, about William – and, if we're honest, about each other – we've been stupid and neurotic and self-obsessed. But he hasn't resigned yet; he can't have signed the contract; there's still a shadow of a chance. Dry your eyes and I'll send him to you – or, better still, put it in writing. Write him a note, and I'll put it in his cello case. I'll even write it for you if you like, no, wouldn't ring true, too artistic. What we want here is the usual bloody drivel . . . like every song in every musical you've ever heard and ever played for. Write it down, Isabel, write it down. It's our only chance.'

It had filled the lungs of Dickens and Eliot and Austen and Greene, and Piotr leaned into the prickly January air, longing to embrace it, feeling energy and nervousness flooding into him, while the wind whipped dizzy snowflakes past his chin. He pressed himself into the side of the railing, waiting, waiting, and the figure underneath the walkway waited too, shivering in the wind.

At last he observed William stepping out from the Festival Hall artists' entrance, crossing towards the underpass and Piotr saw with a wonder that admitted no surprise that he'd noticed Isabel, he'd caught her up, he'd gathered her to him, his lips closing down on hers in full view of every passing car and hurrying stranger, his white head bowed over hers in wordless confession, expiation, forgiveness. Piotr felt infinitely old as he watched them, as if the twists in their lives were bound up with the very muscles of the earth, the endless cycle of cold and warmth, death and renewal. They looked small from this distance, delicate as Dresden, but they were real, fibrous, fellow sufferers. 'Protect each other,' he wanted to cry, but they were still kissing, moulded together as completely as snow and sky.

Piotr forced himself to tear his eyes away from them, from the triumph of Will's defeat; he left them alone again, as alone as on that first night, while the snow swirled wildly around them. Under his shoes the walkway felt harder, more solid; his footsteps more solitary. Piotr drew a deep breath of iced January air into his lungs, then expelled it as a mist which hung suspended for a second on the frost before it faded.

Forgiveness – so basic, so human a thing. He had his forgiveness too, his second chance. He turned and walked sharply away from the concert hall, towards the broken arc of the new city.